SUMMER BREAK

Summer Break was written by Kenneth Hunter

Edited by Laura Neeter

Cover art by Kylah Woods - kylahwoods.myportfolio.com

Hunter publication

Bringing the world a new generation of entertainment

Anything is possible if you don't know what you are talking about

Green's Law of Debate

"I could kill you!," roared an irritated feminine voice through Todd's cell phone. Todd tensed at
the fervor with which his wife Sharon shouted on the other end. The fiery conviction in her tone led
Todd to believe his wife. Her words were not to be taken as a euphemism, they were a premonition.
This was not a threat, he thought. It was a declaration. Todd's 6-foot-2 inch, 200-pound frame dwarfed his 4-foot-11-inch, 110-pound wife's frame. However, her volatile attitude savagely dwarfed Todd's solicitous personality.

Her bite was infinitely more vicious than his bark. Todd also knew better than to bark in her presence unless he quickly followed it by saying he was just kidding. Sometimes, the occasional "I love you" backed up with his most endearing smile would soothe her savage beast. Even then he had to tread lightly.

Todd impatiently looked at the clock on his car's dashboard. He desperately wanted to use the time as an excuse to end the call prematurely. Damn! Only 7:26 am. Todd had scheduled a meeting with his boss Amell for 8 am. Todd was preparing to propose an idea that would benefit both him and his employer financially. If today was going to be like most other days, Amell was going to be late. Todd arrived early to prepare for his meeting in peace and quiet, something he never gets at home. 7:26 means he has to spend the next 34 minutes on the phone being berated by his wife. So much for

4

peace or quiet!

Sharon only communicates with Todd when she wants something. Mostly she wants money. Mostly?, Todd chuckles to himself. That's *all* she ever wants from him. He's pissed her off. Again. Her form of communication when infuriated with Todd is throwing verbal haymakers and low blows. Conversely, Todd's approach can be likened to blown kisses and hugs. Todd often uses humor to try to lighten tense situations, but it's never worked with Sharon. Quite the opposite, in fact. Sharon often took his humor as him sounding like an uncaring jackass, a term she would regularly use to describe her husband around others. Todd thought his jokes and puns were hilarious. He would induct himself into the Dad Jokes Hall of Fame, if there were one.

They're complete opposites in every sense of the word. Todd is tall with an average build; Sharon is short, and extremely fit. He's black. She's white. Todd comes from a peaceful, loving, nuclear family. His family are like the Huxtables from *The Cosby Show*. Todd was like Theo Huxtable: clean cut and possessed a well-developed moral compass. Sharon's upbringing, on the other hand, was tumultuous and scarring at best. Her upbringing was like a horror movie. Her parents like Norma Bates and Michael Myers. As a result, Sharon's character bore a striking resemblance to Stephen King's Carrie.

Todd is timorous in uncomfortable situations; Sharon is venomous. Todd tries desperately to be liked and respected; Sharon hates that he's liked by everyone. He strives to be accepted and to abide by society's norms while Sharon is aroused by shock and awe. She doesn't care what others think about her …or her actions. In his mid-thirties, Todd is five years younger than Sharon. He has a babyface and looks younger than his age. Sharon — due to decades of chain smoking — looks much older than she actually is.

Sharon views Todd's age as a disability. She assumes that since she's lived five years longer than he has she not only has more life experience, but also more knowledge, even though she has no education beyond high school. Nor has she traveled more than 50 miles from where she was born. Still, she has street smarts. Todd is book smart, has a college degree, and has traveled out of the country on numerous family vacations.

If "don't tread on me" were a person, it would be Sharon, while Todd's a pushover. When the two started dating, Sharon described herself as a psycho killing bitch from hell. Todd thought she was joking. Now he sees her description as her warning label: side effects include irritability, mood swings, and acts of violence. Though he once loved her, Todd can't remember why anymore. He also believes she no longer loves him. He questions if she ever did or if he was just a convenience. The spark of whatever love might have been there has long been extinguished. Now they're in each other's lives out of habit. Like drinking to excess. You do it, but you know it's bad for you.

In the back of his mind, Todd always suspected he would die an early death and that his wife would be involved somehow. Thanks to his life insurance policy, Todd is worth more to her dead than alive.

Knowing this, Todd would always take extra safety precautions, never taking a shower without first locking the bathroom door. He feared she would one day come into the bathroom and kill him with a knife. Sharon has plenty of old boyfriends on the local police force. He suspected they would hide any evidence for her and make it look like an accident. She was *that* addicting. People would do stupid things for her if she asked them to and not understand afterwards why they did it.

6

Todd knew he should run very far away, but everybody has a weakness. Unfortunately, Sharon was his. An addiction to meth would be healthier than staying connected to her. In the beginning, their relationship was based on sex. Lots of sex. Eye popping, toe curling sex. He really liked her but was never sure he was in love with her. Sharon went through a depressive stage at one point in their relationship. Like a clueless idiot, Todd tried to fix her problems with a kind gesture. He proposed marriage as a way of cheering her up. There was a limo, dinner, and a moderately expensive ring (two, actually, since he had zero clue about her taste in jewelry). Sharon was so thrilled she became the loving, compassionate woman Todd longed for. But this lasted a few weeks. Todd has been "chasing the dragon" ever since. On the phone now, Todd knows his best bet is to agree with everything and say as little as possible. If he speaks, Sharon will ignore his comments, talk over him, or attack. Anything he says would be used against him in a future argument. His life with Sharon has been one continuous squabble. She never lets anything go.

"I never get time to spend with you!" she exclaimed, in a failed attempt to sound
cute, loving. "You're always working. "I miss you," she continued sweetly. Todd often described his conversations with Sharon as sweet and sour. She'd start off sounding tender but end with something detestable.

"If I wanted to be lonely I never would've gotten married a third time," Sharon argued. "I thought you would be different," she complained. "Remember when we were dating? We would go to concerts, shows, dinner...fun stuff," she reminisced. "How can we do all that if you're trying to get another job this summer?"

Todd completely blocked out her complaints. Instead, he rehearsed what he was going to say to Amell. It was going to be a chess match. Amell would complain about Todd's proposal while Todd would try and find a way to argue its merits.

For the past four months Todd had been teaching a life skills elective to teenage students at a private school after school program. Teaching and mentoring youth was a passion of Todd's. He loved to be involved in the betterment of society. He felt teaching aided the process. Unfortunately, this came at a cost. The institution he worked for doesn't pay well, and Todd and Sharon needed money desperately. The After-School Activity Program – or ASAP – was Amell's brainchild. Amell had always fantasized about turning the program into a conglomerate but had never the time, resources, or creativity to excel over the thousands of other
programs like it in the St. Louis area. The private school they worked for approached Amell with the opportunity to run their after-school program, and Amell's goal was to turn the glorified babysitting program into something more. So he'd reached out to Todd, a successful coworker at their warehouse night job. Amell was impressed with Todd's creative methods of motivating his employees, an often daunting, unachievable task.

Working in the warehouse was hard on employees. It was physically taxing. There was no air conditioning in the summer or heat in the winter. Most of the employees had daytime jobs or were also going to school . Other than the fact that they were getting a pay check and medical benefits there was zero motivation for anyone to go beyond their menial tasks. Still, Todd always found a way to motivate his employees. They regularly led their region in production. Since Amell had approached him about ASAP, Todd had gotten really excited about its potential. Todd's meeting with Amell this morning is meant to convince Amell to go to the superintendent and convince him to start a summer camp at the private Christian school.

8

In two months, the school would be on their summer break. This meant no work…and no pay for Todd beyond his meager earnings from the warehouse, and his weekend job. Convincing the influential school trustees that they needed to start a summer camp and hire Todd to manage it would ensure a paycheck during the summer months. Todd hated starting a new job at a new company. Feeling lost during training and waiting an extra week to get paid was not something Todd was interested in doing this summer. Plus, companies were not bending over backwards to hire a man in his mid-thirties to work for just a couple of months. The jobs that would, usually felt that Todd was overqualified. Building a new program at a job he already had was his best bet at maintaining a steady paycheck. Extending his employment at the school was more of a convenience for him. His part-time teaching job would become a full-time camp director position during the summer months. The school knew him, and he knew the school. As an added bonus, he'd be viewed as a hero if the camp was successful and became a financial windfall for the organization.

The easy part was convincing Amell to run the camp. The hard part was persuading Sharon that his working longer hours was their best financial option.

She'll just have to understand, Todd thought. The alternative - convincing her that she either needs to get a job, stop spending so much, or both - would be Mission Impossible.

Todd was currently working four jobs and was his family's only source of income. He hated it. It was emotionally, mentally, and physically taxing. Todd would often find himself falling asleep behind the wheel of his second job as a delivery truck driver. After working all night at the warehouse, he was exhausted, and would drift off while making deliveries. Worse, that would sometimes be all the rest he'd get some days.

He shared the danger – and his concerns – with Sharon. Her response? "It is what it is." He felt she was often disappointed when she would call and he hadn't died in a fiery crash because he'd fallen asleep behind the wheel. Most people would daydream about winning the lottery. Not Todd. He dreamt of naps. One day sleeping 8 hours. Eight hours in a row.

"Why the fuck aren't you saying anything?!" Sharon snapped, breaking Todd from the thoughts running
erratically through his mind. "Do you even *care* that I'm lonely? You say you work all the time because we're broke, but we're still broke. Why are you *really* working all the time?"

She'd been sweet(ish), Todd thought, so here comes the sour.

"Which bitch are you wanting to work overtime with?" she probed. "Is it a fucking teacher? They aren't smarter than me, you know. Is it a bitch from the warehouse? Better not be. That's where you met me," she continued. "She's not better than me, either, because I left that place. Who are you delivering
shit to? I've seen porn, I know women want to have sex with the delivery man. I'll kill you **and** that bitch," she threatened.

"What in the hell is she talking about?," Todd wondered. "If I'm having a secret affair with anyone, it's with Bill," he joked. "Light bill, electric bill, gas bill, water bill, and trash bill." The fear of having their house foreclosed on kept him in a constant state of anxiety. To lose their house or have a utility shut off would make him feel as if he failed his family. Paying all the bills was the reason he was always so tired. He literally worked day and night and was angry that his sacrifice and hard work were in vain. Sharon mismanaged their finances. Though he made the money, she controlled the funds. She overspent constantly, and overdrew the account regularly. Todd was constantly being ignored by Sharon and his stepson. They had zero understanding of the value of hard work.

"Do you think I want to spend my life working 18 hours a day?" responded Todd, as peacefully as he
possibly could. "Do you think I enjoy working nights in a dark, dingy, depressing warehouse, only to rush to my delivery job before I work another couple of hours at a private school? Do you think I *like* working another 12 hours a day at my weekend job?" he asked guardedly. "I'm exhausted." He didn't want to anger her, but he desperately wanted her to feel sympathy for him. He wanted her to feel they were in this together, to admire and respect him – her husband – for sacrificing everything. Todd was doing this for her and her son, and he wanted her to recognize and appreciate that. She didn't. Todd knew it, and it angered him to his core.

"Don't forget we're in this mess because you. You wanted to spend money you didn't have on a wedding, instead of on paying your bills," Todd pointed out. "Remember that *you're* the one that quit your job as soon as you said 'I do,'" he added.

Todd remembered moving into Sharon's home after their honeymoon. There was a foreclosure sign on the door. Sharon hadn't told Todd that she neglected paying her mortgage during their entire engagement. Instead, she spent that money on the wedding.

Through Sharon's silence, Todd quickly realized that his comments had just flushed any teamwork rhetoric completely down the toilet. The eggshells he had cautiously walked on turned to land mines.

"Have you gotten any leads on jobs?" he asked.

BOOM! Todd practically felt the landmine explode as he finished asking the question.

"There you go, blaming me for everything!" Sharon barked. "*My* bills are now **our** bills, sweetie," Sharon noted sarcastically. "I *deserved* the wedding of my dreams, even if it **was** to you," she spewed. "Now I want the marriage of my dreams, and my dreams don't include a husband throwing guilt at me because we're struggling financially. A man, or some semblance of one, should provide for his family. A real man would take care of his house and everyone inside it. And if you can't, I'm sure I can find one who can take your place," she threatened.

"Wait. Are you saying I don't provide for you and your son?!" His blood began to boil. "You have food in the fridge, don't you? A roof over your head, clothes on your back, gas in your car. I provide you with your needs, but what you want is Gucci and gold!"

Todd took a deep breath. He desperately needed to diffuse this argument.

"Sharon, some people work for a living and some people work for fun. I just work for you. Marriage is a give and take. Well, you've shown me you can take. You've got some giving to do."

"Mother fucker," Sharon barked. "Are you singing a fucking Wham! song?

12

Listen, jackass, I don't have time to work right now. If I did, I would shoot from the heart, because you are to blame. You, asshole, give love a bad name."

The call ended. Relief poured over Todd. Claiming victory also helped him calm himself down. He didn't want to go into his meeting with Amell angered by his fight with Sharon. Todd went back to outlining his list of reasons in support of a summer camp. But, just as Todd began to re-focus, his phone rang. Glancing down, he saw it was Sharon calling him back. He really didn't want to answer. Thousands of excuses as to why he should ignore the call flooded his mind. Todd ignored them because of one. What if there were an emergency? Reluctantly, he hit the button to answer.

"Fuck you for not answering the phone sooner," greeted Sharon. "Why didn't you call me back?" she demanded. "In the movies the husband runs after his wife when he fucks up."

Todd rolled his eyes. "What's wrong?" He didn't want to be a part of his wife's rom-com movie fantasy.

"I'm tired of you diminishing my role at home," she started. "There is a lot that needs to be done here, you know."

"Like what?" Todd retorted. "Watch the dust and dishes race to see which will pile up fastest? Finding out who the baby's father is on *Maury*? Watching Springer interview a man who married a horse?"

"No, asshole!" Sharon thundered. "My son needs me," she responded, trying – but failing – to sound like a damsel in distress. "He's going through a difficult time right now. His dad just had another kid with his new wife. My little boy needs me more than ever."

"Really?!" replied Todd sarcastically. "*Little* boy? In case you hadn't noticed, your newborn is 16 years old. He needs to get a job, too," he added. "He could come work at the camp I'm about to propose to the school. He could go around cutting grass in the neighborhood, or he could bag groceries at the market. He could do anything other than spend all his time watching porn.", catching all your grandkids inside of his socks.

"You're disgusting," Sharon responded. "Besides, he's working on his profession this summer."

"His *what*?"

"He's going to be a professional gamer," Sharon retorted.

"Video games??" Todd asked, incredulous. "He's going to have to take summer school for failing both math and English. How do you flunk English when that's the language you speak on a daily basis? If he can't read, how about you buy him some pop-up books instead of video games."

"Watch it," cautioned Sharon, "That's my baby boy you're insulting" she warned angrily. "Those games are his future."

"His future!" Todd exclaimed. "How is he going to play games when there's no electricity to power them when the company turns it off because we haven't paid the bill?"

"He is *going* to be a professional gamer," Sharon responded. "He's going to analyze the games and tell other gamers how to beat them."

"He's going to do *what*?" roared Todd. "Who's going to pay him to sit around playing video games? And if somebody *did* pay him, he couldn't critique the games the way you're saying because he can't communicate in English! How is he going to write reviews if he can't read?"

"Why don't you call in tonight," proposed Sharon, completely ignoring Todd's points. "We can go to a Blockbuster and rent a movie," she suggested.

Sighing in frustration, Todd took a deep breath before responding. He was tired of having the same discussion with Sharon. When an unexpected expense pops up she'd suggest he work more hours to pay it, then she immediately complains that he works too much. It was a never-ending battle. Yet, once again, he tried to explain:

"One, you and I both know that if I don't work I'm not going to get paid. Two, we're so broke we can't even afford to watch *other* people rent movies. Three, I'm tired. If I was going to do anything tonight besides work it would be sleep," he added. "Sharon, you have a lot of skills from previous jobs. Do you have any thoughts as to what you might want to do for a living? Any extra income would truly help us out."

"I told you I have a lot to do around here!" Sharon screamed. "I can't concentrate on anything, much less finding a job with you berating me and calling me lazy," she continued.

"I never…" started Todd.

"I knew I never should have married a black man," she continued. "All I ever hear is how black men run
the streets and have whores of women."

"It's *hordes* of women," Todd interjected.

"What, Mother Fucker?!" Her fuse was lit. She was now officially mad.

"If you're going to accuse me of being a man whore I want you to at least get the terminology correct."

"Todd? Go fuck yourself." And she abruptly hung up the phone.

Whew, Todd thought. At least now I won't have to listen to her yelling at me for the next 15 minutes. There'll be hell to pay when I get home.

Todd pondered the repercussions of upsetting his wife this time. Though they'd only been married for a year, he'd already experienced the full gambit of her anger. He's been threatened, hit, yelled at, cursed at, talked about, and had objects thrown at him. Even the house has experienced Sharon's wrath. She's
punched holes in walls, kicked the doors off the hinges, and ripped doors off the cabinets. Todd is too embarrassed to have people visit because of the destruction the house has experienced. Todd hoped for
the silent treatment. It can be a welcome relief from being verbally assaulted.

But as much as Todd is welcoming an elongated silent treatment, it could last weeks. And Sharon not only stops speaking to Todd, she tries to force Todd to talk to her by being petty. Just last month she'd removed the

16

mattress from their bedroom because Todd left water on their bathroom floor
after a shower. Sharon went into a tirade when her socks got wet. She gathered all his clothes, placed them in the tub, and soaked everything he owned.

Eight twenty. Late as always, Todd thought, as he witnessed Amell finally pulling into the parking lot.

When eating an elephant, take one bite at a time.
- Bishop Desmond Tutu

"You want to do *what*?!" exclaimed a puzzled Amell

"Let's start a summer camp!" repeated an excited Todd.

"I don't know if I can survive these last couple of months of the school year let alone a summer camp!" Amell sighed. "I need a break," he added. "It's bad enough you have me on campus early in the morning during Spring Break," he complained. "And now you have the audacity to propose that we spend more time at the place I'm trying to get away from during a time I'm getting paid to be away from it?! You must be out of your mind."

Amell was a bald, middle-aged, African American male. The only hair on his head was on his face. He wore a pencil thin mustache and scruffy goatee. He was shorter than Todd, standing only 5'9". He weighed more than Todd, though. Todd guessed he was around 230. Amell always dressed as if he were going to an important meeting; it was extremely rare that you would catch him without a sport coat and tie. For Amell, dressing down was a sport coat, no tie, and dark tennis shoes. Usually, this attire was saved for coaching basketball games. Todd always imagined Amell as the type of person who cut his grass in slacks, a Brooks Brothers shirt, and a pair of white New Balance tennis shoes.

Amell was well-liked around school. The older kids called him "Preach" because of his propensity to give long-winded lectures. Amell's speeches also reminded Todd of the many pastors he'd visited growing up in black churches. The preachers would always ignore the time and take hours to deliver sermons while Todd dreamed of being anywhere but in church. In more recent years, Todd has been caught listening to many of Amell's "discussions," all the while wishing he were anywhere but there.

For their part, the younger kids, especially the girls, would call Amell their second daddy. This made Todd cringe as many of the younger students would wipe their noses on the teacher's shirt as they came in for a hug. Todd also felt it inappropriate to hug a student, especially one of the opposite sex. He thought it looked inappropriate to an outsider. Gave the wrong perception.

"This semester has been unbearable," Amell continued. "I don't know if there's tension at home causing students to act out or what. Or maybe the recession is keeping parents distracted from focusing on their children's behavior. Whatever the reason, the kids seem to be blowing off a lot of extra steam at school. I've given out so many detentions this year, broken up so many fights, I'm ready to quit teaching," he continued. "Maybe I'll do something less stressful like remove mines for the army, or be a marriage counselor for you and Sharon" he joked.

That comment struck a nerve with Todd. He'd sought marital advice from his friend and didn't think Amell would use Todd's troubles as a punchline. He stopped himself from voicing his displeasure, though; he needed Amell's blessing for the summer camp. He decided to allow Amell to continue venting:

"I even had a student try to sell me drugs! Weed!" he exclaimed. "He told me I needed to chill out after I gave him a failing grade on a paper he turned in a week late. He even offered me discounts for every grade I gave him above a D. I had another student ask me for a condom and the keys to my car. He wanted to make out with his girlfriend during lunch. If my fiancée has cut me off until after our wedding, I am *defi*nitely not going to help others get laid," Amell joked.

"Amell," Todd pleaded, "I – we – can make this camp successful," Todd persisted. "We could manage it just like the after-school program. We can make it an all-day thing," he added. It'll be better than the after-school program, though, because we'll be making the school money. What parent doesn't want to have their kids doing something productive over the summer? Anything is better than sitting at home playing video games, watching cable, or getting into trouble. Parents want to have peace of mind that their child is okay while they're at work."

Todd used every persuasive argument he could think of, but Amell's body language told him it was all falling on deaf ears.

"Are you nuts, Todd?!" Amell exclaimed. "I became a teacher so I could have the summer off. I'm so burnt out," he Amell. "Between teaching, coaching basketball, running an after-school program, AND working a night job, I need time to relax. What's my fiancée going to say when she hears I'm even *thinking* of working this summer instead of helping plan our wedding?" he asked. "Not a thing!" he added, answering his own question. "She's going to kill me. And it won't be a quick and easy death, either. She'll make it slow and painful. Then she'll nag me over and over, reminding me of every mistake I've ever made during our relationship. It won't matter how big or small, she'll dwell on it. She'll remind me of all the things I was supposed to do, meant to do, forgot to do, or hadn't thought about doing. She'll list everything I've put before planning our wedding."

20

The summer could be over before Amell finishes his rant, Todd thought.

"She'll stick a knife in my rib cage, tickling my lungs while she turns it slowly. She asks all the time why we haven't picked out a caterer," Amell continued. "She'll ask why I didn't help decide on a band or a DJ. Or why seating arrangements for the reception still aren't finalized. Who cares where they sit?!" Amell shouted. "These people are there for a free meal and alcohol! They don't care where they sit! And then...*then*, as she's taking a baseball bat to my ribs, she's going to ask whether we should go with a buffet or server-style reception. What type of flowers are we going to use? Well how am *I* supposed to know?! There are over 250,000 kinds of flowers in the world. They all smell the same! Want to know what they smell like?" Before Todd could respond, Amell continued. "They smell like sinus problems. I have to visit every florist in the city to help pick them out by next Thursday. It's March! The wedding's in
November! The only flower I care about is the flour in the cake. Oh, and don't get me *started* on cake. Martha Stewart just *had* to have an article on twenty-five new takes on traditional wedding cake flavors. Why are there twenty-five new takes? What happened to good old fashioned chocolate and vanilla?"

Todd glanced down at his watch and wondered how much longer Amell's tirade was going to last. Interrupting his thoughts, Amell continued questioning every aspect of planning his wedding.

"Tell me why I made the mistake of mentioning my first wedding to my fiancée?" he asked. "Now everything has to be bigger and grander than that one was. More flowers, more guests, more food. All
I see, is more money spent," he complained. "I accidentally mentioned having a destination wedding and I almost lost my life for suggesting we

diminish our special day by not having all 200 of our closest family and friends there. You haven't seen hell until you look into the eyes of a woman after you suggest wedding plans that differ from the vision she's seen in her dreams. Vows, groomsmen, a tux, invitations…. ***Invitations***, Todd, are just pieces of paper inside an envelope. Why do there have to be so many variations of them? Tell me who on earth is going to rip through this expensive envelope and say, 'Wow, what a lovely font. Let me frame this in remembrance of this free meal they're going to provide me!'" The sarcasm cascaded from his words the way water flows from a waterfall.

"I suggested we get a wedding planner, but noooo, my future wife thinks planning it by ourselves is fruitful, that it'll be a testament to the lifelong journey we're about to embark on and blah, blah, blah," he continued mockingly. "I'm knee-deep in wedding planning hell, and you want me to be the director of a summer camp? A summer camp?! Brother are you crazy?!" he snapped.

"Summer is the time of year where I only have one job. It's time for me to catch up on some sleep," he added. "Not to mention that the school's tried this before – several times – and failed. Miserably. What makes us any different from those who've tried before us? And you want to do this during a recession?! Who would it be open to?"

"Anyone in the area willing to pay the fees to have us entertain their child (or children) this summer," Todd replied.

"That's nuts!" Amell said. "Our school is private for a *reason*," he added cynically. "These people claim to be Christian, but they only like Christians that look like them. Todd, your black butt better be thankful we have a job here. We're only here so that our co-workers can tell their friends that they're not racist because they have black friends. Us? We're the token black employees that help the school check off the diversity boxes."

Todd sat there and thought about what Amell was saying.

"When enrollment started to decline, I suggested the school reach out to the residents in the community to see if any families wanted to place their children here and they looked at me as though I was the anti-Christ. They actually told me that they do not want any element of the surrounding community at this school because the surrounding community isn't a 'good fit.' When I reminded them that *I'm* part of this surrounding community, I was quickly reminded that I'm one of the 'good ones.'"

This revelation did not shock Todd. He knew that, for some, Christianity ended as soon as their church service did.

"If we weren't on campus," started Amell, "I would be cursing a blue streak right now. Besides. What would make us different from the hundreds of other summer camps in the area?" he asked.

Excited that the monologue was finally over, Todd replied confidently, "Me!" *I'm* what sets us apart from every other camp in the area. I need this to work, for it to be a springboard to financial success for the school so I can get a raise. I'm tired of being paid minimum wage, of struggling financially."

"Todd, everyone is struggling," Amell retorted. "Banks and car companies are failing, and houses are going into foreclosure faster than they ever have before, so why would anyone come to our camp just because *you're* struggling financially?"

"Because our camp will offer course preparedness," Todd replied.

"Course **WHAT**?!," Amell countered. "Don't put lipstick on a pig, Todd! Are you trying to say Summer School?" then, laughing heartily, "You want me to take my summer break to TEACH STUDENTS?!"

"Well, sort of," Todd said. "Except the courses we offered would be ones they hadn't failed yet."

"So it would be Summer School with perks?" Amell teased.

"We present it as one hour of learning to keep the students' minds fresh," Todd said defensively. "We'd help campers get a jump on the next school year and the rest of the day would feature the regular fun stuff that goes with all summer camps."

Todd could see that he'd piqued Amell's curiosity and tried reeling Amell in. Amell was Todd's big fish. If he could feed him bits of information that Amell wanted to hear, enough to get him into the boat, he could serve as bait to help Todd get an even bigger fish: the superintendent.

"I will plan it, organize it, and run it," Todd promised. "I just need you to oversee the operation," he implored. "Oh. And *possibly* propose it to the superintendent."

Todd watched Amell stand there and ponder the pros and cons of Todd's idea. What seemed like hours of contemplation were mere seconds.

"Give me one good reason why I would even consider this proposal," Amell asked defiantly.

"Money," Todd responded matter-of-factly.

"Money, huh?" Amell repeated to himself. He looked up, rubbing his chin. To Todd, he looked like he was pondering all the benefits of running a successful business like a summer camp. Seeing his fish almost in the boat, Todd yanked on the reel.

"Amell, this is the perfect opportunity to show the superintendent and the school board that you have what it takes to be a principal: the ultimate goal in your profession. I want to help you achieve that," Todd offered. "Use me to show them your business sense. The success of the camp will not only better prepare the students for the school year, the financial aspect may be just what's needed to help fix the place up a bit. Plus," Todd continued, "the school will be paying us to run it. It's the perfect opportunity to give yourself a little, much-deserved raise. I'm pretty sure you could use the extra money right now to help pay for your Lifestyles-of-the-Rich-and-Famous wedding," Todd taunted.

He's almost in the boat, thought Todd.

"I honestly don't think you can organize the camp in less than two months," Amell said. "And I expect nothing less than excellence," he added. "Especially if you have my name attached to it."

Todd was now even more motivated. He hated being told he couldn't do something. He promised himself long ago he could succeed with anything when he worked hard enough at it. This was also his weakness, of course. You can't win them all, especially if not everyone shares the same level of commitment. He thought again about his marriage. He was working so hard on making her happy that he was ignoring his own lack of it. Perhaps foolishly, he believed making more money for his family would make everyone happy.

"Amell," Todd began, "I have a deadbeat wife and a mountain of debt. When I have doubters I become extremely motivated. I will do everything in my power to make sure this endeavor is successful. That or die trying," he declared.

"Yeah? We'll see," Amell replied dubiously.

Successfully in the boat, thought Todd, celebrating his little victory.

"I'll consider this on two conditions," Amell interjected. "One: no one calls me before 10 AM with any problems, and two: you plan it with Bianca." And just like that, the fish jumped out of the boat and swam away, pulling the rod and reel into the water with it.

If you don't like the answer, you shouldn't
Have asked the question.
- Unknown

"How did I get myself into this mess?" Todd pondered. He always viewed his life as good followed by bad, as though his life was the embodiment of Murphy's law: if something can go wrong it will. If he lost something he would find it only after he'd replaced it. He got married, but it was to the devil. He has a job – four of them, actually – but the recession has made it impossible to stay above water. And now, although he's convinced his boss that a summer camp is a great idea and has an opportunity to create extra income, has to deal with Bianca.

Bianca was a stubborn young woman. The generational gap between her and Todd made it difficult for them to see eye-to-eye on anything. Todd felt he knew more than Bianca because of age and experience. Bianca felt she knew more because she could see things from a new and fresh perspective. Todd felt cultured because he knew the classics in movies, music, and literature. Bianca felt the same way, since she knew current events, newer music, and newer movies. They were both right, but they were also both stuck in their own ways; neither of them was willing to step into the other's world to experience something new. Todd mostly didn't like her because certain aspects of her temperament reminded him of Sharon.

He, Amell, and Bianca scored a meeting with William Franklin, the superintendent of the school. And Bianca was late. Franklin was definitely old school. Everything in his life was done with a purpose. He followed the unwritten rules of etiquette to the letter. If you weren't fifteen minutes early, you were late. The weirdest, most Draconian rule display of power happened during impromptu meetings. If a teacher arrived late, even by only a few seconds, he would lock them out of the meeting and forbid the rest of the staff from sharing what was discussed. Tardiness simply wasn't tolerated. If you didn't dress to impress he considered you slovenly. And if students left a table without pushing their chair in there would be hell to pay. He ran his school with an iron fist, there was no bending of the rules, no leniency. If a parent was a day late paying tuition, Mr. Franklin would not allow the student to attend class until their bill was current. Any tests or assignments missed during their absence could not be made up. His reasoning? If you can't get away with it in the real world it should not be allowed in school.

Knowing this about Mr. Franklin – and knowing that Bianca knew it, too – Todd could not fathom how Bianca could be late for their meeting with him. He grew impatient with each passing moment. Even Amell was on time, and he's *never* on time, Todd thought.

Finally, Todd saw Bianca's car pull onto the school's parking lot. Relieved that she'd finally arrived, Todd was irritated when she was still in her car a few minutes later.

"Should we go get her?" Todd asked Amell, who was standing next to him. The two were waiting just outside the administration office. Their meeting wasn't until nine, but they'd agreed to arrive fifteen minutes early so as to present a united front when proposing the summer camp to Mr. Franklin. That plan was shot as it was now 8:55 and Bianca was still in her car. As Todd approached it, he could hear her music blaring. He didn't know what was playing, nor did he care. To him it sounded like organized noise with somewhat of a melody.

28

Peering into her car, Todd saw why she was late. Bianca was applying her makeup. I wonder if she has mirrors at home, he asked himself. He never understood why so many women would take their time in the shower, washing their hair, take just as long drying it, curling or straightening it, and applying perfume and makeup, just to finish applying *more* makeup in the car.

"Hi guys!" she greeted them. "Sorry I'm late."

The two men waiting in the parking lot greeted her halfheartedly. Amell was visibly nervous about the meeting. Sweat poured down his face in the balmy seventy-degree sun and rings of sweat were pooling under his armpits. Todd was visibly annoyed by Bianca's tardiness.

"About time you arrived," he complained, not bothering to hold back his anger. He has a lot riding on this meeting, and Bianca's lack of punctuality could derail everything. He shot Amell a look that said "She's going to mess this up."

Bianca was an attractive young woman. She 5'5" and weighed close to 130 lbs, but the heels she always wore added two inches to her frame.. Her nails were always perfectly manicured. Her eyebrows and eyelashes highlighted the contours of her face, punctuating the hazel sparkle in her eyes. Though it took forever to put on, her makeup was applied impeccably, and her nail color always matched her outfit. She was beautiful. She was noticed by everyone everywhere. Everyone except Todd. Todd never noticed. He only saw a spoiled kid when he looked at Bianca. At 19, she *was* still a kid in his eyes, a high school student in an adult world.

Bianca had landed her job at the school because she was related to Amell through a marriage that no longer existed. Her schedule consisted of class half the week and work the other half. However, she rarely was on time for either. She wanted to be rich but had no idea how to achieve that goal. This aspect of her personality reminded Todd of himself at that age.

At nineteen, Todd had been a good baseball player. However, he didn't work at being great. He let life pass him by. He expected things to work out in his favor naturally. This meeting with Mr. Franklin is proof that he was wrong in making that assumption.

Todd surmised that Bianca's tardiness stemmed from her getting lost in her closet. While Todd's wardrobe consisted of four slacks, two pairs of blue jeans, and maybe five shirts in constant rotation, he never remembered seeing Bianca wearing the same outfit more than once. Her clothes were probably the only aspect of her he'd ever noticed: they were always outlandish and impractical for her duties at the school.

Bianca's role was to keep students entertained during their stay in the after-school program through
various electives, crafts, tutoring, and sports. The majority of the time the students wanted to play
basketball. Todd loathed Bianca's unwillingness to partake in activities that required her to sweat, or get dirty. He recalled a time when Bianca assisted a bunch of high school students staining their
woodworking projects. They were supposed to be Christmas gifts and Bianca had worn a designer apron to keep from messing up her outfit. Underneath the apron was an impractical designer cowl neck cashmere sweater. While applying a cherry wood-colored stain to a set of candlestick holders, Bianca stained her apron.

Though Todd barely noticed it, Bianca became enraged that the apron was now ruined. She took it off to examine the damage and, in the process, backed into a project that was still wet, ruining her sweater. Todd chuckled that wearing a t-shirt would've been a better idea, and much cheaper if it got ruined than the one she'd chosen. Bianca scoffed at the notion that she had anything "basic" in her closet.

"I couldn't find the right bag to go with my sundress," Bianca said, trying to justify her tardiness.

To Todd, Bianca was a walking mannequin, modeling the latest in fashion. Her well-designed sundress was a Vera Wang. Her stylish shoes were Jimmy Choo. Her chic sunglasses were Bvlgari. Her fashionable purse Lana Marks. Her intoxicating scent Hermes. Her classy watch Cartier. Her outfit cost more than what Todd made in a month, maybe two!

Bianca was the product of a woman getting pregnant by an athlete and her mother used her child as an American Express card with no spending limit. Her monthly child support payments were more than Todd made in a year. Unfortunately, the card reached its limit when Bianca turned eighteen. Bianca needed a job, too. Todd was pretty sure that Bianca could retire on the spot if she sold all the clothes, shoes, and purses in her closet. Her baby blue BMW 6 series M6 was definitely out of Todd's budget. But while her possessions were nice – very nice – Todd saw them as a waste of money. Todd dreamt of having life experiences around the world: exploring different cultures, eating lavish foods, and gazing at picturesque horizons, not collecting expensive jewelry and clothes. It was just another thing he and Bianca did not see eye to eye on.

"We're going to a meeting to pitch a summer camp, not help you catch a sugar daddy," he snapped.

Her spoiled little self just doesn't understand the importance of this meeting, he thought. He wanted the three of them there so their proposal seemed orchestrated and organized rather than some piece of crap thrown together at the last minute. The proposal was, in essence, a business plan. They needed facts and numbers to present to Mr. Franklin. To Todd, Bianca's extreme self-preparation would only have been needed if they were trying to entice a dirty old man in Hollywood. Precious moments that could have been used to prepare for their presentation had been wasted so Bianca could paint her face and match a bag to her fingernails.

"What are you talking about?" Bianca asked, puzzled. "The meeting's at nine. I'm early,!"

Todd glared at her and spoke through clenched teeth. "We were *supposed* to arrive early," he said.

Bianca twirled in a circle as though she were on a runway. "Do not get mad at me just because I'm the finest thing you see day in and day out. And don't get mad because you can't afford to look as good as me," she sang.

Todd stared her down. "You know," he said, "putting a price on your body makes you a...."

Amell interjected before Todd could finish his sentence. "Hey!," he shouted, fed up. "You two are on the
same team! Todd, you came to me about this camp for a reason," he scolded. "Remember that. Bianca, I'm sure Todd's reason for wanting this approval can also benefit you, so I want you two to go in there and act like

adults. Let's sell this camp as if our lives depend on it."

Claim victory and retreat.
- Aiken's Solution

"NO!" shouted the man sitting behind the desk. William Franklin was an acrimonious older man. He appeared to be in his late sixties, so Todd had been shocked when he'd learned that Mr. Franklin was only fifty-nine.

He looks stressed, thought Todd. Mr. Franklin's frown lines and the dark circles under his eyes were deep. Years of stress from working in the educational system had taken their toll. Strategic decision-making, hiring and firing, and the coordination of what Todd thought were unnecessary meetings added to the many wrinkles on his face. His job was even more difficult this year because of the recession. Students were leaving the school like it was the second exodus; tuition had become too much of a financial burden for parents. Trying to find new students to enroll in their place had probably caused Mr. Franklin to age even more rapidly.

And students were not the only ones leaving. Teachers and counselors were also abandoning the ship. There was no green grass on this side of the fence. The school board had frozen employee wages, which were already the lowest in education. Much needed supplies, textbooks, and computer expenses were put on hold to keep the lights on. The school's endowment had dried up. The building itself was old. Pipes burst in the winter and mildew formed in the spring. Paint was chipping off the walls, the carpet was frayed, and the linoleum floors were marked up. The campus required a lot of expensive maintenance and renovation. Everything was outdated and had been for decades. Parents were abandoning it for fancier, updated schools.

34

Unfortunately, those repairs cost money the school did not have. They could not increase the cost of tuition to afford the upgrades because families were already having difficulty paying. This meant that repairs were made with duct tape, glue, and prayers. Like many older buildings, the roof leaked when it rained. Classrooms were cold in the winter and sweltering in the summer. To keep costs down, the heat and air conditioning were only ever turned on in extreme conditions.

Younger students affectionately called Mr. Franklin Mr. Frank. And he did have an angelic side to him. Sometimes. Unlike the staff that worked under him, Mr. Frank treated everyone equally. He hated them all.

Todd was shocked by the nasty attitudes those in the administration building had given that the school was a Christian organization. When Todd started working there, he'd expected a heavenly environment. He thought the staff would be angels. But he was wrong. *No one* was pleasant; they all had a foul attitude. I would have a permanent scowl on my face, too, thought Todd, I had to be around Mr. Frank all day.

Unless you were a child, Mr. Franklin was crotchety toward you. His affection for his students
came from the bible. Since Jesus told his disciples not to hinder the children Mr. Frank had a soft spot for them. In moderation. However, it was mostly forced. The smile he pasted on his face when he was around students was reminiscent of the Grinch's smile after his heart began to thaw. Mr. Franklin claimed his door was open to everyone; you just had to make an appointment. However, doing that was an impossible task. His calendar was always booked, or that was what he told his secretary to tell anyone who wanted to take advantage of his open-door policy. He would say he's open to new and exciting things yet was stuck in his same routine. Mr. Franklin

would shoot down anyone else's ideas if he hadn't been involved in its development.

Today, though, Todd, Amell, and Bianca had an appointment. Even then, they were at the mercy of Mr. Franklin's lack of desire to meet with anyone. Todd overheard him tell his secretary he didn't have time for them, and only relented when he heard her say they were there with a business opportunity.

Todd, Amell, and Bianca were ushered into Mr. Franklin's office. There was a collection of clocks hanging on his wall with a sign that read 'time waits for no man.' A poster hanging directly behind Mr. Franklin's read 'Patience.' Todd was shocked at how little Mr. Franklin displayed.

"Mr. Franklin," Todd started, "I understand that times are rough. Especially financially. Believe me I know. So do many of our students' parents. With the economy being the way it is, I suspect people will be looking for part-time jobs to supplement their incomes. Our summer camp can help."

"Summer camp can *help*?" questioned Mr. Franklin, sighing. He was visibly miffed. Setting his pen on his desk with frustration, Mr. Franklin leaned back in his chair and exhaled.

"What? Are we going to hire every parent affected by this recession?" he asked sarcastically. "Which one of you has a business degree? Running a program like a camp is a lot more than planning field trips and games. Now kids," he started, opening his laptop. That angered Todd. He was in his 30s and Amell was in his 40s. Being called a kid in a business setting was highly disrespectful.

36

"I have a lot on my plate," Mr. Franklin continued, focusing his attention on his computer screen. He began typing something vigorously, completely ignoring the trio's presence. An eery, awkward silence filled the room. The only sound was Mr. Franklin's fingers pecking away on the keyboard.

Todd waited patiently for a break in the typing so he could continue his argument. Mr. Franklin sensed Todd was going to ask another question, though.

"Enrollment for the next school year is already down 30% compared to this time last year, which was down 40% from the previous year. We have several students whose tuition payments are already past due more than 60 days. Several more families are more than 45 days behind. Still others are 30 days past due. We've only had two families inquire about attending next year, and they're asking for discounts. We can't offer incoming students the amenities other schools offer, nor can we afford to match other schools' prices. The roof leaks like a sieve. Our school bus leaks oil worse than our roof leaks water, and my coffee from this morning is requiring me to need to visit the restroom." He shifted uncomfortably in his seat

"So if you don't mind..." Mr. Franklin stopped typing and stared at the door, attempting to use polite nonverbal communication to tell them to get out.

"Thank you for your time," Amell said, recognizing it was time to leave. He gave Todd a look that said *let it go* look. Todd ignored it. He refused to take no for an answer, especially since this was something he believed in wholeheartedly.

He realized he needed to pull something out that would change Mr. Franklin's mind. He was upset that his grand plan wasn't given the respect

37

he thought it deserved. This is why we needed to have had a meeting before our meeting, Todd thought. He felt he was the only one who had a clue to what was going on between him, Amell, and Bianca. Deep inside, he knew the others didn't share his dedication to the project since they weren't as desperate as he was. The awkwardness in the room and their refusal to interject was evidence of this.

"No sir, we are not hiring parents," Todd replied. "The summer camp can be an open house to *this* school."

Todd purposely said "this school" rather than "our school." He'd never felt welcomed by any of his white coworkers. In Todd's eyes, minority staff members were only hired as glorified babysitters. He felt the school viewed them as capable of only working as after school program directors, music teachers, choir directors, coaches, or electives instructors. No candidate of color had ever been interviewed, much less hired, to teach any of the core classes. Being allowed to run an entire program like the one they were proposing was going to be a major step forward for him and Amell. This was their opportunity to earn the respect of his peers, and become saviors of the financially failing school, Todd lied to himself. He knew deep down inside this was the best chance of him financially saving himself. While being petty, and giving the school a big HAHA look, I did something you couldn't *slap in the face*. He really needed to say something to pique Franklin's interest. A daunting task that will take a lot more than arguing every excuse Mr. Franklin was throwing at them. So far he hadn't even looked at them. Todd thought the least the man could do was make eye contact with them, and he couldn't shake the thought that it was because of his race. He's white, I'm black, but we both need some green, he thought.

"Mr. Franklin," Todd began, "our camp would be a hybrid of fun and education. "We'll be doing something no other camp in the area is doing so we could generate enough revenue to pay for the school's many expenses. We can advertise the camp at the many different churches the school's families attend. Let them come to our camp that features preparedness classes and see how wonderful this campus and school is."

A smile started to spread across Mr. Franklin's face. He was interested!

"Preparedness classes?," he questioned. "Are you trying to say summer school?" he asked, laughing. "Amell, is he serious? We can barely afford to pay our staff throughout the school year let alone the summer. Tell me who wants to work during their summer break," he continued. "You, Amell? Do **you** want to work this summer? Don't you have a wedding to plan?" Todd felt a tug of war to persuade Amell brewing.

Leaning back in his chair Mr. Franklin took off his glasses and set them gently on his desk. It was obvious he had become tired of this discussion. He inhaled deeply and the group knew this was going to be his final comment on the matter. "It's not enough to come up with a sort of nebulous idea of what you want your camp to be and what you want it to encompass. Have you three actually thought this through?" he questioned. "I know you all look at me and think I'm some crotchety old man who's losing his mind and would fall for your half-thought-out scheme. But I'm not. I've been doing this job for over forty years," he declared, banging his fist on his desk. The force shook the room, including the trio standing in front of him. He was making his point and it was being heard.

Gathering his composure, he continued, "I didn't just fall off the turnip truck yesterday." I know the ins and outs of my job. Have any of you thought of the budget you'll need to operate and maintain your camp moving forward?

The staffing situation you'll find yourself with, the kinds of campers you're hoping will attend?"

"Of course we have, sir," Todd lied, hoping Mr. Franklin did not ask for figures. "We plan to charge an application fee to be used to pay for any start-up costs," he said. Amell suddenly looked perplexed; he hadn't heard of such a plan. No one has, Todd thought Todd

In truth, Todd, Amell, and Bianca had absolutely no idea what the answers were to any of Mr. Franklin's questions. Even worse, Todd knew they hadn't even thought of them. Fortunately for them, he'd just come up with how to start planning the summer camp, Todd thought, hoping for a miracle approval.

"We can hire college students or use the school's students as staff," he suggested. "Everyone needs work experience for their resume," he continued. "Most camps' cut-off age is twelve, but we can charge parents to send their pre- and early teens to ours. Not as campers, but as volunteers. Isn't community service a requirement for graduation? We'll just charge parents to help their children get the hours they need to graduate."

Todd was impressed by the way he was coming up with good ideas in pitching the summer camp. And all off the top of his head! He felt confident.

"I know you don't believe in us," he started. "To be honest, Amell and Bianca aren't 100% sure that we can pull it off themselves, but I believe in us. I believe in myself. I cannot afford to fail. I *won't* fail," he declared emphatically.

A second passed in silence. Then two. And then Mr. Franklin started

40

laughing. Hard. He wiped a tear from his eye.

"You have guts, kid. You remind me of myself when I first started out. Your ambitious nature will either be your springboard or your downfall."

The comment left an uneasiness in the pit of Todd's stomach. Having returned his focus to his computer screen, Mr. Franklin saw something he didn't like and closed his laptop violently. Several moments of intense, awkward silence filled the room. Todd, Amell, and Bianca were too terrified to move. Todd could feel his heart racing and a cold sweat began to pour down his face. The moment reminded him of many interactions with his wife.

"I know when someone has a solid business plan and when someone is blowing smoke," Mr. Franklin continued. His voice was calm and broke the tension in the room. Making eye contact with his guests he pointed at each one of them and said directly, "In the future, make sure you have all your ducks in a row. Don't try to sell me a pipe dream developed in 'your' reality," he warned. "A lot of livelihoods will be affected if this school fails, including mine. It's been around for more than 75 years, and I refuse to allow the doors to close on my watch." He paused. "I'll give you the green light to start, run, and manage the camp."

Todd couldn't believe what he'd just heard. They did it! **He** did it. He looked at Amell and Bianca. Both had blank stares and mouths agape. Todd knew they couldn't believe it, either.

"Obviously none of you seem to have a clue what you're doing," continued the superintendent. "This is a Christian school. I'm desperate; the school's desperate; and, judging by your persistence, Todd, you are *very* desperate.

Any extra revenue we can generate is a welcomed blessing. We're barely treading water, he continued. "I see your camp as a spark that can help us. It's the only idea we haven't tried in a while and you three are the only ones foolish enough to try to make it work. I pray your spark doesn't burn the school down, though the money we'd get from the insurance claim would be kind of nice," he joked dryly.

Forcing himself to smile, Mr. Franklin continued, "I pray that you three can provide this school with a miracle," and, for a second, his voice was warm and caring. But only for a second. His face turned cold, callous, and a deep scowl set in.

"If you fail," he cautioned ominously, "It will be the last thing the three of you do in affiliation with my school, or with any religious institution in the bi-state area."

His words sent shivers down each of their spines. The pressure was on. Not only did Todd need to make this successful for his benefit, but also for the benefit of the entire school. Instead of feeling scared, though, Todd felt motivated. He knew no one believed in his ability to succeed and the thought of being the school's savior, its superhero, was enticing.

"Now if you'll excuse me, I need to use the restroom, and you need to organize the pile of crap you just presented to me."

And just like that, Mr. Franklin ushered the trio out of his office.

There is no job so simple that it cannot be done wrong.

-Perrussel's Law

"The zoo?!" whined Bianca disappointedly, "Who wants to go to the zoo?"

"A field trip to a zoo is a great way for campers to observe animals and feel a connection to wildlife," Todd noted. "Plus, ours is free!"

All the painstaking planning they were doing was beginning to wear Todd down. He, Amell, and Bianca had spent the past 3 hours arguing at a time when they needed to be organizing the summer camp Superintendent Franklin had approved a couple weeks ago. Time was running out and the group had yet to agree on a single activity. Frustrated, tired, and annoyed Todd was starting to regret suggesting the idea of a summer camp. As desperate as Todd was for money he was starting to wonder if it would just be easier to go work for a summer camp somewhere else. The answer was a resounding yes. There was so much more to the planning aspect that he hadn't thought of.

Besides suggesting a summer camp and getting it approved, Todd was getting overwhelmed by Mr. Franklin's questions concerning the camp. He realized he hadn't even considered a lot of the business aspects of running the summer camp. At the beginning, he'd been confident he would be able to
figure it out, but he'd become less confident in less than two months. He had zero confidence
in his coworkers' commitment to helping. He was growing frustrated with Bianca's lack of compromise when it came to agreeing with the field trips the campers would take, and with Amell's lack of leadership in making

suggestions. Nevertheless, the comfort of a situation he knew and the ease of manipulating
the system and stealing extra hours by finishing tasks slowly was an added bonus.

Unfortunately, planning the camp wasn't a task he wanted to take his time doing at the moment. He was tired. He had a busy night ahead of him at the warehouse. His stomach was doing flips, and his nerves shot worrying over the potential mood Sharon would be in when he got home. There were a lot of lesson plans, activities, and budgets the trio had not begun to plan. And time was running out. Todd worried his co-workers didn't have the same sense of urgency he did. Todd had a lot riding on this. He needed the money. He *always* needed the money. A financially successful camp may lead to a raise for the upcoming school year.

It had already been a long day. The three of them had waited until the end of the school day to work on the camp. Todd had to be at his warehouse job in less than four hours. He needed to be using this time to rest. Worse yet, after three hours, the trio were no closer to having a concrete plan than they'd been when they started.

"Who wants to spend the hottest part of the day sweating and smelling animal poop? Why can't we find a field trip indoors, like a mall?" Bianca asked.

"Well, Bianca, for two reasons," Todd said patronizingly. "One, unless they just window-shop, a trip to the mall will cost parents more money. And two, our field trips should have a little education mixed in. A trip to the zoo means the campers can learn about the animals' habitats. Besides, he added, "Who doesn't want to see a bunch of cute, cuddly animals?"

44

Todd himself didn't really care to see any cute, cuddly animals, either. His idea? Plan the field trips and stay on campus with the campers who hadn't gotten their permission slips signed. Maybe rest inside the library. Todd hated going to the zoo mostly for the reason Bianca had just given. The smell! He also hated playing the where're-the-animals game. Many of the animals on display were nocturnal; they hid during the day. Trying to find where they were hiding did not interest Todd at all. He wanted entertainment from the animals. He wanted to see a tiger chase down a rabbit or squirrel. He wanted to see the monkeys swing from limb to limb. If he wanted to see a mammal being lazy, he could just stay home and observe his wife and stepson. Plus, he thought, zoos are for kids. The food and the face painting were there to attract and entertain children. Even the shows are geared for kids. Todd also hated the amateur zoo photographers. There always seemed to be paparazzi parents willing to knock over someone else's kid to take a once-in-a-lifetime picture of an animal doing absolutely nothing. Or those adults who found it funny watching animals having sex. Who cares?, Todd thought.

"If you really **must** know, Todd," Bianca replied, "Those 'cute, cuddly animals' actually suffer adverse effects from unnatural conditions. Zoos are psychologically and physiologically damaging to animals," she continued. "Zoo breeding programs create dependencies and changes in animal behavior due to living in captivity. No animals have ever been harmed shopping at a mall," she said sarcastically.

Amell snickered, but Todd was speechless.

"How about bowling?" Amell asked. He felt changing the subject was the only way to broker a peace between Bianca and Todd. "It's indoors, it's cheap, and it's fun! he continued"

Bianca shrieked. "YUUUUCCK!! You want me to put my manicured toes inside a pair of communal shoes that someone *sweat* in?! Ummm…no. Those shoes have bowling alley wax buildup, chalk chemicals from the spray they use on them, cigarette butts and ashes on the soles, greasy fried food, old chewing gum, and other disinfectant sprays permeating the faux leather. And sweat. Did I mention sweat? I will **not** have someone else's foot sweat on my feet," she declared. "Duh, that's how people get athlete's foot," she added. "No way," she concluded.

"Maybe we can see if Christian Louboutin makes red-bottomed bowling shoes," Todd shot back.

"How about the Botanical Garden?" Amell suggested.

"Allergies!" Bianca replied.

"Okay…" he sighed. "We're not getting anywhere with the field trips. Let's move on to staffing," he suggested. "Where are we going to get workers for this camp?"

"I've been thinking about this," Todd said. He was growing impatient with Bianca and Amell. Their inclusion was holding him back. The interruptions and disagreements were delaying any progress in the camp's development. If they needed to be involved there was going to have to be some sort of compromise or the camp isn't going to work.

"We can ask teachers if they'd be interested in working this summer. I know they'll probably say no, though, so we can look for potential employees who need extra money since we can't pay anything over minimum wage."

"How many people should we hire?" asked Bianca.

"That depends on the number of campers we have," Amell answered. "I think the law states we have to have one adult per every ten kids."

"That doesn't sound like enough. Who are we going to have to clean, cook lunch, be a nurse, work front desk, and teach your glorified summer school," she teased.

"I've been thinking about that, too," Todd replied. "Remember what I suggested to Mr. Franklin?" he continued. "Most camps and daycares have a cut-off at age 12, right? But most parents don't feel comfortable leaving 12-, 13-, and 14-year-olds by themselves, right?"

"I guess," Amell said.

Todd continued, "Adults who lost everything in the recent market crash are taking most of the summer jobs because they have work experience and an established work ethic, right?"

"Where are you going with this?" Amell asked. It was clear he wanted Todd to get to the point.

"Let's open our camp up to early teens. We charge them to be volunteers," Todd suggested. "They'll be our cleaning crew, front desk personnel, and our go-fers."

"Gophers?" asked Bianca. "Like the animal?"

"Yes, Bianca. Like the animal," Todd answered, rolling his eyes. "No. they 'go for' this, they go for that. So they're called go-fers. We charge parents for the opportunity their kids will get to garner work experience and a work ethic while we provide them with a safe environment for the summer. Plus, they can use their volunteer hours as community service hours."

"I love it, I love it, I love it!" Amell said excitedly.

"Why would any kid volunteer to do this?" Bianca asked cynically.

"Because their parents would make them,!" Todd responded. "Plus, it adds to our customer base while
setting us apart from other area camps."

"I like it," started Amell. "It's settled," he continued.

"Wait!" Bianca interjected. "I designed a t-shirt for the campers to wear!" She pulled a navy blue t-shirt from her expensive Hermès Birkin bag, proudly displaying her design. The school's logo was on the upper right lapel and the back read A.S.A.P. Summer Camp. The phrase "Walk in faith, Lead by example" marched across the shirt under the camp's name.

Todd was upset. He wanted to continue to complain about her lack of participation, but she'd actually contributed something meaningful. In truth, he was more upset with himself that he hadn't come up with the idea of campers sporting a t-shirt that advertised both the camp and the school.

"I also have some that read "Staff" on the back so campers can tell who to

48

go to if they need assistance" Bianca added. "And I can design one with the word "Volunteer on it."

"I love it!" exclaimed Amell. He paused for a moment, then said, "I think the best way to operate the camp is for Todd to be our activities director and Bianca to be in charge of staffing. Good meeting!" he said as he headed for the door. "I'm on my way to do some more unnecessary wedding stuff."

Before Todd could argue Amell's decision, he was out the door with Bianca in tow.

What was *that*?!, he thought. An **activities** director?! What even *is* that? Todd was mostly mild-mannered, but he became enraged after hearing Amell's decision. I teach career development. I manage a staff of teamsters at night. Bianca has never even had a real job! Why does *she* get to be in charge of staffing instead of me?! Even though he was fuming over Amell's decision, Todd decided to head home.

He normally spent his commute thinking about how many work hours he'd put in for the day, how many he has left at his warehouse job, and how many more hours he needs to work in order to be able to pay his bills. His main focus usually centered on how long he could nap before he had to go to his next job.

However, today all he can think about is Amell's decision to make him the camp's activity director. Has he
forgotten the camp was *my* idea? he wondered. Who better than me is qualified to find the staffing we need for the camp I'm envisioning?

Staffing! How does he think BIANCA is more qualified than I am to be in

charge of staffing?! She can barely get to work on time! Even when she *does* get there when she's supposed to she either leaves early or hides so she doesn't really have to do anything. What type of staffing boss could she possibly
be if she herself is a poor example of an employee?! Todd continued to fume over the issue, but as he got closer to home another thought took its place...

Sharon!

Suddenly, his feelings of anger gave way to dread. The closer he got to his house the more Todd wanted to puke. His hands turned cold, his stomach became unsettled, and he couldn't breathe. He was hyperventilating. Todd was having a panic attack. Tears flooded his eyes. He was shattered. Tired. Tired from work, and tired of his marriage.

It had been a couple of days since he and Sharon last talked. The tension in the house was thick, suffocating, even. The silent treatment she was giving him was deafening. Living with Sharon had become unbearable. He thought of leaving her constantly. But Todd was stubborn. He thought he could make it work, *should be able* to make it work. Most of his friends and family argued that it wouldn't work and he wanted to prove them wrong, not because he was in love with Sharon, but because no one believed they could have a successful marriage. Todd took it as a personal challenge. He was determined to find success where others saw inevitable failure. He used the vows he made in church as an excuse to fight. He was fighting *for* her, but she was fighting him. Rolling with the punches isn't the best strategy when your spouse throws brutal haymakers.

It was the same with the summer camp: no one seriously thought it would be successful, and this motivated Todd to prove everyone wrong.

Todd hid how unhappy he was with Sharon. He was depressed, but he generally didn't open up to others about his issues at home. It wasn't anyone else's business. If he was being honest with himself, though, he was mostly embarrassed. Men rarely show signs of weakness, he thought, and expressing his feelings was a definite sign of weakness. He needed the task of organizing the summer camp as a distraction from his home life.

Lately, Todd was having thoughts of being the bigger person and apologizing to Sharon for whatever it was he'd done, but the blame he accepted often led to Sharon wanting to reiterate why she was right. Worse, she wouldn't stop bringing up how he was wrong. How she knew more than him because she was older. Sharon loved to fight, and Todd's refusal to engage with her made matters worse. Todd couldn't understand how not fighting with his wife would result in a fight, but it happened all the time. Sharon would usually complain while Todd sat there and let her berate him. He wanted discussions and compromise. She wanted to win.

"Say something!" Sharon would demand, but Todd was cautious about sharing his feelings with her. If he
expressed how troubled he was by something she said or did, she would get upset. She'd play the victim. Todd would then have to console her and apologize for making her feel bad because he didn't want to share his feelings. If he was right when they quarreled, Sharon would continue the fight until she beat him into submission. And if he surrendered Sharon gloated over her victory, making him feel crappy. Todd hated the phrase "happy wife, happy life." It left no room for the man to have any happiness.

He tries to remember that Sharon had been abused most of her life. She was abused as a child. She was abused in school. She was abused in previous relationships. It's all she knows. And she thinks his reluctance to fight, yell, and scream means that Todd doesn't love her because he's not fighting for her. This baffled Todd to no end. She claims that fighting shows emotion so Todd surmised that her putting holes in the walls and kicking down doors meant she loved him a whooole lot. Maybe he could convince Hallmark to make a card that said "I'll kick down doors to be with you."

Because he was scared of his wife, Todd would leave rooms to get away from her. He simply didn't know what she was capable of, and didn't want to hang around to find out. It just wasn't in his nature to argue with her. Not all the time, anyway. It was exhausting, and all it did was add more tension to his life. He understood matters had to be dealt with, but not by having the same argument over and over again. He barely had enough energy as it was; being with Sharon drained the last bit he had left.

Todd saw his wife as a vampire: she was sucking the life out of him. She sensed when he was too weak to fight and that's when she'd put the pressure on. Todd would walk away. He needed to breathe. He needed to decompress. He needed to get his thoughts together so they could attempt to have a civil conversation. He was being attacked. He would run, she would pursue him. She wanted to be heard and would force her argument upon him. The more withdrawn he became, the more she'd attack. Finally, when he could take no more, Todd would say whatever his wife wanted to hear. An argument with Sharon was like sinking in quicksand. He was trapped with no one around to rescue him. The pressure of the quicksand pushed on his chest. It became harder to breathe. The more he struggled, the worse it became.

Todd would often fantasize about his wife passing away and leaving him in peace. He'd taken a vow of 'til death do we part. But since she was a heavy smoker Todd hoped she would part sooner rather than later. These thoughts sickened him. This was his **wife**. He shouldn't be looking forward to her demise.

Maybe her anger is my fault, he thought. Maybe if I had better jobs she wouldn't feel so lonely. Maybe if I yelled back, she would know I loved her. I should help her stop smoking, not hope it kills her. Todd suspected his wife was an alcoholic, too. Since he was always working, though, he couldn't be sure. His only clues were the bottles of Jose Cuervo he'd find lying around the house. That part he didn't mind.
Much. But the only time there was any intimacy in their marriage is when she tasted of liquor. Actually, he *did* mind it. All Todd wanted to do is sleep. An intoxicated Sharon was wild in bed.

Pulling around the corner, Todd could see his house. And her car. Dammit!, he thought. She's home. The carport was littered with car parts, tools, antifreeze, and transmission fluid. Another one of Sharon's impromptu projects. Todd could say one thing for his wife: she was crafty. If there was a manual she could figure most problems out. This week she apparently wanted to be an auto mechanic. Todd was weary of letting his wife work on his car. He feared she would cut his brake lines and claim the resulting crash was an accident. Todd also feared that if the outside of the house was cluttered the inside was probably much worse. Todd didn't have the energy to deal with any of this.

Sharon was standing in the doorway wearing nothing but a smile and holding a shot glass. Great, thought Todd despondently. Just great.

Things get worse under pressure.
-Murphy's Law

Whap! The sound of Todd's head hitting the desk filled the teachers' lounge at school. Todd was beyond tired. Beyond exhausted. Everything hurt. He was struggling to keep his eyes open. Todd had missed his much-needed nap time last night. Sharon had decided they needed to "spend time together." That "time" was followed by another stressful night at the warehouse. After his shift, his last-ditch chance at sleeping between jobs had been foiled by his wife, who'd kept drinking while he'd been at work and apparently had decided that she wanted to have a baby. Todd may have had thirty minutes of sleep before Sharon said she wanted to "talk." Talk should be a code name for fight. Her talks meant she was going to voice her displeasure about something. If Todd didn't respond the way she wanted him to – something that felt impossible – she would get upset. In Todd's mind, talks always led to a fight. This time, Sharon was dismayed that Todd only lasted half a round before tapping out. His head pounded, his eyes crossed, and his body ached. Todd's whole body was going on strike.

He sat alone in the teachers' lounge waiting to meet with Amell and Bianca. He hoped it would be productive since the others had been anything but. They needed to *plan* something, not bicker, he thought. Time was running out. They had less than two months to organize something. Even so, Todd prayed Amell and Bianca would continue their trend of being late. Their tardiness would give Todd 15 – 20 minutes of peace, quiet, and rest. He relished any time that he had to himself with no one bothering him. At home, Sharon was always upset over something he did, didn't do, should have done, or was going to do. At school, students wanted him to think for them because they were too lazy to find the answers for themselves. At the warehouse he had to answer questions for upper management or give answers to his employees.

Todd thought of how divine it would be to nap right here, right now. It would definitely be more satisfying than last night's activities with Sharon. He longed for a moment to close his eyes. A quick nap right here, he proposed. But no, he decided. He's at work; he needs to be professional. He feared being labeled lazy. But he was so sleepy he almost didn't care what people thought of him at this point. He considered walking to the parking lot and taking a nap in his car but immediately nixed the idea. He didn't have the energy to walk that far.

His main focus should be organizing the summer camp, yet distracting thoughts of his dysfunctional marriage occupied his mind. Those thoughts along with nightly pressures at the warehouse were beginning to take their toll on his health. His most recent fight with Sharon began after Todd failed to perform during their private moment together. Todd tried to put himself in Sharon's shoes and wondered how he would feel if his partner just quit in the middle of intimacy. It was bound to happen, though. He wasn't engaged in the act at all. He couldn't focus on anything besides bills, the warehouse, and how little time was left to get the summer camp up and running.

Ever since the meeting with Mr. Franklin, Todd had realized no one shared his desire to make the camp a success. And last night with his wife, he had just lain there, thinking about all the things that still needed to be done. His mind also began to wander to the next warehouse audit. He tried to stay focused on Sharon, but he couldn't. He was pushing himself past his limits. His failed attempt to engage with his wife was another example of his putting others' happiness above his own. He should had been open and honest with Sharon, but the façade he put up led to another argument, and a left hook to the jaw. Rehashing the events in his mind now drained him so much that he had to fight the temptation to drift off to sleep right there in the lounge.

WHAP! Todd's head hit the desk again. Was he dreaming? He got up to walk around the room. He considered doing some jumping jacks to get his blood flowing but his body quickly vetoed that. He needed to conserve all the energy he could.

Trying to keep his eyes open Todd glanced around the teachers' lounge. Just like the rest of the school, it was nothing special. In its former life, the room was an extended janitor's closet. Its walls, like every wall in the school, were a bland bluish gray. Prison walls were probably more vibrant. Fluorescent lights buzzed depressingly overhead. There was an old couch in the corner, but no one sat on it. It looked as if it would fall apart if anyone put any weight on it. There were two round tables in the middle of the room with seven mismatched chairs circling them. There was a coffee pot that Todd was pretty sure had never been cleaned. Between the unimpressive walls and the buzzing lights, Todd was starting to drift off again.

Todd tried to refocus himself on the types of activities he would plan for the campers. He thought about how he'd handle the preparedness portion, what the campers would do when they first arrived and were in the classroom. He thought about how they'd go to lunch or line up for field trips. Every detail needed to be attended to. Todd even thought about the lesson plans for each age group and how he'd align them to state educational standards. He was hoping the class preparedness portion would be the catalyst for students to become honor roll recipients. He envisioned the campers working on core classes. They'd start with simple math and reading assignments then progress to harder assignments. That should be easy!, he thought. I can search the internet for worksheets or pillage the supply closet for older-edition workbooks.

When it came to field trips, Todd organized a swimming outing every Monday. The local pool had group rates, and he surmised that every kid likes to go swimming. Every Thursday would be their bowling outing. It's an activity that's cheap and indoors.

Todd intended to have a theme for each week, complete with a corresponding field trip on Wednesdays.
Week one's theme was going to be animals. A trip to the zoo was his first choice even after Bianca's
animal rights tirade, to further spite Bianca, Todd added a person that brings exotic animals to schools. Let the campers hold the animals, he planned. The handler could teach the campers, through hands-on interactions. Learning and exploring, up close, you can't beat that thought Todd.

Week 2's theme would be Mother Nature. Staff could teach the campers about climate change, plants, and ecosystems and take a field trip to the Botanical Gardens.

Week 3's theme was water. The field trip would be a riverboat lunch cruise.

Week 4....

WHAP! Todd awoke after violently slamming his head on the desk. Drool ran in a path down his face. Embarrassed, Todd realized he had been sleeping for quite a while. The back of his throat was sore. Todd guessed that meant he had been snoring, too.

"Late night?" asked a voice from behind.

57

Startled, Todd sprang up, fully alert now with his adrenalin pumping, but he could only catch a glimpse of a person walking out of the lounge with a cup of coffee in hand.

How long was I out?, he wondered Who caught me napping? But before he could try to figure it out he heard voices coming from down the hall.

"Todd, we're going to need your help!" exclaimed Amell as he entered the lounge.

Here it comes! Todd surmised, now fully alert. Ever since Amell placed Bianca in charge of staffing, Todd has been waiting to be asked to assist her with her job. Todd was excited that he was about to get to say "I told you so" to Amell.

"We're going to need you to interview the potential volunteers and staffers," Amell said.

Todd was shocked! He could not believe what was being asked of him. Not only was he not placed in charge of staffing – a position he thought he was best-suited for – *now* he has to pick someone else's staff'!

"You have a knack for reading people," Amell continued, interrupting Todd's thoughts.

Did Amell just say 'interview' or '*assist* with interviewing'? Todd questioned. Infuriated, Todd thought of hiring the worst staff he could find. He wanted Amell to see how inadequate Bianca is at her job. Todd wanted her to fail. Then he came to his senses. If Bianca fails, the camp fails. He couldn't afford failures.

"You want me to pick out her stuff?" Todd asked, puzzled. Amell's request was idiotic.

"Bianca has a lot on her plate," Amell explained. "She needs to devise a training program for the staff she hires," he continued. "And time is of the essence!"

A lot on her plate?? Todd thought. What about *my* plate? Sensing Todd's unhappiness, Amell placed his hand on Todd's shoulder.

"Reading people is your gift," he began. "We need all the help we can get, and I think your gift will help us find the perfect candidates to develop an excellent summer camp," he continued. "I know whoever you decide is qualified enough will make the camp successful."

Bravo! Todd thought. Way to stroke my ego as you screw me with Bianca's work.

"Can I count on you?" Amell asked.

Todd's gut instinct was to tell Amell to go eff himself. But his phone rang before he could get the words out, and when he saw it was Sharon, he knew he had to answer.

"Hello?" he answered.

"How are we supposed to have a baby if you can't last long enough to get the deed done?" Sharon questioned.

"I have to go," Todd replied and promptly hung up on his wife. He knew he was going to pay for it, and, sure enough, his phone began ringing again immediately. Again, it was Sharon. Todd ignored the call and tried to focus his attention on Amell.

Hesitantly, Todd said "Yes, you can count on me." He wasn't happy accepting this added job responsibility, but it gave him something to think about other than Sharon's insistence that they have a child. Todd wasn't even sure he *wanted* a baby, and now more than ever he needed to take control of every aspect of the camp to ensure its success.

Maybe it won't be so bad, Todd tried telling himself. What's the worst thing that can happen? Maybe one or two bad applicants. It could actually be fun, he thought, though he was pretty sure he was lying to himself. In the back of his mind, he knew all the good applicants had already accepted jobs with other camps. He knew that with less than two months before the start of camp, they would be scraping the bottom of the barrel.

Nothing is foolproof to a sufficiently talented fool.
-Stephen Hawking

Standing at the front of the classroom with Bianca and Amell, Todd was eager to address the group of students and adults that were there to be interviewed for the summer camp. It was almost a month since they'd been given approval to start and it finally felt as if things were progressing.

Today was to be the camp's career fair. Todd didn't quite agree with calling it that since the camp was only going to last 8 weeks, but he didn't make a big deal of it. Most of the applicants were former students who had taken his career development class. He taught his class so his students would be prepared for moments like this. Todd envisioned himself not as a teacher but as a guru imparting wisdom about how to build an attractive resume, how to fill out a job application properly, and how to market yourself during an interview. He spent a good chunk of each semester training his students on what to say; how to say it; and, of course, when to say it.

He painstakingly articulated the importance of body language. "Your nonverbal communication speaks
louder than verbal communication," he would say. And now here they were: so many of them coming out to apply for a position in the summer camp he'd developed. Todd couldn't wait to see how well they'd shine in a real-life scenario.

Despite his excitement, Todd was still perturbed that Amell put him in charge of the interviewing process after proclaiming Bianca the head of staffing. Todd thought that if someone was going to be in charge of staffing, that that person should also be in charge of hiring her own staff.

He was also distressed that he'd only had a week to organize the career fair. To his way of thinking, if he was going to be interviewing everyone the least Bianca could do was find prospective job seekers.

Luckily, he'd had enough time to send fliers home with students and advertise on job boards at grocery stores, libraries, and churches. He was disappointed with the setup, though. Everyone was herded into one classroom and had to wait there for a big introduction from the executive staff before they'd be brought into the library for their interviews. Todd had envisioned something a little more organized. He wanted the interviews to be conducted in an office setting, with appointments, and not in the first-come-first-served style he was having to settle for.

There were day-old donuts and juice left out for the guests, and only 15 chairs for the 30 interviewees who showed up. The classroom felt crowded.

Applicants segregated themselves by age: the adults stood on one side and the middle- and high school-aged kids on the other. Everyone was there for the same reason but no one really wanted to be. The students were forced to attend by their parents; and the adults, slightly desperate because the job market had been drying up, are there out of necessity. The students grew louder the more impatient they became. This angered Todd. He'd always taught his students that the interview began when you stepped onto the potential employer's property.

"Consider the possibility that they might be watching you," Todd would say. "They might watch to see how you conduct yourself when you think no one is watching." Based on their current conduct, the student applicants had either forgotten what he'd said or hadn't been paying attention to that lesson.

All the reasons he felt irritated were really just excuses. Todd was just in a bad mood. As usual, he
was tired from work and his life with Sharon. He didn't want to be at school all day, and judging from the group in front of him, the day would be a long one, especially without any help from Bianca or Amell.

I need to get this started, he thought as he made his way to the front of the crowded room.

"AHEM!" Todd cleared his throat to gather everyone's attention. "Good morning!," he said, mustering up the most authoritative voice he could. "My name is Todd Bethel . I'm the Activity Director for the ASAP Summer Camp. I would like to thank you all for attending our first-annual summer camp job fair." Todd turned, directing everyone's attention to a bunch of papers and pens neatly stacked on the table to his left. "I have a stack of applications here as well as some pens if you didn't bring one," he said.

A rush of students charged the table, grabbing applications and pens and making Todd's stack a disheveled mess. It was the first indication that they'd even been paying attention. Todd gestured for them to sit back down; he was angered that so many of the applicants were his former students, and yet they'd come completely unprepared. He made a mental note of those who took applications. Strike One, he thought.

"I would like to take this opportunity to Introduce you to Amell Jackson, our camp director, and Bianca Jackson, our camp staff director. Guys, would you like to say a few words before we begin?" Todd gestured for Amell and Bianca to address the room but hoped they would turn down the opportunity to speak. Todd was forcing his eyes to stay open and was desperate to get started. The sooner we begin the sooner it'll end, he kept telling himself.

But Amell was headed to the front of the room, so Todd could only hope that he'd keep it brief. He'd been watching Amell in front of crowds for years, though, so Todd knew his prayer wouldn't be answered.

In his best Robin-Williams-in-*Good-Morning-Vietnam* imitation, Amell shouted, "Gooooood morning, ASAP Summer Camp applicants! I would like to quickly say a few words."

"Quickly?," Todd whispered to himself. "Strap in! He never says anything quickly!"

"Thank you all for being here today," Amell said. "For those who don't know me, I teach Business Applications here."

Amell turned his attention to Todd. Pointing in his direction, Amell continued, "When Todd came to me to sell me on the idea of this camp, I was extremely hesitant," he started. "Having time to do things like swim, travel, and relax are one of the benefits of being a teacher," he continued. "Last summer, I went to Columbus, Ohio," he started, but Todd interrupted with a look and a quick clearing of his throat. "But that story will have to wait for another day," he concluded. "If you're hired to work with us this summer you will go through an extensive training program designed to prepare you for a successful camp."

"Do we *have* an extensive training program?" asked a confused Bianca.

"Seriously?" Todd started Todd angrily. He took a deep breath, looked at Bianca, and said, "you'd better hope to God we do since the staff is your responsibility."

"How detailed a training program do we need to have to help a bunch of brats play Red Rover," Bianca asked. "What type of extreme activities are you planning to have them do?," she questioned.

Todd rolled his eyes, wondering if he might actually see his own brain in the process.

Amell continued, "I expect a camp of excellence. Those hired to work in the educational preparedness portion will teach the subject matter with precision." He placed extra emphasis on the word 'precision.' "We need our campers to run through our doors every morning excited about what they're about to learn," he added. Todd was witnessing why they called Amell "Preach." "I want them to have the same excitement about reading, writing, and learning that they do with swimming, running, and jumping. Can I get an 'Amen?'" he crowed.

The room erupted with a robust amen. Ain't this something?, thought a jealous Todd. This man is hyping up the room talking about working hard. I couldn't even get a *cough* with my greeting!

"I demand excellence from the cleaning crew," Amell declared. "**My** cleaning crew will clean until the building is spotless!" and he jumped back as if he'd caught the Holy Ghost. "From the front to the back, you will clean every crevice and crack," he preached. The roomful of people hung on his every word, clapping and cheering with everything he said.

Todd felt like he was back in his grandmother's church. There the preacher would elongate his words, praise everything, and rhyme. He'd jump and turn, anything to keep the congregation engaged. And here was Amell, doing the same thing. And it was working, Todd thought.

"Everything you clean should look as fine as a sweaty bald man's head in the sunshine," Amell sang. Todd
wondered if Amell's head glistened in the sunshine the way he expected the floors to.

In a low tone, Amell launched into another scenario. "We have younger campers who will attend our camp, bless their hearts. They don't always have the best aim." Raising his voice, Amell shouted, "They aim for the bowl, but they hit the floor."

Todd was getting tired of Amell's poor rendition of a rapping preacher. In the time he'd spent preaching he could have passed the collection plate around four times *and* helped me with these interviews!

"Cleaning crew!," Amell started as he wiped the sweat off his brow, "You will mop up that yellow demon and have my floors smelling like a lemon," he preached.

Todd winced at that unnatural verse. This is getting ridiculous, he thought, but the applicants are eating it up.

"Bleach will be our bathrooms' best friend, if you know what I mean. Cleaning crew, everything from the
windows to the wall will gleam. Volunteers! You are like our interns. Too young to be staffers, too old to be campers. You're here to be mentors.

You'll be like older siblings to our campers, a shining example of how to act. You will lead by doing on field trips. You will correct any unruly behavior. Through your behavior, you will show other camps what they can truly be."

"He's doing your job," Todd whispered, deviating from his plan to stay silent.

"He's not helping me!," Bianca whined. "He's just standing up there making a fool of himself and whatever church he's mocking," she continued.

Drawing closer to Bianca, Todd positioned himself close to her ear. "He's telling everyone in the room how to do their job," he whispered harshly. "Any training you provide them will be a non-rap version of everything he just said," Todd continued. He gave her a sharp, angry look and walked a few steps away, just far enough that Bianca couldn't reply without interrupting Amell's sermon.

"High schoolers," Amell continued, "A lot of you are just joining the workforce and probably have zero job skills or experience, am I right?," he asked rhetorically. "By the time the summer is over, any job application you fill out will have years' worth of experience obtained in just 8 weeks. What I mean is that you're going to learn a lot under Bianca's expert tutelage," he added, gesturing in Bianca's direction.

"If this is your only job in life, how are you going to teach anyone anything?" Todd asked just loud enough that Bianca could hear.

"Still upset that I'm the staff leader?," Bianca probed with a slight grin on her face. "Besides, Old man, you can learn anything online," she retorted. "I got this job, didn't I?"

67

"You only got it because you're related to Amell. Eventually you're going to have to prove yourself in a real-life scenario," Todd said.

The truth was that although Amell and Bianca *were* technically related – through a marriage that ultimately failed – Bianca's employment started through her high school's Co-op program. She'd since graduated and Todd has been adamant about the school replacing her. He has regularly let it be known that he's not a fan of her constant tardiness and unprofessional behavior.

"I hope you kept the AOL CD-ROM discs you had as a kid because you're going to need to do a lot of that online research," Todd replied.

"AOL? Really?," Bianca retorted. "Where's the time machine you use to go back in time to dig up your outdated references?"

Amell quickly shot an evil glance at both Todd and Bianca. Neither had realized that their verbal sparring was getting increasingly louder. The look he gave them reminded both Todd and Bianca that he was still the boss.

Turning back to his audience Amell adopted a more welcoming expression and continued with his speech. "My activity staff," he began, "If you're hired, what do I ask you to provide our campers?"

Everyone in the classroom shouted excitedly in unison "EXCELLENCE!"

"NO!," Amell corrected." From my activity staff I expect creativity," he shouted. I want campers to have fun, exciting days. If this happens every day, I'll know the camp is being run with excellence."

68

Bianca whispered to Todd, "His wrapping up this *supposedly* short speech would be an example of
excellence."

Finally something she said I can totally agree with!, Todd thought. He hoped this was the end of their bickering. They were going to have to put their differences aside and work as a team if this was going to be a success.

"Bianca, is there anything you'd like to add before we get started?" Amell asked.

"Yes, Your Excellency," Bianca mocked. "Potential employees, Todd will be conducting interviews
next door in the library," she continued. "I hope everyone signed in; Todd will be calling your name in that order. Have a wonderful day!"

"Wait!" Todd exclaimed, confused. "Are you both leaving? I thought one of you would stay and
orchestrate this mess while I'm in the library."

"Unfortunately, I have to interview several photographers for my wedding," Amell answered. "But Bianca's here," he coddled.

"No I'm not!" Bianca interjected defiantly. "I have to get my hair braided."

I can't believe this!, Todd thought. "Not only do I have to plan eight weeks of activities, I also have to interview everyone who might work here?!
Dejected, Todd decided to rush through it so he could get home and take a nap.

The ideal resume will turn up one day after the position is filled.
-Murphy's Law

"Good morning!," Todd greeted the young man sitting in the chair across from him. The strong, herbaceous odor emanating from him made Todd sick. He held his breath, but feared the redolent odor of the weed he'd clearly been smoking was going to give him a contact high.

"Do you do drug tests?" the young man asked. Todd wondered if he could even see him through the deep redness in his eyes and was surprised he could form complete sentences being as high as he was.

Todd was taken aback by the question. He should have told the truth and said 'no,' but decided to lie and say 'yes.'

"Awwww, man! That's messed up!" the young man complained as he got up. He stumbled around a bit and then left.

Todd fanned the air, still holding his breath and hoping to clear out the smell. The last thing he needed was for the former students who'd come to apply to think he did drugs. Once he was sure the smell was gone, Todd asked for the next applicant to join him in the library.

"Good morning!," he greeted another young man. The young man handed Todd his resume and sat down. "Welcome to our job fair, Chad," Todd said as he looked it over. Todd knew of the young man but hadn't had him in class. He'd been popular among his classmates, though, especially the girls. Todd looked him up and down; something seemed off. *I don't think this is who I* think it is, Todd thought.

"Do you go to this school?," he asked, confused (and very embarrassed).

"Yes, sir, I do," Chad responded.

"Oh my gosh. I am so embarrassed! I've been calling you Jake all year!" Todd exclaimed.

"That *is* my name," the young man replied.

"Then who's Chad?," Todd asked.

"That's me!" the young man said.

Todd's head was spinning. He didn't know the name of the applicant sitting across from him, and the kid was frustrating him because he wasn't elaborating on any of his answers.

Finally, Todd asked for clarification. "Who **are** you?," Todd demanded

"It's me, sir!" the young man answered.

"What is your name?," Todd asked impatiently. "Is Chad a nickname? A middle name?"

"No, sir," the kid said. This time silence filled the room as Todd waited for an elaboration. Nothing. "Then **why** does your application and resume both say 'Chad'," he finally demanded. "Can you please explain why you don't appear to know your own name?"

71

"Well, sir, I copied and pasted the resume off the internet. It belonged to some guy named Chad. I didn't have time to change it because my mom was yelling for me to do the dishes. It was just easier to
write Chad on the application since the resume says Chad."

Todd had had it. He now regretted fanning away the previous applicant's aroma of weed; he needed something strong to calm his nerves after the round of *Who's on First?* he'd just played with Chad. Or Jake. Or whatever this kid's name was.

"Do any of the highlights on this resume belong to you?," Todd asked, deflated.

"Nope," Jake replied.

Todd continued inspecting the resume, which listed "Jake's" address as being in California. They were, of course, in Missouri.

"We'll be in touch," Todd said, hurriedly ushering Jake out of the library. "Next person, please!"

Another young man walked into the library. Todd didn't recognize him.

"Good day, sir," he said.

"Your resume says your name is….," Todd hesitated before he read the name: Chad. "Chad, Is this your real name?"

"No, sir" the applicant responded.

"Both your resume and application say 'Chad'," Todd sighed wearily. He felt a sense of Déjà vu come over him.

"Yes, sir," answered Chad #2. Silence filled the room. Is he going to say anything?, wondered Todd. He waited....and waited....and waited, wondering if he should say something or just wait him out. Glancing at his watch, though, he wondered if he'd be waiting all day.

Finally he couldn't take it anymore. "So are you going to tell me who you are?," he asked, exasperated.

"I'm Ryan," responded Chad #2.

"Do you mind telling me why your resume and application say 'Chad'?" Todd asked.

Ryan tensed in his chair before answering. "I...umm...," he started. Todd was growing ever more impatient and gestured for Ryan to hurry up with his answer. "I forgot to bring a resume so I copied someone else's."

"Thank you, Ryan, we'll let you know," Todd said, perturbed.

Todd was almost at his wits' end. He walked into the classroom where the potential employees were waiting to be called for their turn to interview. "Listen up!," he started. "Any of you young men who copied and pasted Chad's resume: throw it away and start over."

Five Chads got up and threw away their resumes.

Todd couldn't believe what was happening. He wanted so badly to share "Chad-gate," as he'd decided to call it, with someone. Unfortunately, his coworkers had abandoned him and his wife was still boycotting him. He felt so alone. He wished he had the type of relationship with his wife that he could share funny stories, share his pain. And Todd *was* in pain. He constantly had a feeling of impending doom. Throughout the day, he would find himself exhaling deeply as the mounting stress threatened to overwhelm him. He wasn't happy, and his zest for life had been zapped.

What was there to be motivated *for*? he would often ask himself. I live to work, he thought. He wanted to complain to someone, but he'd convince himself that men aren't supposed to do that. When he struggled to get up for work he would tell himself to man up. When the stress would cause him to lose his appetite and his shoulders to ache (pain killers had stopped working long ago), he'd push harder to make it through the situation he was in. He wouldn't slow down; he'd move faster. He was past his breaking point, but it didn't matter, so he swallowed his unhappiness.

"Next!," he shouted.

A young lady walked into the library. She looked like she was thirteen years old. Todd guessed she was applying for the volunteer position. He remembered thirteen being a much simpler time in his life, a time in which the stress of his responsibilities wasn't slowly killing him. He wanted to tell the little girl in front of him not to do it, to run away. Enjoy her youth.

At least her name won't be Chad, Todd chuckled to himself. He looked down and read the name on her resume. It was Chad. Peering intently at her, Todd spoke very slowly.

74

"What is your name?," he asked.

"Lori," she answered.

"Well, Lori," Todd started patronizingly, "Were you in the classroom a moment ago when I asked anyone who had Chad's resume to throw it away and start over?"

"Yes," she answered meekly.

"Why didn't you do as I instructed?," Todd asked.

"Because you just asked just the guys to do that," she answered matter-of-factly.

Todd wanted to snap. He no longer cared about Lori's youth. Let her suffer like us adults, he thought. Antics like these are what is causing adults to age faster than we should, he concluded. But he couldn't crush her spirit. The precious smile plastered on her face and her look of innocence were far too charming.

"Fine," he responded. "It says here you have experience with childcare," he said, deciding to continue with the interview.

"Yes, sir," Lori responded. "I have to watch my little sister. I do everything for her," she continued. "You know, help her get up in the morning, play the games she wants to play. And I have to sacrifice my time to help her get ready for bed at night. You know, bathe her. Do I have to bathe anyone here?," Lori asked Lori

"Definitely not," Todd answered.

"Oh, that's good," Lori replied, though I could definitely do it," she added. "I'm getting really good at it, too. I almost drowned my little sister a couple of times, but she survived," she said proudly.

"Okay!," Todd shouted uncomfortably. "We'll let you know," he said.

Raking his hands through his hair Todd started to question if he truly wanted kids anymore. The several kids he'd interviewed so far had been a more effective form of birth control than any prophylactic on the market.

"Next!," Todd shouted.

A new applicant walked in the door. He was dressed formally, sporting a dress shirt, clip-on tie, neatly-pressed slacks, and polished shoes. Finally!, Todd thought. Someone who shows some promise!

"Hello!," Todd said to the young man.

"Hello," he replied, handing Todd his application and resume. Todd was ecstatic when he looked down and saw the name 'John.' Whew! No more Chads.

"John," Todd started, "If I hired you, what could you provide to the team that displays excellence?"

John stared blankly at Todd, not saying a word. After a few moments, Todd

76

restated the question in a different way.

"John, why should I hire you?"

"Why do you keep calling me John?," the young man asked.

"Isn't that your name? That's what your application and resume say," Todd responded.

"No, my name is Chad," John said. "You told all the guys whose resumes said 'Chad' on them to throw them away, so I did. I found this guy named John's in the classroom and decided to use it. See?," he emphasized, "I can follow directions. That's why you should hire me."

Todd was dumbfounded. "Oh!," he said mockingly, "Is *that* why I should hire you?," he asked.
"I mean... I don't know," Chad replied, annoyed. "I'm only applying because my dad said I had to get my lazy ass up this summer. He said that since I sleep a lot in class I should have a lot of energy this summer," he continued. "If I don't have to be here early I think I can stay awake my entire shift."

"Do you have a hard time staying awake?," Todd asked. He wondered if maybe John suffered from narcolepsy. He wanted to ask, but knew he couldn't legally.

"Nah," John answered nonchalantly. "I just get bored listening to teachers talk," he added. "Like that summer school portion of the camp? I *know* I won't stay awake for that boring stuff."

"NEXT!," Todd shouted. "John, you can go," he said, irritated.

As John exited the library, an attractive woman entered. John looked like he was going to start drooling. "Ooh! Can I work with *her*?!" he asked.

The woman sat down across the table from Todd. She wore a tight white blouse that was only half buttoned. Todd fought to keep his eyes focused away from her chest which meant making eye contact a challenge.

"Good morning!," the woman started. "My name's Terri."

Todd greeted her with an awkward grin. "Hi, um, Terri," he said, his voice squeaking as if he was going through puberty. Todd cleared his throat and started again. "I see you have your degree in education. Will working at a religious institution be a problem?," he asked.

Todd was ecstatic to be interviewing someone not named, or affiliated with the name, Chad. But he needed to address Terri's comfort level when it came to religion to see if she would be a good fit for the school. Todd remembered how the school board had bombarded him with religious questions until someone finally blurted out, "We want to know if you're a heathen before we hire you."

Todd presumed the board would probably call Terri a jezebel because of her attire. The women they usually hired dressed ultra conservatively and they were forbidden from showing too much skin. Shorts and skirts had to come to the top of the knee. No form-fitting or revealing attire was allowed. This included leggings, jeggings, and plunging necklines.

Todd wasn't exactly sure why this rule had been enacted. Far from being a fashionista, or even looking physically fit, Todd preferred comfort to style. If it were up to him, he would wear sweatpants to teach.

Thinking back, he's heard principals recite 1 Timothy 2:9-10, 1 Peter 3:2-5, and 1 Corinthians 11:2-16 to female students at nauseam. He'd never paid enough attention to know why, but he knew being too revealing was bad.

Todd wanted to shield Terri from these kinds of questions and so tried to determine if she was there to teach or to be a temptress.

Bianca's attire has been the topic of many discussions, too, so Todd kept his simple: khakis and a collared shirt. He didn't want to draw any more attention to himself than he had to.

"Definitely not," Terri responded, bringing Todd back to his original question about working in a religious setting. "I believe in the Spirit," she continued.

"Welcome aboard!" Todd exclaimed Todd. "I'll keep in touch."

Todd was eager to put someone with Terri's credentials to work in his educational-preparedness program. He figured she was too qualified to pass up.

An excited Terri jumped up and ran around the table, hugging Todd appreciatively. Todd couldn't help it; he felt comforted, even though he knew that's not why Terri was offering the hug. He could feel his stress melt away and didn't want to let her go.

It had been ages since someone had held him affectionately. The last hug Sharon had given him had been a side hug, and he couldn't even remember

79

why she'd given him *that*. There were no romantic feelings between him and Terri, of course, though Terri's embrace made Todd long for the comfort of someone to love, who'd love him in return. He craved someone who would hold him up when he was down, who'd say 'It'll be okay,' or 'I support you.'

He ended the hug abruptly and sat down. Terri flashed a smile and waved goodbye. Todd was saddened by her departure but called in the next applicant, a student named Teresa.

Why her?, he groaned to himself. Todd knew Teresa from the school year. On paper, she was the perfect applicant. She was the student council vice president, was on the honor roll, was involved in several clubs, and was taking all honors classes. The only knock against her, was, well... her personality. If "she's a Karen" could be a person, Teresa would definitely be her. She was an obnoxious, angry, entitled young woman. Todd couldn't remember ever seeing her with any friends, and she never smiled. She was an extremely focused student who was determined to achieve her goals by any means necessary. Todd thought Teresa was exactly what the camp needed; he just didn't want to deal with her.

Teresa's mother was the same way: Her mother would come to every event, cheer Teresa on, and provide an analysis of everything she could have done better. Teresa was biracial, sixteen years old, and parked her brand new Land Rover in the teachers' parking lot. Her reasoning? She tutored the basketball team and felt as important to students' success as a salaried teacher. Todd had even overheard Teresa once tell Superintendent Franklin that she deserved to be on the payroll. Her argument was that a tutor is essential when a teacher has failed to communicate the material in a way that the recipient was able to retain it. Her tutoring was instrumental in allowing several star athletes to participate in their respective sports, thus ensuring winning seasons. She argued that winning sports teams generate additional revenue for the school, that since she made the school money that they should invest in her, as well.

Teresa had been so convincing that Superintendent Franklin had actually considered her request. He then fired the teachers whose students needed tutoring. This motivated Todd to step up his teaching methods.

"Good morning," Teresa greeted Todd nonchalantly.

Todd didn't want to waste any time and Todd jumped directly into the interview questions: "If I hired you, what could you provide the team that displays excellence?," he asked.

"Tooooodd!," Teresa whined, disappointed. She acted as if they were colleagues. This angered Todd. She was a **student**. In his eyes, calling a teacher by their first name was extremely disrespectful. "Is that the most challenging question you can come up with?," she asked. "I'm an honors student with a 4.0 grade point average. I am the vice president of my student council, the president of my Speech and Debate Club, in Choir, Orchestra, and part of National Honors Society. I volunteer with the Red Cross, am in Latin Language Club, Drama Club, Photography Club, Yearbook Club, Book Club, and I play on the Mathletes and Robotics teams. I think I can handle a more mature question for this interview," she snapped.

As Teresa was spouting off the list of organizations she was involved with Todd realized why she didn't have any friends: she was too busy for them. He also surmised that she was able to be the president of so many clubs because there was such low enrollment and interest in those clubs at school.

Feeling challenged, Todd thought of the most difficult interview question he could. He respected her zeal, but hated her criticism of his interviewing techniques. I got it!, he thought. Smirking, Todd asked "What's been your biggest failure?"

Not a hard question, he thought to himself. He was hoping to trap Teresa into revealing job-related mistakes that could cost her employment consideration.

With a huge grin on her face, Teresa replied confidently - and with more than a little arrogance - "I don't view anything I do, correct or incorrect, as a failure. Every moment in life is a teachable moment. And gaining knowledge is always a positive experience," she concluded.

Todd was amazed at how quickly Teresa was able to come up with such an intelligent response. She was able to articulate it without stutter, stammer, or filler words.

Teresa stared at Todd knowing she had bested him. Todd remained silent and shocked as if the two of them were in a chess match and Todd was trying to get out of checkmate.

"Thank you," Todd said. "We'll let you know."

"I'll anticipate your call," Teresa replied.

Todd knew Teresa was qualified to work the camp, but he was concerned about having her as a staff member since she wasn't 18. He worried about the legal ramifications of having a minor alone with other minors. He was

82

also apprehensive about her one day taking his job. He could see that she was destined for greatness, and had the determination to be a legend.

Teresa stood, placed her hands on the table, leaned over, and looked directly into Todd's eyes. "My age will not be a problem," she declared as if she could read Todd's mind. "I'm wise beyond my years and plan to run my own school one day. I'm going to be a superintendent. Teaching is my passion. Your summer preparedness program is the experience I need to get started achieving my dreams. I will NOT let anything stop me," she said emphatically.

He wasn't sure why, but Todd felt threatened by her declaration.

"Remember what I said!" Teresa called as she exited the library.

Todd wondered if Sharon had acted like Teresa at her age. They both have that get-out-of-my-way, explosive demeanor about them. Maybe the similarities between the two were why Todd wasn't fond of Teresa.

Frustrated, Todd leaned back in his chair, and glanced down at his watch. Shit!, he nearly said aloud. I've spent all morning interviewing a bunch of clueless brats and only one of them had a smidge of qualification. Amell would be insane to hire any of them to be volunteers, he thought. I wouldn't hire any of them to babysit a blade of grass.

Sitting there thinking, Todd struggled to find answers as to how the teens he'd interviewed functioned in their daily lives. They'd take everything so literally and couldn't think for themselves! Todd wondered if he'd been that bad as an adolescent. Nah, I doubt it, he decided. Todd wondered if grumpy old men were grumpy because of the next generation. I can't believe these parents pay all this money for their

kids to go to this private school and they have the audacity to walk around as clueless as they are! Kids today have all the answers readily available, but they're too lazy to do the research. I hope they all win the lottery and hire someone to care for them, Todd thought. Otherwise they're all going to have a pretty rough life.

This revelation motivated Todd to work even harder to teach his students to be better prepared for the workforce. He wanted his students not only to learn how to conduct themselves in an interview, but in life, even though Todd was still trying to figure that part out himself. I understand them being nervous, but those kids were utterly confident in their moronic incompetence. How could you copy and paste a resume and not even read it or change it so it had **your** name on it?! Todd was beyond himself. He was so frustrated and so lost in his thoughts that he didn't see the couple approach.

If the shoe fits, it's ugly.
-Golds Law

"'scuse me! Sir! Excuse me!"

Todd's thoughts were interrupted by a middle-aged woman and a slightly older man. Todd was so deep in thought that he was actually startled by their presence.

"Is this where I come to interview for the summer camp counselor position?," the woman asked.

A part of Todd was thrilled that someone with life experience finally came to interview, but that excitement was quickly extinguished by the woman's attire. Throughout the school year Todd would teach his students how to conduct themselves in an interview. His first lesson on the subject was that appearance equals perception. If you want to impress your prospective future employer you should dress for success. Dress as though you're interviewing for *their* job, he would teach.

Apparently, this lady hadn't taken a course like his. She was dressed in a wrinkled t-shirt that featured Nirvana's *NeverMind* album cover, the one with the uncensored baby. Todd could not believe that this older lady missed the signs on the campus alerting visitors that this private school was a Christian organization. Maybe she and her escort missed the various religious emblems displayed
throughout the campus, or maybe the scriptures that graced the hallways of the building were somehow camouflaged by the crosses hanging every ten feet.

How she could continue to walk past all those relics and still think wearing the t-shirt was the proper attire for this event baffled Todd. It showed her complete lack of attention to her
surroundings, and it meant that watching kids wouldn't be an environment she was well-suited for. Maybe she just didn't care. Ballsy, and still not a position she would excel in.

The woman's jeans were worn and torn, and not in a stylish way. And to top it off, she wore flip-flops. The footwear clearly hadn't been chosen to show off her perfectly-manicured toes, however. Quite the opposite was true, actually, as her feet were in desperate need of moisturizer and nail clippers.

Her companion wasn't dressed much better. He, too, wore an offensive album cover on his t-shirt: the one of David Bowie as a half dog, half naked man flanked by two blue women. On his bottom half, the man wore camo cargo shorts and Crocs. Why are they dressed like this, Todd wondered? Were these the only clothes they owned? Are they seriously here for a job? Maybe they're on parole and just need to go to a certain number of interviews per week to stay out of jail.

Nah…. This was a prank; it **had** to be a prank. Todd waited for someone to jump out and yell "We got you!" But then they sat down. Strike Two, Todd thought. Even his students knew to continue standing until they were offered a seat.

"How may I help you?" Todd asked.

"She's here for a job," the man said.

Wait. Todd thought to himself. Did he just answer for her?

"Do either of you have any experience working with kids?," he asked. He waited for one of them to hand him a resume or application. Nothing.

"What type of kids?," the woman asked.

This is definitely a prank, Todd thought. Who asks what type of kids? How do I even answer that question? Ignoring her question, Todd started to go over the job details, secretly hoping the couple would realize they were in the wrong spot.

"We're a Christian-based summer program," Todd started. "Our program combines summer camp with course preparedness to…"

"Are you trying to say this is a summer school job?," the older man interrupted with a hearty laugh? "Did you hear that, honey?," he continued. "He's suckering parents into paying for summer school!"

Todd sighed, trying to think of a polite way to end the interview. Looking in the woman's direction, he spoke. "I forgot to ask your name."

"It's Gerri," the older man replied, giving Todd a slight smirk. He was a tall man, possibly in his 60's, Todd guessed. He stood around 6'3 and weighed close to 300 pounds. His salt-and-pepper hair was cut short but still managed to be disheveled. He spoke with an exaggerated sense of arrogance.

By stark contrast, his partner, aside from the fact that they'd arrived together, showed zero signs of being a partner. She appeared bashfully

demure, so much so that Todd guessed it was her partner who'd dressed her in her pornographic shirt. She carried herself as a former tomboy whose days of athleticism had long passed her by. All that remained now was her highlighter-yellow blonde hair, cropped into a tomboy style and parted on the side, and a nose that was slightly off-kilter, possibly from having been broken a couple times. Todd guessed that she was in her mid-40s. Judging by her frame, Todd surmised that she'd been a softball player, or had maybe done field events. He chuckled to himself. She reminded him of the headmistress in the movie *Matilda*, Miss. Trunchbull. He could see her as a former shot
putter or hammer or javelin thrower who had now been relegated to throwing bad students over fences.

"What qualifications do you have that would be an asset for our summer program?," Todd asked, continuing with the interview.

The older man reached into his pocket and pulled out a folded piece of paper and handed it to Todd. Todd unfolded the paper to reveal Gerri's resume. Strike Three, he thought. Not only was he unsure which of the pair was Gerri, who folds up a resume? A resume was supposed to be a piece of paper that showcases your work experience and best qualities, not something you fold and hand to an interviewer as though you're passing a note to a friend in class.

Glancing at the resume, Todd realized Gerri had quite an extensive education. "I see that you went to several prestigious universities and studied a variety of subjects," he said. He forgot how disappointed the couple had made him feel up to this point. The list of achievements on the piece of paper washed them away.

88

"Oh SHIT!," the woman shouted, once again forgetting (or not paying attention to) the fact that they were in a religious institution. "Are those still on there?" She paused, then confessed, "I don't actually have a degree. My last job required one to get in the door, so I made it up."

"Don't tell him that!," her partner exclaimed. "These jobs don't ever research that stuff! Sir?," he asked, turning to Todd, "Do you ever research this stuff?"

"Actually," Todd started...

"But Sebastian," the woman cried, interrupting him. "I don't want to lie to a man of the cloth!" she exclaimed.

Finally, Todd realized who he was actually supposed to be interviewing. She's Gerri, he's Sebastian, and they were sitting there in front of him arguing about lying on a resume. Gerri had anxiously admitted to her discomfort at lying to a pastor inside of a church.

"Ma'am," Todd interrupted, "I'm not a pastor."

"Oh! Sorry, Reverend!," Gerri corrected herself.

"No, I'm not any sort man of the cloth. This is a school and..."

"Get your mind right!," Sebastian snapped at her, interrupting Todd. "He's not wearing a robe or a roman collar. He's clearly a deacon or a bishop."

"He's trying to recruit for a summer school so I just assumed he was a youth pastor," Gerri argued.

"I'm not affiliated with a…," Todd tried to explain. But Sebastian interrupted again.

"At the least he's a secretary or Sunday School director," he said. "Sir," he said, addressing Todd, "Tell her your summer school is for a Sunday School."

Convinced neither of these two was qualified to work with the camp, Todd wondered how successful the camp could be with Terri as the only qualified candidate. Todd wondered if he could do all the rest himself (Amell and Bianca weren't going to be much help). Yes, he answered, but deep down he knew it was a lie. He was tired from planning and organizing the camp, running it was going to be a different beast altogether. He didn't have the energy, and he surmised that wasn't going to change any time soon. Sitting here conducting interviews had drained him. Worse yet, his day wasn't over. He still had to go home and contend with Sharon and then face a night at the warehouse.

"How many weeks' vacation will we get a year if we accept this job?," Sebastian asked.

"And how many hours a week do we have to work?," Gerri asked. Todd felt tag-teamed.

"Do we get a paid lunch break?," Gerri continued. "And what type of health benefits does the job come with? Do we have to change diapers or wipe noses? Because I get sick really easily," she added. "I don't want any of these carrier monkeys' germs attacking my immune system."

"If I can become an ordained minister online would you pay me more to

90

work here?," Sebastian asked.

Todd felt himself becoming overwhelmed. He cleared his throat loudly. "I'm sorry," he started, "This is a temporary position; the program only runs for 7 weeks."

"We'll let you know if we're interested," Sebastian replied, interrupting Todd again. And just like that the two were off to harass someone else.

Just as Todd began to celebrate the peace and quiet left in Gerri and Sebastian's wake, Gerri came running back.

"I couldn't find the collection plate," she confessed, setting a $10 bill on the table in front of Todd.

Is this a pathetic attempt at bribery?, Todd wondered. Or is she really this clueless about what goes on here?

"I'll say a couple of Hail Marys on my way out," Gerri declared.

Todd was convinced. She was clueless.

Experience is a good teacher but her fees are "High".
-William Ralph Inge

"What up, my nigga?!" greeted the young man entering the room.

"Excuse me?!," Todd replied, annoyed at the disrespect. "Don't you **dare** use that type of language in my presence again!" he scolded

Fuming, Todd had to remind himself he was an educator dealing with an uneducated student. He needed to teach, not threaten.

"I was just saying hello!," argued the young man.

"Then just say 'Hello,'" Todd responded, turning his nose up at another applicant that reeked of marijuana.

"Come on, man!," exclaimed the young man, rolling his eyes at Todd's contempt of his vernacular. "It's not bad anymore when *we* say it," he said, as if one person of color calling another person of color that name could somehow reclaim the word. "It's good now," he concluded.

"Who is 'we'?," Todd questioned. "No one asked me if I was good with that moniker," he argued. "I didn't get a vote, and that word will <u>never</u> be good in my eyes. It shouldn't be in yours, either."

"Why not?," the young man asked, clearly not understanding Todd's outrage.

"That word," Todd began, "whether it's pronounced with an -a or an -er at the end was just one of the countless psychological tools used by slave traders and slave owners to break slaves into submission. Every time you use it, you need to think about the 12 million people who were ripped from their homes and stripped of their language, culture, and identity as they were transported across the Atlantic Ocean like animals. Millions died in the process. When you use that word, think of the millions who would have been scared to death of their slave masters after they'd witnessed others be whipped or lynched for daring to attempt to reach freedom, or to get an education. Think of every rape, murder, and beating performed by perpetrators using that name. It wasn't that long ago that African Americans were called that deplorable name as they were turned away from businesses, water fountains, restrooms, and schools."

As he spoke, Todd hoped his words were reaching the young man in front of him. He knew he didn't carry the same street cred as the rappers the young man was probably trying to emulate, but he still needed to try. He longed to make a difference in the lives of the next generation.

"Like George Orwell said," Todd continued "If a thought corrupts language, language can also corrupt thought."

"Nigga **WHAT**?!," the young man cried, smirking.

Todd shot him a stern, menacing look. He was peeved that his argument, his attempt to wake this kid up to how offensive his word choice was, was not only being ignored, but mocked. Slowly and deliberately, Todd continued speaking, even though he was pretty sure his words would continue to fall on deaf ears.

"The words you speak enter another's mind and create thoughts based on the words the original thinker said. Simply put, words are powerful and can either do great things or cause great harm. Until everyone can say that word without offending anyone it will continue to be a vile description and reminder of a despicable time in human history. Now take a seat," Todd all-but-commanded.

He reached for the young man's resume. Todd was very familiar with the applicant. Derrick Mott. Derrick was considered the school's celebrity: star of the school's basketball team after having been kicked out of an inner-city school for what was rumored to be just about everything, he had a bad boy demeanor that the girls were smitten over and the boys idolized. Todd himself wondered if any of the rumors of Derrick's exploits were actually true, but because he was a minor at the time of his enrollment, his records were sealed.

Derrick was the lone exception to the school's we-don't-accept-outsiders rule. This tends to happen when your athleticism instantly exalts the school's sports programs. Derrick was incredibly different from the typical student here. Todd jokingly referred to him as the Fresh Prince of Bel Aire, though it was rumored he'd done a little more than get into one little fight like Will Smith had on the show. Also unlike the show, Derrick didn't go to live with a rich uncle upon his expulsion from the city school; he became the responsibility of his hardworking grandparents. Desperate to build a more stable foundation for him, they'd enrolled him in the first affordable private Christian school they could find.

Derrick was 6'3" and 180 pounds of pure athletic talent. He had a naturally muscular physique, one that comes from doing hard physical work, not from working out in a gym. His strong jawline and thick, wavy hair were qualities Todd surmised Derrick used to get his way. His arms were covered with tattoos, but Todd was never able to distinguish what they said since the school had a no tattoo policy and forced Derrick to keep them covered. The only time they were visible were during basketball games, but even then Todd couldn't tell what the images were since Derrick's dark complexion hid their visibility.

Glancing at Derrick's resume, Todd became intrigued with some of the entries . Most of the information listed were of typical high school activities: basketball, a couple of classes he'd taken, various clubs. But the section on job history caught his eye. Derrick's one and only job began two years ago and ended right before he started attending the Christian school. He described himself as a small business owner. In the description he wrote he invested $50 and grew that into a $5000 per week profit. Todd dismissed that as a typo. Derrick then wrote that he'd met and exceeded customer expectations, successfully managed multiple suppliers, worked well under pressure, and excelled in a fast-paced environment, that he was great at networking. Todd was intrigued.

"Derrick," he started, "It says here...."

"Whew! Sorry I'm late!," Bianca interrupted, pulling up a chair right next to Todd.

Todd stared, amazed. Bianca's outfit was exquisite, and – shockingly – appropriate for work. Still, he once again felt she was overdressed for the occasion. She wore a berry blue slim fit Fenice jacket with structured shoulders and a tailored waist. It featured high-notched lapels and a single jet chest pocket. Her pants matched, and her feet set on top of platform sandals crafted from smooth Italian calf leather. Todd couldn't help but wonder why she'd decided to show up during the very last interview.

"You look amazing," Derrick complimented.

"Oh, this old thing?," Bianca responded, blushing. "I figured my Altuzarra business suit would be perfect for the job fair."

"The job fair you basically missed," Todd muttered under his breath.

Bianca and Derrick ignored the comment.

"You look nice, too," remarked Bianca to Derrick, who was wearing a simple long-sleeved t-shirt and basic Levis. The only thing exceptional about his outfit were the extremely expensive Jordan 6 Retro tennis shoes he wore on his feet.

Like Bianca, Derrick wore something Todd could neither afford nor justify spending his money on. He was starting to feel like a wing man as the two began fawning over each other. Todd wondered if Derrick was the young man Bianca had gotten caught making out with. Todd had never asked Bianca about the incident, he just knew she had been written up for inappropriate behavior. Bianca discussed her various love interests so often that Todd struggled to keep tabs. Not that he cared. But her truancy, tardiness, and the write up were all major strikes against her in the eyes of the administration.

Initially, Todd had been shocked at the thought of a staff member doing anything inappropriate with a student, but he had to remind himself that Bianca and Derrick were virtually the same age. She was still on the clock when she'd done what she'd done, though, which made the act inexcusable.

"Can we get back to the interview?," he asked, interrupting the flirting. "As I was asking before CEO Barbie interrupted us," he joked, "It says here you owned a small business. What was the commodity?"

"What?" asked Derrick, puzzled by Todd's use of such a big word.

"He's asking what product you sold," Bianca interjected.

"Ohhh, I gotcha," Derrick replied. "I, uh, sold, uh...." he started, struggling to find the right words. "I sold crystals and organic leaves," he said softly.

"Sounds very holistic," chirped Bianca excitedly.

"I see," Todd responded. Weird combination of products to make such a substantial profit, he thought. "It says here you managed multiple suppliers, but I don't see any names – of suppliers *or* references – on your resume," he continued.

"The thing is," Derrick said, "It's important that our clients' identities remain confidential. We upheld that to the highest standard."

"How honorable!," Bianca threw in.

"Umm...ok....," Todd started.

"Derrick, what are some of your strengths and weaknesses?," Bianca asked.

Wow!, Todd thought, surprised. She's finally contributing something to the hiring of her staff.

"My strengths?," Derrick began. "I can walk onto the sales floor and bring a level of street smarts and hustle like you've never seen before. My determination and hard work would often force my competitors away."

"I, uh, see," Todd replied. "And your weaknesses?"

"I'm a take-charge type of person, and I never take no for an answer," Derrick replied.

"That sounds like another strength to me," Bianca said, gushing.

"It may come off as a little intimidating," Derrick added.

"Thank you, Derrick," Bianca began, clapping and smiling at him. "You're hired!," she exclaimed, running around the table to embrace him.

I guess we'll both have eye candy, Todd thought to himself, thinking of Terri. Though he would never entertain the idea of making out with her, or doing anything else that would be inappropriate. To Todd, Bianca's flirting with Derrick during an interview danced on the line of inappropriate behavior.

"I'm out of here," he said, gathering his things and walking out. Derrick and Bianca forgot he was even there. They quickly transformed from business associates to personal friends as they exchanged numbers.

The more you fear something the more it will happen.
-Murphy's Law

As Todd headed home, he thought about the day's events. He knew he needed to call Amell and review the staffing candidates with him, but he didn't have the energy to relive the frustration the applicants had put him through. Todd's biggest fear was having to perform another round of interviews. Besides Terri, Derrick, and Teresa, no one was even close to being qualified enough to work any aspect of the camp. It was like starting at square one. He also didn't want to be stuck on the phone with Amell, who could be long-winded at times.

As Todd pulled up, he saw Sharon's car in the carport. Knowing his wife was home gave Todd butterflies in the pit of his stomach. Coming home to Sharon was like playing a game of Russian Roulette. Wondering which attitude Sharon would have caused him debilitating, often paralyzing fear. One mistake and Sharon would apply the seven pounds of pressure needed to fire a fatal shot. Even on good days Todd felt she would spin the chamber and threaten to shoot if he did something wrong.

Reluctant to enter the house, Todd decided to stay in his car and call Amell, even though he didn't really want to do that, either.

"Thank God you called!," Amell exclaimed. "I'm in wedding planning hell," he complained. "We're meeting photographers, and let me tell you I am in the **wrong** career. What these people are trying to charge us.... Let's just say they'd be doing us both a favor by just using a gun and ski masks and getting it over with, because either way I'm getting robbed."

99

Todd immediately regretted calling Amell. His friend was in the beginning stages of a rant and it was probably going to continue for quite a while.

"Can you believe someone wanted to charge us *five thousand dollars* to take pictures at our wedding?!"

"That doesn't sound unreasonable," Todd answered.

"But they want us to supply the camera!" Amell retorted. "Another company said they reserve the right to kick guests out of the ceremony if they interfere with their artistic vision. Who cares about vision?! I just want pictures of the event!," he continued. "Oh. And an*other* company wants us to provide food and drinks for all fifteen members of their crew! If I'm paying ten grand for them to take pictures then they should bring a brown bag lunch. The people here now keep saying the word 'optics.' They want us to have wardrobe changes and are color-coordinating our wardrobe for the best optics. Who says '**optics**'?!" he complained. "Say pictures, for crying out loud. I think they use that word to justify us paying them an arm and a leg. This photographer actually has my fiancé contemplating changing our wedding colors so we can have the best *optics*. She also told us not to get any darker because it'll interfere with her artistic vision. It's about to be summer and you're telling us not to get darker?! I'm one more mention of the word 'optics' away from handing all the guests disposable cameras and asking them to shoot the wedding themselves. Todd," he continued, "We even had a photographer suggest we change the time of our ceremony for better lighting. Really?! Better lighting?!! Just use a flashlight if you need better lighting!"

By this time Todd had stopped listening to Amell altogether. He'd make a sound every now and again to feign interest, but he was really counting the moments he was wasting on the phone when he could be napping before he had to be at the warehouse. He was also annoyed that Amell had yet to ask him about the interviews. Further proof, he thought, that no one shared his dedication to this summer camp. Though Bianca had arrived to assist with an interview, it was only to help use a candidate to fill her social calendar.

"This other photographer wants us to run all activities past them for approval so they know what pictures to plan to take," Amell continued. "She actually said she doesn't take unnecessary pictures. This photographer says she refuses to take pictures of the wedding party getting ready for the ceremony, because she deems it unnecessary. If that's what my fiancé is hiring you to do…if that's what we are **paying** you to do, then, guess what, picture lady, that's what you're going to do," he concluded.

Todd, still sitting in his car, still only half listening, and still very much regretting making this phone call contemplated just hanging up, turning off the phone, and telling Amell later that the call dropped and his battery had died. I'd better not, though, he thought. That excuse never worked on Sharon.

"My fiancé's yelling for me to come back in there," Amell said. "I've been at this all day!," he complained. "Todd, you have no idea what it's like sitting through horrible candidates one after another," he grumbled.

"That's actually why I was calling," Todd interrupted quickly. "I don't really like any of the summer camp candidates."

"I have to go," Amell said suddenly, and he hung up the phone.

"AAAARRGHH!" Todd exclaimed, exasperated. He sulked as he thought

101

about how badly he wanted to share how bad his day had been with someone. I guess Sharon will have to do, he conceded.

Entering the house, Todd scanned the kitchen nervously. He really didn't want to interact with his wife, especially since the tension between the two of them had continued to grow. His home, what *should* be his sanctuary from work, had become what he escaped when he went to school.

As per usual the dishes were piling up. The ever-increasing number of cats were running rampant over the furniture. Cat dander filled the room with each movement they made. Todd already longed for a frustrating day at school if it meant escaping his repugnant living conditions. At least his life at school was purposeful; he felt as if he was making a difference in the world. At home he felt as if his world was turned upside down. The house was dark; the only light came from above the stove. Todd assumed his stepson was at a friend's house doing one of the two things he did best: playing video games or looking at raunchy magazines.

Todd entered the living room cautiously, his eyes still struggling to adjust from the dusk of the outdoors to the pitch-black house. Feeling against the wall for the light switch Todd stepped directly into an overflowing litter box. As he removed his foot, the overwhelming stench of ammonia filled the room. The dust he kicked up tickled his nose unpleasantly. The toxic gas gave Todd a headache instantly. As he flipped on the light, Todd noticed movement inside the litter box. He moved a little closer and was horrified to discover little roundworms squirming in and out of the cats' feces. He fumed over the condition in which Sharon, who was home all day, kept the house. What did she do all day?!

Todd quickly turned away from the putrid litter box when something else caught his eye. She was on the floor, motionless. Sharon. Was she dead? What do I do?, he thought. Did she fall? Was she attacked? Should I call the police? If I do, will they think I hurt her?

Questions and hypothetical scenarios continued to flood Todd's head as approached her body cautiously. He was scared; he'd never seen a dead body that hadn't already been prepared by a coroner and he didn't want to see one now. But as he inched closer he realized that Sharon wasn't dead; she was crying.

Never stand between a fire hydrant and a dog.
-Murphy's Law

The sudden revelation that his wife was still alive disappointed Todd, and that in and of itself horrified him. , For just a moment, though, he'd felt free from her tyranny, and that feeling was hard to let go of.

He bent down to touch her. Sharon flinched. In her distraught state, she hadn't noticed that Todd had gotten home and she didn't want him to see her in that state.

"Get away from me!," she snapped.

Todd could see the pain in her eyes, even through her tears. Her agony permeated Todd, and he felt sorry for her. He wanted to shed tears for her, too.

Sharon continued to cry. Her red eyes, runny nose, flushed face, and swollen eyelids revealed that she'd been at it for some time.

"What's wrong?," Todd asked softly. He'd never seen her this vulnerable before. She looked frail. Defeated. Todd knew Sharon hated the way Todd was looking at her. She was used to being feared, to being a rock. Powerful. But her power was gone now.

Sitting up quickly, Sharon pushed Todd away. "Nothing's wrong!," she yelled. Hurriedly, she began wiping the tears from her eyes, desperate to put on a strong front.

104

"Sharon," Todd started gently, "you're lying in the middle of the floor crying. Did you fall? Are you hurt?" He searched her body for any obvious injuries.

"It hurts," she sobbed. "I hurt all the time."

Todd scanned her body for the source of her pain.

"Can I get you some ice?," he offered. He was desperate to help her but at a loss for what to do.

Weeping, Sharon wrapped her arms around him. She needed him, needed him to hold her tight. To console her and to tell her he understood her pain. She needed him to take it away. Repeating "it hurts, it hurts," Sharon tightened her grip. Todd *wanted* to ease her pain, to understand it and protect her from it, but he couldn't do any of that. He had to know what was going on first.

"Do you want some aspirin?," he asked, but Sharon did a 180 and threw him off her, demanding he leave her alone. She was infuriated because he didn't understand what was going on. Todd could sense that she didn't know how to express the pain she was feeling and that his ignorance was making the situation worse.

"You're such a buffoon! I'm not in *physical* pain. It's....it's deeper than that."

Great, Todd thought. Another roadblock in their relationship.

Sharon flung herself back onto the floor and curled up in a fetal position.

"What do I need to *do*?," Todd asked. He kept trying – and failing – to

105

understand. And then it finally dawned on him: Sharon's pain was internal. He **was** a buffoon. He was mortified. How could he have been so blind to her agony? Still, realizing the pain wasn't physical didn't help clarify anything. How do you fix someone that was broken inside?, he thought. How can I comprehend what she's going through if she herself can't even explain it?

He began to feel guilty. Was *he* the cause of her pain? Was she this unhappy because he was never home? Had he triggered this by calling her crazy?

"I'm here," he said, digging down deep for the most caring, considerate voice he could muster. His words were so cliché, though, and he knew they carried no weight.

Finally, Sharon sat back up slowly. "Find me Xanax," she demanded. "I want this pain gone; I don't want to feel anything anymore."

"I didn't know you had a prescription for Xanax," Todd said.

"***GET. ME. XANAX!!***," Sharon screeched. "That bitch Amy sells me hers," she said. Her tears of pain had turned to tears of rage. "She went out of town," Sharon whimpered.

Todd didn't know what to do. He wanted to help, he truly did, but was finding her pills really the answer? Where do I even begin to get drugs?, he wondered. What if they're not what she needs?

"Numb this pain," Sharon pleaded. "Please." She again curled into a fetal position, crying, shaking, and rocking herself back and forth. "I don't want to feel the emotions," she admitted. "I can't take it."

106

Todd could not comprehend what was happening. It was clear Sharon was having a mental breakdown. He needed to call someone. He knew finding her drugs was *not* the answer. He wondered how long Sharon had been taking drugs not prescribed to her. Surely that had to be dangerous.

Suddenly, the phone began to ring. Sharon jumped off the floor and ran to answer it.

"You *do*?," Todd heard her say excitedly. "How much? For **one**?!," she exclaimed. She sounded shocked. "I'm on my way," she said, darting out the door.

"Wait!," Todd exclaimed, running behind his wife. "Where are you going?"

Sharon ignored his question as she fumbled with her keys, trying to put them in the ignition. She wasn't in the right physical state to be driving, Todd observed.

"Wait!," he demanded., but Sharon started the car and put it in reverse. Todd sprinted to the rear of the car. He tapped on the trunk to let her know he was back there, but it didn't matter. Nothing was going to stop Sharon from getting what she thought she needed. He realized too late that she wasn't going to stop, even for him. He tried to get out of the way but was just barely holding on to the car's trunk. He tightened his grip as he felt the car's inertia begin to increase. She was going to run him over! Todd was terrified, sweating, and then his fingers started to slip. He was losing his grasp!

Sharon drug Todd twenty feet down the driveway. When she stopped to switch the car to drive, Todd slid onto the pavement and tumbled a good ten feet. He looked up just in time to see Sharon glance down at him as continued her trajectory out of their neighborhood. She only narrowly missed running him over.

The pain Todd felt at his wife not even checking to see he was okay hurt much more than his flesh dragging along the pavement and the gravel now embedded in his arm and side. His legs burned from the road rash left where he'd once had skin.

He could only see her taillights now. She was racing down the street, ignoring every speed limit and stop sign. Her speed increased and Todd could hear her tires screech with every turn. She was gone. The thought that she'd gone to meet her supplier did nothing to mask the pain he was feeling. He struggled to pick himself up off the ground. Dirty, bloody, limping, and in searing pain, Todd hobbled up the driveway.

I m going to take a nap, he concluded.

> *Smile. Tomorrow will be worse.*
> *-Murphy's Law*

"OUUUUUCH!," Todd bellowed. A sudden, spontaneous muscle contraction had hit, leaving his hamstring in excruciating pain. Todd was used to waking up on Mondays in this kind of pain, the result of the Charlie horses he got from constantly standing and walking at his weekend job.

His pedometer usually registered close to a dozen miles every time he was there. He didn't mind being on his feet all day, though; the menial tasks allowed his mind to wander, and focus on ideas for the summer camp.

But all Todd was able to do now was lay still. Every movement caused the muscle to constrict, resulting in searing pain. Maybe this wasn't the normal post-weekend-job pain. Maybe this was the effect of surviving his wife's hit and run. Unable to move for the moment left Todd stewing over what Sharon had done. He couldn't believe that she'd left him there on the pavement without even checking to see if he was okay.

The birds were chirping outside and flowers were in bloom. It was going to be a beautiful day. Todd wondered if he was going to be able to get up and enjoy it or if he'd be stuck in bed, squeezing his eyes shut tightly in a vain attempt to absorb the pain coming from the back of his leg.

Finally it began to subside, and Todd was able to begin adding more and more movement. He peered out the window. The sun was starting to rise and he wondered what time it was. He glanced at the clock. 5:12 AM. Yes!, he thought excitedly. I still have another hour before I have to get up. He grabbed his pillow, fluffed it, and closed his eyes. But he couldn't sleep. The first day of summer camp was today and Todd was giddy with excitement. Finally, all his hard work is being put into motion. He knew the camp was going to be a success, and it would all start today.

***

"Who is she?," he heard Sharon ask accusingly.

Drowsy and confused, Todd wiped the crust from his eyes. He strained to focus, but saw his wife standing
next to their bed. It hadn't dawned on him that she wasn't in the bed next to him. Why wasn't she in
bed? Todd's mind began to race; he wondered if he'd accidentally kicked her out during his most recent bout with muscle cramps.

THWACK! Todd heard the sound of Sharon's dainty hand making contact with his face before he felt the pain. When it hit, the sharp sting zapped any wooziness that was left in his body. He was awake now!

"I asked you a question," Sharon said. Her deliberate tone both scared and confused Todd.

"Who is *who*?," Todd asked, confused. Ever since he'd found Sharon on the floor the night of the hit and run, Todd had noticed changes in his wife. Sometimes she'd be numb, almost zombie-like. Other times she was like a raging bull in a fine china shop, yelling, screaming, and damaging anything in her way.

Today was supposed to be a great day!, he thought. He'd been able to quit his delivery job since the income from the summer camp would pay what he

110

made there. He was excited about that, and about the first day of camp. He'd spent so much time planning, and he was anxious to see his creation come together. He'd hoped Sharon would be excited for him, too. This didn't appear to be the case; her bullish side was making an appearance.

The pain on the side of his face made him come to the realization that today was not starting off well, and probably wouldn't improve until he got to school.

"Sharon," Todd began. "I have no idea who you're asking about."

He did a quick internal assessment to be sure he was telling her the truth. Nope! There was no affair. He was too busy to have one! He was too busy to even *notice* another woman. If he **had** noticed another woman, he would've passed up sleeping with her for a nap.

"The woman that had you moaning in bed," Sharon finally responded.

Todd was even more confused now. He looked around, but there was no mystery woman in his bed.

"I don't know," he said, "but if she can make me moan, tell her to come back when I' awake," he joked.

THWACK! Wrong answer, he thought as the second slap connected with his face in the same spot the first one had.

"Will you *please* stop hitting me?," he begged. "I honestly have no idea who you're talking about."

111

"I've been standing here for the past two hours watching you smile and moan in your sleep," Sharon said. "You're obviously dreaming of another woman and I want to know who in the hell she is."

"There's no other woman...," Todd started.

"You vowed to be with only me," Sharon interrupted, "Yet you moan in your sleep and spend more time planning some silly camp or preparing for audits at the warehouse. If you aren't cheating on me with another woman, then you're two-timing me with your jobs." She sighed. "If I hear you moaning in bed again I'm going to cut it off," she threatened.

I need this alarm to go off and wake me from this nightmare, Todd thought.

"Are you crazy?," he asked. "Seriously," he continued. "Are you crazy? I am not having an affair with another woman. I don't have any desire to. You are my wife, for better or worse," he continued.

It's mostly been for worse, he thought as he gingerly rubbed the side of his face. He waited for Sharon to reply. She blinked hard, cocked her head to the side, and stood there staring at Todd for a moment. Todd started back, trying desperately not to blink or look away.

What is going on?, he thought. Sharon just stood in place as if she were a buffering video that hadn't quite finished downloading. Then she just turned around and walked off.

Did she say she watched me sleep?, he wondered. For two HOURS?? Who **does** that?, he questioned. Todd felt violated. What an uncomfortable feeling it was knowing you were being watched when you were in your most

112

vulnerable state.

With his face still stinging, Todd pondered whether he should go back to sleep for a brief moment or just get up and get ready for the first day of summer camp. As excited as he was, Todd elected to go back to sleep.

"I'll show you crazy!" a voice said. Todd's eyes caught the glint of metal as it hit the reflection of the sunlight pouring in through the window. Sharon hastily thrust a knife in his direction.

Startled, Todd rolled toward the middle of the bed. Sharon plunged the knife into the exact spot Todd had been laying just a second ago. The sudden movement revived the muscle spasm down the back of Todd's leg. Paralyzed by fright and agony, Todd could only wince in pain and fear as Sharon slowly crawled into bed next to him. She inched toward him gradually and deliberately, her movement mimicking a big cat stalking its prey. Her eyes locked in on Todd, anticipating any sudden movement he might make, ready to pounce if he tried to escape.

Despite the tremendous pain his leg was causing him, Todd moved away from his wife cautiously. The pain pulsated with every movement. Trapped between a wall and his wife, Todd squirmed. The muscle spasm meant he could only wiggle away slowly in his attempt to escape Sharon. Is this what an injured gazelle feels just before a lion rips it to pieces?, he wondered. The back of the bed was positioned up against the wall, so Todd had nowhere to go. He struggled to sit up, pain throbbing in his leg, his heart pounding.

Sharon continued to approach ever so slightly, a faint, devilish grin appearing on her face. Her eyes cut

113

through Todd as if she was vividly picturing finishing off her prey. She stopped mere inches from his face
taking in the scent of his fear as if she was becoming aroused by it.

"Do. not. call. me. crazy.," she instructed in a terrifying whisper. She enunciated each word, sending fear coursing through Todd's body. She was serious in her threat. A fiery rage filled her eyes, adding to the seriousness of her words. This wasn't a request; it was a warning.

Sharon gripped her weapon tightly in her right hand and used its cross section to gently outline Todd's throat, followed by his neck. Back and forth, back and forth, Sharon guided the blade across his skin as if allowing it to hunt for his most vulnerable spot. With her eyes fixed on Todd's throat, she brought the point of the blade to rest just below Todd's jawline. The blade was cold and made him shiver.

Sharon stared at Todd icily, then took her left hand and thrusted it violently into his Adam's Apple. Todd's head crashed into the wall and would have dented the drywall had he not happened to hit the wall's stud. He almost blacked out.

The morning sun continued pouring its warm rays into the room, but Todd struggled to see any light at all. Tears filled his eyes, and the pain made him see stars.

Sharon was nose-to-nose with him now and continued staring right through him. Todd was frozen in painful fear. He gulped, closing his eyes tightly as he could feel the prick of the blade with every movement. Praying silently that this ordeal would be over soon, he could feel Sharon's grip around his throat slowly tighten as she attempted to cut off his oxygen.

The emotionless stare she'd plastered to her face disappeared, replaced now by one of rage. And suddenly, Todd understood. All the years of suppressing anger, of not being in control. All the pain caused by her ex-husbands, the fear caused by her abusive father, the frustration of Todd never being home were erupting into this act of violence. Months without having any motivation or ambition evaporated. Living a dull, emotionless existence while the man in front of her left every day to serve his life's purpose angered her more than anything else ever had. Nothing ever felt real in her life, and Sharon was tired of feeling nothing and everything all at the same time.

Todd guessed that Sharon was finally feeling something. She was able to vent so many things that she'd pushed deep down inside. Choking the life out of Todd made Sharon feel alive. Todd was trying to stop from incurring a puncture wound from the blade Sharon held while, at the same time, taking shallow breaths so he wouldn't lose consciousness. He began to wonder how his marriage had gone from 'I do' to 'I don't want to do this anymore.' Looking back, Todd never thought the two of them would ever get married. They had fun together in the beginning of their relationship. But now their life goals were too dissimilar. Todd wanted to explore the world while Sharon was satisfied exploring cable channels. Though it was a shared desire at one point, realistically Todd wants children, while Sharon just wanted more cats.

Todd wondered how long Sharon had been depressed. All he could see when he gazed into her eyes now was fury. Her eyebrows drew together to form a 'v' just above her nose. Her lips were pressed tightly against her teeth as if the act of clenching was helping her bite her rage at having been called crazy. The muscles in her forearms flexed as she continued to squeeze Todd's airway shut.

Sharon inched closer to her husband and unexpectedly thrust her lips against Todd's, kissing him in a way that suggested she was turned on by the power she had over him. Todd was sure Sharon was trying to seal off the oxygen to his lungs.

Moaning with each movement of her lips, Sharon released the grip around Todd's throat and began caressing his head gently. When she didn't feel Todd kiss her back – since he was struggling to breathe – Sharon applied pressure from the knife's blade to the underside of his jaw as a means of motivating him. Todd could taste her anger and obliged unwillingly. Her kiss was bitter. Todd wanted to run and hide from this woman, not make out with her. He felt nauseous. He imagined how she would gut him like a fish if he threw up in her mouth. A death like that would be worth it if his last act demonstrated how truly sick she made him. Choke on it!, he thought. How far would she take this?, he wondered. Thoughts of any form of intimacy with her made him cringe.

As if she could sense Todd's disdain for her, Sharon suddenly pulled herself off him, licking the wetness
she'd left on his face. The act disgusted him. As he moved to wipe it off, Sharon cautioned, "Leave it," and she laughed at the power she possessed over him. She leaned in close, grabbed his throat with her left hand, whispered "'til death do we part," and then slapped his already bruised cheek as she repeated each word again:

"'Til" *SLAP* "death" *SLAP* "do" *SLAP* "we" *SLAP* "part" *SLAP*.

Then she stood up, picked up the knife, and pierced a hole in the bed where she'd just been sitting.

116

"Would you make the bed, sweetie?," she asked. And she left the room as if nothing had happened.

Todd sat in her wake. Do I call the police, he wondered. If not the police, I need to call the looney bin, he concluded. He had to fight the urge to vomit as he thought about the noxious kiss he'd just shared with his wife. He started to feel responsible for Sharon's actions, to blame himself for the way she behaved. Maybe if I didn't work so hard... he began thinking.

His excitement about the summer camp dissipated after realizing the time away from home he'd taken to plan it almost cost him his life. Was she trying to kill me for the little bit of life insurance he had? Did she stop when she realized she wouldn't get paid if she murdered him? Was she trying to replace the vulnerability Todd had witnessed during her mental breakdown with extreme ferocity?

Todd's thoughts were interrupted. The high-pitched sound of his alarm was ear-splitting. And even though it was less than five feet away, Todd could not move to shut it off because of the spasm in his leg.

"Turn that loud shit off!," Sharon demanded from another room.

Too scared about what might happen if he didn't do what she said fast enough, Todd mustered the ability to ignore his discomfort and follow Sharon's direction immediately.

117

You will never run out of things that can go wrong
-Murphy's Law

Apprehensive thanks to his wife's abusive hands, Todd was both excited and relieved to arrive at school for his first day of summer camp. Not only was he anxious to see the results of all his planning and hard work, he also needed a distraction from all the chaos at home.

He limped through the parking lot, expecting to see fanfare announcing the camp's first day, but there was nothing. No balloons. No streamers. No staff members waving or welcoming guests. Nothing. Todd only had himself to blame. As activity director, he supposed he needed to direct someone to do each and every activity, including preparing a welcome mat and fanfare for the first day. He just hadn't had time.

Todd *had* made sure every field trip was planned out and paid for. He'd purchased board games, movies, puzzles, and cards, all to ensure campers had activities to keep them busy. He'd purchased Dodge balls, soccer balls, and softballs for the athletes in the camp. For the coordinated campers, there were beaded skipping ropes, outdoor skipping ropes, skipping ropes that would record how many times you jumped, metal skipping ropes, PVC-coated skipping ropes, nylon-coated skipping ropes. Paper, pens, pencils, paint, markers, and rulers had been purchased for the preparedness courses. Lesson plans had been written for reading, writing, arithmetic, and geography for each age group, and there were a whole host of science experiments ready to go.

Todd was proud of his efforts; he felt as if he'd planned every moment of all seven weeks of the camp. He'd worked tirelessly to make the camp

118

foolproof. After a series of failed interviews, Todd hadn't been able to find anyone who could do the job the way he wanted it done; it was all up to him. He'd worked
harder planning the camp than he had in all his other jobs combined and he was tired. Adrenaline was the only thing propelling him through his days.

When Todd, Amell, and Bianca had gone over which potential candidates to hire, Todd was ready to inform the others that only Teresa and Terri were qualified. Unfortunately, Amell surprised Todd and hired everyone who applied. Even the stoner. Flabbergasted, Todd had politely asked Amell why. He wanted to shake some sense into that brain of his, but Amell responded that everyone deserves a chance.

Noble as that was, Todd was angry that he'd gone through the entire interview process for nothing.
However, he did take pleasure in knowing that those applicants were now Bianca's problem, though he feared it would become his problem, too, since she didn't have the best track record and no management experience.
Walking through the campus, Todd mapped out the best places for signs or balloons welcoming campers.
Missing opportunities to display exciting events would normally upset him, but Sharon had slapped (and nearly cut) all the excitement out of him. Todd only hoped no one would notice the handprint she'd left on the side of his face.

"High five!." Bianca shouted, holding a high-five gesture toward Todd's face. Less than a minute after arriving on campus and Todd's hopes were already dashed.

"I guess your wife had to tell you something twice," Bianca teased. Todd

119

would normally have been infuriated by such a comment, but the noise in the cafeteria was making it impossible to focus on anything she said.

It had been decided that the cafeteria was the perfect spot for starting camp each morning. It was centrally located and aesthetically pleasing. It was also the coolest building on campus and would provide a respite from the hot, humid summer days St. Louis was known for. It was also big enough to split into sections so campers could play, socialize, or even watch a movie without every other section being disturbed. At least that's what Todd and the others had theorized.

This morning was proving that working theory wrong, though. The entire building was in chaos. The camp had received a grant from the city to provide campers with a free breakfast. The school board, ever wanting to make a dollar from fifteen cents, tried to find a way to charge parents for it, anyway. The cafeteria was where students would pick up and eat their free meal.

For his part, Todd would not eat any free meal the school provided, no matter how many double dog dares he was given. As he looked at what he thought was eggs and bacon, he realized the school had gotten what they'd paid for.

Todd scanned the room, beside himself at the chaos unfolding before him. Near the front door of the cafeteria, a line of parents waited impatiently to sign their campers in before leaving for work. Unfortunately, the room was so loud that volunteers couldn't hear the names parents were giving them. And finding each camper's name on the sign-in sheet was a painfully slow process. The level of frustration grew as each parent realized they had no choice but to wait in line. They'd already paid for the week and had nowhere else to take their children.

Realizing Bianca was not going to assist her staff, Todd began to make his way to the sign-in table.

"I'm going to kill you!," bellowed a little girl with gum in her hair as she shoved Todd out of her way. She was holding a pair of scissors and chasing a little boy who was running away from her and giggling. Observing it all triggered a flashback of Todd's traumatic morning. He could feel his pulse rate increase; nervousness consumed his entire being. He inhaled deeply, then exhaled in an attempt to control his anxiety. The little boy threw chairs as he and the girl darted around the cafeteria, creating obstacles to aid his escape. Closing in behind him, the little girl smacked directly into a parent who was waiting in the sign-in line. Without so much as an apology, the little girl scowled, annoyed that the parent had been in her way. Then she ran off, intent on exacting revenge on the boy.

Am I the only one seeing this?,Todd wondered. Todd became increasingly frustrated as he waited for one of Bianca's staff members to say anything, do anything to bring order to this mess. He focused his attention to their boss: Bianca.

Bianca seemed oblivious to everything going on around her. She appeared deep in thought as she inspected each of her perfectly-manicured nails. They did look impeccable, he thought, but definitely not worth the attention she was paying them. If she continues to pay more attention to her nails and ignores the chaotic camp environment, we're bound to get shut down. Sensing his annoyance, Bianca, without diverting her attention, kicked Todd's leg lightly to get his attention.

"These kids are making me rethink my decision to work this summer camp!," she yelled.

"And I'm starting to rethink having someone who acts like a kid work *with* me at this summer camp," Todd smartly replied. He knew his response was over the top and rude. All the toxicity in his life was changing him into a more negative, grumpy person. But at the moment, he didn't care. Everything he'd worked so hard for was in shambles; this was not what he envisioned.

Bianca was three feet away from him but they had to yell to hear one another. This ruckus was uncalled
for. Todd wanted to take charge of Bianca's staff. He needed to guide them. He wanted the chaos
to stop. His camp needed to be organized, but he also wanted Bianca to fail, for word of this mayhem to reach Amell. It would be sweet justice for Amell putting a kid who'd never had a real job before in charge of staffing.

Alas, Todd thought. If she fails, the camp fails. He wondered who in their right mind would continue to wait in line to leave their child in this turmoil.

"Are you so old that you forgot what it's like to have fun?," Bianca yelled. "Let them burn all their energy off now, before your summer school prison session starts," she continued, chuckling as if she was the only one who understood her joke. "That's what being a kid is all about!," she added, waving
her hand around the room.

Complete. opposites., Todd thought. I see lawsuits, and she sees an amusement park.

122

"I understand that your Gossip Girl mentality can't comprehend this, but if you don't fix this mess, this mess that you and your staff are in charge of, parents are going to rethink spending their money here. And if someone from the superintendent's office sees the cafeteria in such disarray? They'll shut us down immediately. No campers, No camp, No money, No manicure. I guess it'll have to be Lee Press-On nails for you," he continued

"Lee who?," Bianca asked. "I don't know who that is. But knowing you, Todd, it's some stupid 80's reference," she snapped. "Newsflash! No one knows what you're talking about half the time. It's 2008," she continued. "Stop with the 80's references. They probably weren't relevant then and they're definitely not now. Coke, crack, and Jheri curl are all you need to know about that fucked-up decade," she concluded. "Oh. And by the way, Pops, here's one for you for your time machine. If you'd take off your BluBlockers, you could've seen that she had safety scissors. You know: safety. As in safe for children, as in not sharp enough to cut construction paper let alone skin. You know. Dull. Like your personality. Your energy is toxic," she said. And she turned her back and walked away. "Too bad whoever slapped you didn't knock some sense into you," she added, "They just knocked your personality out of you."

"You'd think a man with six other jobs could afford a personality," she chided.

A crowd of campers started to gather around the two. Bianca carried on, feeding off their energy. She became more and more animated. A finger wave here, a head twirl there, Bianca was playing a role for the crowd.

123

"You always act as though you know more than me, Todd. You don't know shit!," she roared. The crowd of campers oooh-ed and ahhh-ed at Bianca's digs. As she inched closer and closer to him. Todd flinched. Placing her hand on his tensed shoulder, Bianca whispered menacingly, "All a person has to do is take one look at you to see that you're in an abusive relationship. Just because you don't have control at home doesn't mean you have the right to come here and try to control everyone else. The bags and dark circles under your eyes are telling you to slow down," she continued. "You keep getting more and more irritable, and I refuse to put up with your shit attitude. Get your life together, Todd," Bianca hissed. "Don't tell me I'm living wrong when it's obvious you're not living at all."

Ouch, Todd thought. Her words stung. Was she right? Of course she was. He tried to tell himself that Bianca didn't know what it meant to be in a serious relationship much less be married. The only relationship he was aware she'd had was the one with the student she got caught making out with. She doesn't know what she's talking about, he maintained. Sharon isn't abusive! She's just going through some things.

Why would Bianca think I'm in an abusive relationship?, he wondered. She doesn't know what goes on in my house! The more he thought about it, though, the less defensive he got. If a kid can see it, why can't I? A nineteen-year-old has life figured out better than I do, he concluded.

"Look what I found outside!," a camper interrupted. His hands full of mud, Bianca ignored him pulling on her exquisite Tom Ford dress. The look of shock on Todd's face must've made Bianca think she was getting through to him because she continued her argument. Todd had stopped listening, though, and started to calculate how much dry cleaning it was going to take to clean her dress.

124

Just as she opened her mouth to speak again, though, Bianca shrieked. A muddy frog jumped out of the camper's hands and flew toward Bianca's face. Only then did she look down at her mud-smeared sundress. She was completely traumatized by its destruction and ran off screaming.

The crowd of amused campers could not contain their laughter. Todd saw it as instant karma, though he knew the arguments she'd made were justified.

The commotion caused the room to fall silent; everyone's attention now focused on the same thing:
Todd. This was the perfect opportunity to corral the campers. Thankfully, the school's cafeteria doubled as an auditorium, though its acoustics definitely left something to be desired. The school staff called it a cafetorium. The multipurpose room featured an elevated platform at its head that was used as a stage. A few steps behind him was a curtain that wrapped around it. Behind that was a soundboard, several microphones, speakers, and a drum set. As impressive as the equipment was, it was all a waste of money in Todd's opinion. The walls were made of cinderblocks and reverberated sound, making everything echoey and distorted.

Todd thought back on the several school concerts the staff had been forced to attend in an effort to support the students. He remembered thinking that some of the performers would have sounded divine if they sang acapella. The musical instruments playing behind them just made organized noise. The sound board operator would adjust the equalizer, but no one benefited.

Remembering all this, Todd still chose to use a microphone to gather everyone's attention. It looked more professional, he thought. Todd tapped on the microphone and cleared his throat. The speakers squealed and Todd

125

was sure people three states away could hear it. Watching his audience cover their ears and moan in discomfort, he decided it would just be best to put the mic down and use his natural voice to address the crowd. Everyone focused their attention in his direction, and Todd couldn't help but they were all focused on the discolored hand print on the side of his face.

"Good morning, campers!," Todd cheered nervously. "Let the fun begin!"

Several campers gave him sideways glances; they were upset that their fun was interrupted by someone saying good morning.

"We'll spend about an hour of every day going over some fun lessons," Todd said, desperate to excite the campers about the class-preparedness portion of the camp. No one approved. A snickering parent could be heard in the background, and Todd was mostly met with the campers' dirty looks.

"We have to do homework at this camp?!," screamed a camper in disapproval.

Ignoring the opportunity to defend his program to those who would partake in it — since that approach wasn't working, anyway — Todd decided to introduce the campers to the staff members who would teach the curriculum. Even though he believed this portion of the camp would set them apart from the other camps in the area, he was still perturbed that he had to introduce Bianca's staff to those in the room.

"Those going into first through third grades will be headed off with Miss Teresa. Fourth through sixth graders will be leaving with Miss Terri, and seventh and eighth graders will go with Ms. Heidi."
"Okay, everyone!," he continued excitedly, "Go line up with your teacher!"

126

No one moved. The campers, the volunteers, the staffers. Everyone stood still. Todd wondered if they'd even heard him. He repeated the instructions, but the only movement came from the campers' heads as they looked side to side, lost. After a few minutes, several campers asked, "What teacher am I supposed to go with?"

Doesn't anyone listen anymore?!, Todd fumed to himself. Frustrated that none of the staff was offering to help coordinate the division of the campers into their respective classes, Todd had no choice but to direct each individual camper to where they were supposed to be. As he did so, Todd took mental notes of which volunteers stood around playing on their phones instead of helping. They could have been cleaning up or assisting the still long line of parents waiting to check their camper in, but they weren't. If anyone from the superintendent's office saw this mess..., Todd started to think, but before he could finish, he saw Ms. Amanda, the head custodial engineer, milling about. Ms. Amanda was in her late fifties and was shaped a bit like an upside down lightbulb. She had a long neck, wide hips, and stubby legs. She was always scowling. Ms. Amanda's grandfather had started the church that started the school. It always baffled Todd that the only position her family felt she was suited for was cleaning up after kids while her siblings all sat on the school board or were principals.

Ms. Amanda had been opposed to the summer camp, and now she stood here shocked at what remained of the once pristine cafeteria. Todd didn't want to confront her head-on so he began barking out orders to the volunteers to get the room back in shape.

"Hey you! Pick up that piece of paper," Todd instructed the volunteer standing closest to him.

127

"Every speck of trash on the ground needs to be picked up. That includes lint!," he added. "This floor needs to be……," he started, but was distracted by a volunteer who was dressed unprofessionally. He thought Amell had told every staffer to dress in the camp's t-shirt that listed their position on the back. That way, anyone who visited would know who the campers were, who the staff was, and who the volunteers were. He'd thought the plan was to have staffers wear khakis and volunteers wear khaki shorts.

"Hey," – what's that kid's name….-- "Tuck in that shirt!," Todd commanded, much like he imagined a drill sergeant would.

This is the job Bianca should be doing, he thought. As he moved about the room he continued directing the volunteers as to what needed to be done. After just five minutes, the room looked brand new, the check-in line was empty, and Ms. Amanda had finally left.

One of the best ideas Amell had thought to introduce was every staffer being equipped with walkie
talkies. This way if someone needed anything, or if a staffer was trying to locate a camper, all they needed was to communicate via the walkie talkie. Unfortunately, they only worked indoors.

As Todd walked the hallways of the school, he felt a sense of accomplishment as he peered into each classroom and saw campers focusing on their preparedness lessons.

Suddenly, his walkie-talkie crackled, breaking the silence and echoing down the empty hallway.

128

"Todd, do you copy?," a female voice asked. "Todd, can you come to my classroom? It's an emergency."

Every solution breeds new problems.
-Arthur Bloch

"Copy," Todd answered. "I'm on my way!"

He felt like a superhero coming to the rescue of a damsel in distress, even though he figured it was probably only Terri needing copies of an assignment, extra pencils, or a bathroom break. As he entered the classroom, he found Terri scrolling nervously through her phone. The campers, without direction, were conversing amongst themselves. When they saw him, they became silent, nestled in their desks as if a show were about to begin.

"Thanks for getting here so quickly," Terri said, diverting her attention away from her phone.

"Is everything okay?," Todd asked empathetically.

Judging by the way Terri had been looking at her phone a moment earlier, Todd wondered if a family emergency had happened and if she'd been made aware of it through her phone.

Terri kept glancing down. She seemed to be awaiting a response of some kind, and she was obviously impatient.

"It's my boyfriend," she said. "Well, my ex-boyfriend, actually," she corrected herself.

"Is he okay?," Todd asked, trying to show concern he didn't really feel.

"He isn't answering my texts," she replied. "He told me he'd moved to Colorado, but my girlfriend said she saw him last night hugged up with some skank at this shitty hole-in-the-wall club."

"Terri!," Todd interrupted. "This is a private religious school," he reminded her. "You can't talk like that when you're with little kids, " he scolded.

"Oh. I forgot kids still believe in fairy tales," Terri said cynically. "Easter bunnies… mermaids… God…… make believe," she continued.

"The Easter Bunny isn't real?!," screamed a little girl from the back of the classroom.

"Miss Terri was talking about the Easter *rabbit*," Todd replied, trying to reassure the child's belief.
Turning his attention back to Terri, Todd moved closer so the campers couldn't hear or see their conversation.

"***Make believe***, Terri?," he whispered. "I thought you *believed* in God," he questioned. He panicked. How do I explain this to the school board?, he pondered. Amell hired Terri on his recommendation, **his** recommendation to hire a non-believer at a religious institution. Todd now understood why they didn't trust outsiders.

"You knew this was a religious institution when you applied! You said you believed in the Holy Spirit!," Todd argued.

"No I didn't," Terri snapped. "I said I believe in the Spirit. The spirit of mother earth.

Todd was confused and wondered if she was being serious. He wanted to laugh, but the expression on
Terri's face stopped him. She meant it! Now he wanted to die. Todd looked deep into Terri's eyes,
checking to see if her pupils were dilated. Is she high?, he wondered. I don't smell alcohol, so I don't think she's drunk.

"Like Arbor Day?," Todd finally asked.

"No, like Mother Goddess," Terri answered, obviously annoyed.

"Who is that?," Todd asked. "Is she like Mother Nature?" He really couldn't believe he was asking for an explanation.

Todd thought back to his memories of Terri's interview, of any signs she was insane. Todd struggled to recall her interview, but he was currently distracted by her cleavage. Unfortunately for him, it had nothing to do with any attraction he might feel for her. Now he had to address her too-revealing manner of dress before Amell, the superintendent, or anyone on the school board saw her.

"No, Todd!" Terri replied, now extremely annoyed. "Mother Goddess is the goddess who represents and is the personification of motherhood. She's equated with the Earth, or the natural world. Such
goddesses are referred to as Mother Earth or as the Earth Mother," Terri continued.

Todd was incredibly confused and wondered if she'd memorized a script. He knew the words she was speaking, but not in the context in which she was

132

using them. I must be getting pranked, he concluded.

"Mother Goose, Mother Nature, Earth Goddess," he started….

"How dare you?!," Terri interrupted, shocked. She placed her index finger on Todd's lips and ordered him to hush. "We do not mention her," she continued.

"Mention who?, Todd asked. "Right now I wish I hadn't mentioned any of them," he continued.

Terri stepped closer to Todd and placed her whole hand over his mouth. Looking around as if she didn't want anyone to hear her big secret she softly whispered in his ear. "Earth Goddess. She's a deity of the underworld. Do not conjure her up," Terri warned.

"So," Todd started, "Mother Nature is some evil chick?," he joked.

"Do not joke about things you do not understand," Terri warned. "Now I need to purge this room," she continued.

Reaching into her bag, Terri pulled out a rag or towel of some sort that had been stuffed with what appeared to be leaves. Retrieving a lighter from the same bag, she flicked it, setting the leaves on fire.

"Whoa! You can't just start sparking up in the classroom!," Todd yelled. "This ain't the 60's!" he continued as he fanned the flames, trying to blow out the fire.

The campers in the classroom were both panicked and entertained. From

133

their perspective, two adults
were acting out a play with pyrotechnics. They assumed the fire was the
finale and began to clap.

"It's not weed, you imbecile; it's sage!," Terri yelled.

"Who brings a *spice rack* to work?!," Todd teased.

"Can I leave to go find out who this skank is around my man?," Terri asked,
finally returning to the 'emergency' that had summoned Todd to her
classroom in the first place.

"Terri, you have to watch your language around these kids," Todd reminded
her. "You cannot go around calling people skanks," he whispered.

"That ho *is* a skank if she's hanging around my man," Terri replied,
completely missing Todd's point and ignoring his instructions.

"What is a ho skank?," asked a camper.

"It's a species of skunk that works in gardens," Todd responded. "Terri, one
last time. Watch. your. language. around these campers," he cautioned.

Still captivated by the content on her phone, Terri ignored everything Todd
said.

"Look, look at this picture my friend sent me of them, Todd," Terri said,
thrusting her phone so forcefull in Todd's face that it almost hit him.

Todd was unable to see Terri's competition; the movement of the phone in

134

her hand made the image blurry. He didn't care to see Terri's ex, or his new "ho skank," anyway. He was becoming more annoyed that Terri was wasting classroom time stalking her boyfriend, or maybe ex-boyfriend, on her phone.

"He's only interested in her because she has a nice rack. Mine is perkier, though," Terri bragged. "Doesn't mine look perkier?," she asked.

"Let me see!," exclaimed a boy camper. Terri turned her phone to oblige.

"No, we do not need to see this," Todd said emphatically. "Terri, this is not show and tell," he added, making sure the class couldn't see her phone.

"What's a rack?," another camper asked.

"It's a country in the middle east," Todd responded quickly. "Terri," Todd whispered. "Speaking of, um, twin peaks, Todd sheepishly described Terri's anatomy, you need to cover yours. Your manner of dress does not leave much to the imagination, Todd continued coyly. Especially with the thin white, partially unbuttoned blouse you're wearing. Todd respectfully ignored gazing at Terri's revealing silhouette underneath her blouse. It made him feel uncomfortable, and he shuddered to think what a parent or the superintendent would say if they were face to face with her. It's inappropriate to be worn around campers this age, and definitely does not adhere to the dress code dress for this school, he argued. That's why we issued you a Camp Staff t-shirt.

Todd's navy blue summer camp t-shirt had been made by Amell's fiancé. She liked crafting and took on making the staff's uniform shirts as a project. Plus, budget wise, she was all the camp could afford. The camp's initials were on the lapel: A. S.A.P. Unfortunately, poorly-applied letters were peeling off.

On the back in bold letters were the words ``Summer Break," except "break" was misspelled. What a great way to advertise a school. It wasn't even what the camp ordered. They'd asked for the back to read "Summer Camp." The quote Bianca came up with was omitted since the cost of the shirts increased with each letter. All the sizes ran small, and tight, and the spots where the lettering was applied were itchy. It was no wonder Bianca and Terri wore something other than the uniform, but rules were rules.

"I need a bigger size," Terri replied. "And I don't like my girls corralled; that's why I never wear a bra. I keep mine liberated," she protested. Men don't have to wear bras, so why do women?"

"Terri, I can't have this conversation right now. What's the emergency that you made me come here for?," he asked. He really wanted to continue to remind Terri how her clothing was not only inappropriate for this Christian school, but for being around children and faithful, married men, but he didn't have the energy at the moment. Terri had valid points, but Todd was just too tired to think about or find a solution for them. It had already been a long morning; he just wanted to crawl back in bed and start the day over. Maybe not *his* bed since there was a stab hole in it, but some bed somewhere.

"I need to go to my ex's old house to see if he's really back in town or if it's someone that looks like him."

"Girlfriend," yelled a camper. "I saw the same thing happen in a movie," added another camper.

136

"I saw that, too!" recalled a third. "A woman was annoying so her man faked moving to another country to be away from her."

"She must be annoying," concluded the first camper, pointing in Terri's direction. The whole classroom erupted in laughter.

"It *was* just a movie," replied the second camper, looking at Terri. "But maybe it's about you!"

The room burst into laughter again.

"Class! Quiet down," Todd demanded, trying to bring order to what was supposed to be his class-preparedness portion of the camp. He was amazed that the campers had seen the movie they'd referenced at their age. Todd had seen it and blushed, and he was twenty years older than most of the campers!

Turning his attention back to Terri and her ridiculous request to leave early, "Are you serious?!," he asked, dumbfounded. "Can't you go after you get off? I'm sure if he *is* back, he's not going to move again in the next couple of hours."

"Fine!," Terri yelled Terri as if she was a toddler who'd just been told she couldn't have a cookie.

Walking out of Terri's classroom, Todd felt as if he'd been hit by a truck. This was the most annoying series of events he'd ever dealt with, all because of someone's ex.

"LISTEN!!," screamed a voice from down the hall."What *now*?!," Todd cried to himself.

He went to investigate and found that the scream had come from Teresa's classroom. Campers were lined up along the wall, their arms outstretched, palms facing the ceiling. On top of each palm sat children's bibles. Struggling to keep their arms extended, campers were crying from the strain they had to exert to keep the books from falling. Todd was shocked.

"Keep your arms out!," Teresa yelled. "If your bible hits the ground, you will go to hell," she warned. A collective gasp filled the room and each camper found extra motivation and strength to keep their arms outstretched.

"What in the name of Pelican Bay is going on here?," Todd asked. "Kids, relax your arms," he said. Not a soul moved. The campers were obviously deathly afraid of Teresa and her threat.

"It's okay," Todd reassured them. "You can set the books down." The books came tumbling to the ground all at once. Fatigued arms fell to each camper's side.

Turning his attention to Teresa, Todd calculated what her punishment should be.

"Why the illegal corporal punishment?" he asked, looking disapprovingly at Teresa.

"They got out of line so I had to show them who's boss," she replied.

"Kids, take a seat," Todd instructed. "Teresa, may I please speak with you over here?," he asked.

Teresa followed him to the other side of the classroom. "When we told you it was going to be hard to get respect from some of the kids because you're still a student, we didn't mean for you to take it forcefully by physical punishment," he started. "What did they do wrong, anyway?"

They ask questions without raising their hands," Teresa declared. "I demand order in my classroom," she said.

"Give them a break! It's only the first day!," Todd replied. "Besides, it's not school. This is supposed to be a fun learning environment," he continued. "I remember when...." he started, but was interrupted by a crackle from his walkie-talking and then Terri's voice:

"It's an emergency, Todd, I need you again," she said.

"Excuse me, Teresa," Todd said as he exited her classroom.

As he walked down the hallway toward Terri's room, he pondered picking up the pace so he could attend to Terri's emergency. But judging from her earlier 'emergency,' Todd began to question whether Terri knew what an emergency really was.

He passed two volunteers in the hallway who were on their phones. Todd was irritated by their lack of work ethic and even more annoyed that they seemed completely oblivious to his presence. He stood next to them waiting for them to see him. After a few moments of being ignored, Todd's patience ran out.

"Aren't you two supposed to be working the front desk?," he asked.

"It's 8 o'clock," one of them replied sarcastically. Todd remembered her from her interview. Her name was Lori. She was a petite fourteen-year-old with long hair and was sweet yet sassy. If she thought about it, she'd say it. No filter. She'd say it without malice or evil intent, but her goal in life seemed to be to push boundaries. Todd was pretty sure she was going to be a headache all summer long.

"I'm glad you can tell time," he responded. "Now, tell me what that has to do with you not operating the front desk?" Todd could be sassy, too, but some of his sass *did* have malicious intent.

"The summer school classes started at 8 so we figured no one else would be coming in," Lori responded. "I also had to text Michelle about Bianca's muddy dress," she continued.

"Who's Michelle?," Todd asked. "And why does she need to know about Bianca now and not after work?"

"Hi there, sir, I'm Michelle" said the young woman standing inches from Lori.

Todd desperately wanted to delve into why the two of them, standing inches apart, found it necessary to text each other, but he didn't have the energy or the patience to process any possible explanation the two adolescents might give him.

"We're in summer camp," Todd explained. "It's not the school year; campers don't have to arrive at a specific time. We have campers signed up for full days, half days, only coming on some days but not others…," he continued Todd. "Therefore, we need someone at the front desk to sign campers in

140

and out all day."

"That sounds boring," Lori said.

"Go back to the front desk, and don't leave it again unless I tell you to," Todd said.

"Okay, okay," Lori relented. "You don't have to be mean about it," she added. "Just let me text Michelle and let her know I'll be at the front desk."

"*GO!!*," Todd bellowed.

Finally reentering Terri's classroom, he was shocked to see her sitting behind her desk with tears streaming down her face. Todd expected to hear another soap opera scenario about her personal life.
As *Terri's World Turns*, or *Days of Terri's Life*, he thought, chuckling to himself.

"What's the emergency?," Todd asked warily.

"What am I supposed to be doing?," Terri asked.

"What do you mean?," Todd replied. From her earlier drama, Todd wasn't sure if this was a life-altering question or if Terri was being practical. "I don't understand the question," he confessed.

"What am I supposed to be doing with this?," Terri asked, throwing Todd's lesson plan across the desk.

"Don't you have a degree in education?," Todd inquired.

141

"Yes, but I've never used it," she confessed. "I student taught in college, but the teachers don't actually let you teach. I spent that semester making copies."

How is it that I managed to find the one certified teacher in the state of Missouri who doesn't know how to teach, Todd thought incredulously.

"How did you pass your certification?," Todd asked.

"I got lucky," Terri said. Todd believed that was true.

"Use the lesson plans as a teaching guide," Todd suggested.

"I did that already. The problem isn't the coursework; the problem is teaching it," Terri said.

"I truly don't understand," Todd admitted.

"I know how to add and subtract, but I don't know how to teach someone else to do it," Terri confessed.

"Is this conversation really happening?," Todd wondered. I feel like I'm in a corny sitcom. This camp needs a better script and a laugh track. If I told anyone about this morning, they wouldn't believe it. I'm living it and I don't believe it.

"It's elementary math," he started, "I'm pretty sure they already know it. Just put problems on the board and let them practice.

"Todd, come in," called a voice from his walkie-talkie.

"This is Todd."

"Todd, this is Heidi from Mr. Franklin's office. A parent is trying to sign in."

I'm on it!," he replied. "Thank you, Heidi. You can do this," Todd reassured Terri as he exited the classroom.

Where in the world is Lori?, he wondered. It's only been ten minutes since I told her to work the front desk. Maybe I needed to text her what I wanted.

"Good morning!," Todd greeted the parent as he arrived at the front desk. "I'm so sorry about this. It's the first day and we're still working out the kinks with the volunteers and everything," he added.

The parent was obviously not in a forgiving mood and shot Todd a disapproving look before hugging their child and walking away.

"Good morning!," Todd said to the camper. "You're going to be in Miss Teresa's classroom, room 355. A word of advice? Be sure to raise your hand before you ask a question!"

Todd was furious. Between lazy volunteers and inexperienced, abusive staffers, he wanted to fire everyone and start over. Camp had only been operational for an hour and it's been one headache after another. His stress level was already spilling over. A paycheck is not worth all this, he thought. He wanted to quit. He wanted to run and hide. Do we *really* need electricity?, he began to wonder. Cave dwellers survived without it, he thought. Man up, he told himself. Real men don't whine and quit.

143

He took a deep breath and composed himself. There was no quitting. No matter how turbulent their relationship, he had a wife to take care of. He had a school to save. He needed to prove to himself and others that he could be successful.

Todd bumped the side of the desk to wake Lori up. "Good morning, Sleeping Beauty," he said in his best sing-songy voice.

"Todd, come in," crackled another voice from the walkie.

"This is Todd," he responded.

"We need you to come to the administration building," Heidi replied.

"On my way!," Todd said, then, turning back to Lori, "I'll deal with you later. Stay awake," he instructed.

What is it now?, Todd thought. He half-hoped Mr. Franklin had decided to shut down the camp. Upon entering the administration building, Todd saw Mr. Franklin walking quickly toward the restroom. He must have just finished his morning coffee, he surmised.

"What's the emergency?," Todd asked Heidi.

"It's Bianca," she responded. In her late sixties, Ms. Heidi had been a staple of the school since its inception in the late seventies. She knew everyone. Parents would visit her to pay tuition, or talk to her to announce their child's absence. She knew every student, as well, from those sent to the principal's office for discipline to those getting awards: every student had to pass her

144

desk first. Ms. Heidi attended every play, sporting event, and concert.

"Where is she, by the way?," Todd asked. "She needs to be helping put out the fires around here."

"She's in the restroom," Heidi replied. "Her dress is ruined and she doesn't want anyone to see her in such filth."

Todd gave Ms. Heidi a confused look. He was aware she had knowledge of every rumor, every piece of gossip, but this was uncanny.

"Amanda informed me of Bianca's mishap," she said, as if she could read Todd's thoughts. "I don't know why that girl has to dress like she's going to Prom every day. Anyway, Amanda thought you might want to know that Bianca's having a meltdown and wants to go home to change clothes. So I guess that puts you in charge of the camp until she gets back!" she added.

As frustrating as this news was, Todd was relieved it wasn't something worse.

"Come in, Todd" came a voice over the radio.

"Have a good day," Todd said as he headed back to the main building, probably to handle another crisis.

"Todd there's an emergency at the sign in desk," cried the voice over the walkie-talkie. It was Lori. Thankfully she's not asleep, Tod thought as he hurried to her location.

"What's the emergency?," he asked, out of breath.

"Can I do something else now? I'm bored," Lori whined, placing her head on the desk.

> *Left to themselves,*
> *things tend to go from bad to worse*
> *-Murphy's Seventh Law*

What a morning!, Todd thought as he ran his hands through his hair and down his face. Massaging
his eyes with the heel of his palms, Todd was trying to wake up from a horrible nightmare. He struggled to wrap his head around all the issues that had happened already on day one. He'd imagined having to deal with campers who misbehaved or not enough assignments, maybe even a camper
forgetting their lunch and not having lunch money. But today had been an indescribable series of Murphy's Laws. Todd longed for someone to pop out from behind a curtain and yell, "You've been pranked!"

BOOM!

Was the sound rumbling throughout the building? Fearing to face reality, Todd hoped the noise he heard
had been an explosion of some sort. That would be a welcome scenario compared to what he was imagining.

Todd walked down the hall with urgency, trying to find a window to look out. As he passed closed-door classrooms, he could see dark shadows escaping through the shade-drawn windows. Through the giant window in the stairwell at the end of the hallway, Todd saw it. His fear realized. Storm clouds. The booming sound he'd heard earlier was the sound of thunder as a weather front made its way into the
region. Dammit!, Todd thought. He remembered the forecast calling for a

miniscule thirty percent chance of rain in the evening; nothing but sunshine during the day. Re-checking the forecast on his
phone, as if he didn't believe what he was seeing in front of him, Todd saw the forecast had changed in the last two hours. His phone now said there was a ninety percent chance of thunderstorms for the next three hours, some severe. Searching the web for weather radars, Todd looked intently for any chance to disprove the storm clouds, dancing lightning, and booming thunder in front of him. Todd dreaded the reaction of a hundred disappointed kids when they found out their field trip to the swimming pool canceled due to rain.

Crack! The sound of lighting violently hitting an object a few miles away. The sound of the strike was glorious compared to the tornado-warning siren Todd now heard echoing in the distance.

A tornado created a completely new list of problems. The likelihood of a tornado hitting the school was
small, Todd thought, but it was still a very real scenario that had to be taken seriously. Time to gather the campers and seek shelter. Then it dawned on Todd: where do we assemble for a tornado? The library or
interior locker bays were where they would assemble during the school year. But during the summer, those areas are under renovation. Assembling there with as many campers would be just as dangerous as facing a tornado. Sarcastically, Todd wondered if he should wait for Bianca. Is she even back from her wardrobe change? Will she instruct her staff where to assemble the campers? His thoughts were interrupted by a scene he couldn't fathom.

"What in the fuck?," he exclaimed. There before him stood dozens of campers with their mouths open, their tongues out, looking up at the sky. As a kid, Todd remembered the delectable taste of summer raindrops on his

148

tongue, the innocence of a time long gone spent singing and dancing in the rain.

This was more than a simple summer shower, though, he thought. This had the makings of a serious weather event. Wind speeds had increased dramatically; lightning lit up the sky; and dark, thick clouds completely blocked out the sun. The rain fell with ferocity.

"Bianca?! Come in!," Todd screamed over the walkie-talkie. No answer. "Bianca! Over!," he repeated. Once again, no response. Then he saw her. Bianca, outside with the campers. Her arms outstretched, her head tilted up with her tongue sticking out. Banging on the window from where he was on the second floor, Todd yelled Bianca's name, hoping she could somehow hear him over the tornado sirens, thunder, and through a plate glass window.

Trying the walkie-talkie again in vain, Todd remembered that they don't work outside. A deafening *thwack!* of thunder filled the air. As if time suddenly ceased to exist, everything and everyone stopped for just a second, then it started again. Frantically, screaming campers ran for cover. The clouds opened up and a deluge of rain poured out of the sky. The tornado sirens seemed to get louder.

Todd took the stairs two at a time to get the campers to safety more quickly.

Smack! Thump! Thud! Whap! The sounds of campers losing their footing as their wet shoes met the dry linoleum at a high rate of speed was not a good combination. As they witnessed their friends wiping out, the remaining campers turned their entrances into an Olympic sport. Soaked to the bone, the campers dove and slid onto the floor. Baseball slides, belly slides, the campers tried to outdo one another with an entrance more spectacular than that of the previous camper. Some had enough momentum that the wall was their only means of stopping.

When Todd witnessed a few of them run back into the storm, Todd had had enough. It was time to put a
stop to this before someone got seriously hurt.

"Line up!," he commanded. Only a handful of the younger campers obliged; they were still rationally fearful of the tornado sirens wailing in the distance.

"Stop! Get back over here!," Todd yelled in his attempt to restore order. He moved side-to-side, looking like a goalie trying to block multiple pucks of many different shapes and sizes at the same time. And then…. *THUMMPP!*

Todd came crashing down on his back. The air escaped his lungs as he hit the ground violently. A
a crescendo of applause and laughter filled the hallway. Bianca had decided to join in on the fun and now stood over him.

"Toooddd!," she whined. "You ruined my slide!" The campers laughed and applauded as Todd lay on the floor, struggling to catch his bearings, and his breath. He contemplated staying there as he gazed up at the ceiling. He wondered, given all that had happened just this morning, if he could even survive the remainder of the summer.

He wanted to be angry, but he couldn't help but smile. The campers' laughter was infectious. Todd felt his cares wash away. The summer camp really was what he needed. He needed to remember how to have a good time.

150

"This is not the time or the place for this kind of monkey business," shrieked a woman's voice. Still on his back, Todd just wanted to lay there instead of trying to explain what was going on.

Fortunately, the campers knew precisely what was happening. Someone was going to be in trouble and now was the time to act right. They immediately lined up and stood quiet and still.

Bianca, already on her feet, reached out her hand to help Todd up.

"Luckily, those sirens were just a warning!," the voice continued. "You two!," it said, pointing at Bianca and Todd.

Oh crap! It's Amanda, Todd thought, finally matching the voice with a face.

"If this type of behavior is indicative of how this camp is run then I hope they shut you down immediately," continued the head janitor. "I knew you people had no business being in charge," she added.

"You people?!," Bianca snapped. "You mean *black* people?," she questioned. "Are you saying black people are incapable of being in charge? If so, that confuses me, because I thought Christians were
supposed to love all people, and that doesn't feel like love. Are you judging us?," she asked. "Because if you are, you should take the plank of wood out of your eye before you judge the speck of wood in mine," she snapped.

Todd had never thought of Amanda as a racist. A bitch definitely, but not racist.

"I-I-I-I didn't mean it like that," Amanda stuttered. I'm not a racist," she continued; my best friend in grade school was black. I take off every Martin Luther King, Jr. Day, and I support you people during Cinco de Mayo."

She isn't racist, Todd thought, just clueless.

"I was heading over this way to unlock a safe area for you to assemble for the tornado warning," Amanda said. "Is everyone safe?," she asked, glancing at the soaked floor and drenched campers.

"We are FINE!," Bianca said. "Just shocked by your statements."

"I honestly meant nothing by it, Amanda replied. "I love you, guuurrrl," she concluded, donning a dialect that was both racist and awkward.

Before hurrying away, Amanda grabbed Bianca, gave her a sideways hug and offered Todd a one-fist salute.

"Huh. I wouldn't have pegged her as racist," Todd said. "I guess you never know!"

"Maybe she is, maybe she isn't," Bianca responded. "I just used her words against her to get us out of trouble. Who could she tell this story to without sounding racist," she asked.

Todd disagreed with her method. Todd couldn't argue with what the results were likely to be.

"I guess swimming is out of the question, Mr. Activity Director," Bianca said sarcastically. "What boring activity do you have planned to replace it?," she asked.

Todd hadn't thought of a contingency plan for swimming. He didn't think he'd need one; he trusted the
weatherman. Scrambling for a quick solution, Todd thought about playing board games, or maybe watching a movie in the gym.

"Don't say a movie in the gym or something dumb like board games," Bianca said. "We should take
the campers to the $1 show, she suggested."

"You read my mind," Todd lied.

Dejected that Bianca had labeled his suggestion boring, Todd grabbed his phone to find the cheapest and most accommodating theater for 100 campers.

"The movies!? Where?," Amell asked, just arriving at the camp. Todd was both miffed and relieved that his boss had missed the morning's excitement. He was more jealous of the fact Amell was able to sleep in, a luxury not afforded to Todd.

"The Plaza," Todd answered.

"*THE PLAZA*?!," Amell and Bianca exclaimed simultaneously.

Never go to a doctor whose office plants have died.
-Erma Bombeck

In its heyday, The Plaza had been an elegant mall. Many Fortune 500 companies were located nearby. But as the companies went out of business or merged with larger ones, they moved away. So did the people who frequented the mall. The meticulously-cared-for neighborhoods surrounding it were now shells of their former glory as more and more people left the area. The mall, which had once housed at least 100 stores as well as several high-end department stores, now only contained several discounted novelty shops, a ninety-nine cent store, discounted jewelry stores, and a movie theater.

The movie theater opened during a time when the focus was on filling seats, not on the comfort of the guests. Where most theaters opened around the same time had updated their seating to larger, more comfortable, faux leather, heated seats, the Plaza's theater had never upgraded from their old plastic chairs.

"It's the only affordable theater that can accommodate a group our size," Todd argued, defending his selection. He wasn't sure if that was even the case. The Plaza had been the first result in his web search for cheap movie theaters, but Todd was tired of searching. With the unexpected thunderstorm, and 100 restless campers, Amell was limited in his options.

"Have the volunteers load up the bus," he said.

Awesome!, Todd thought. The theater will be the perfect spot to take a nap!

154

The Plaza reminded Todd of a movie scene when the desperado came into town. The townsfolk hid in their homes, locking the doors, shutting the blinds, and not making a sound. But instead of tumbleweed rolling across the prairie, trash blew in the wind across the Plaza's parking lot. Instead of dirt at
the cowboys' feet, weeds grew in the cracks of the street.

"Maybe we should have stayed in the gym and watched a movie," Bianca said.

"Is this the hood?," asked a camper.

"No," Lori replied emphatically.

Todd gasped at Lori's response. That was the most energetic he'd seen her all day!

"What do you know about being in the hood?," he asked.

"I used to live in the hood!," she responded gleefully. "There were drive-by's at night," she boasted as if it was a point of pride. She was soaking up the attention and admiration from the campers.

"Have you ever been in a fight?," asked a younger camper.

"MANY," Lori bragged. "People know not to mess with me," she continued. "I've had guns and knives pulled on me," she said with a flourish.

"We should just put *her* on the stage," Amell said. "Her story is way more entertaining than anything that's out in the theaters!"

155

"Isn't she from Riverside, California?," asked Bianca.

"I'm not sure," Todd responded, "but I don't think she's ever seen any drama in her life. I honestly think she's reciting lines from a movie I saw a while ago," he continued.

As the group made their way into the lobby, Todd could smell mildew from the carpet. Several leaks in the ceiling were dripping onto the floor.

"Look! It's raining in here, too!," pointed out a camper.

Making his way toward the box office, Todd wondered if anyone was working. The concession area smelled of stale popcorn. The floor had more popcorn on it than the popcorn holder did.

"Welcome to the Plaza," said a kid wearing a wrinkled Plaza Theater Uniform.

"Good morning, sir," Todd responded. "I need 108 tickets for the 11:30 showing of…"

"Hold on man," the kid interrupted, pulling out his phone. "Hello? Nah," he said to whoever was on the other end of the phone. "Hold up, I'll be right back," he continued, walking away to finish his conversation.

"Did you see that?," Todd asked.

"Kids don't have manners anymore," Amell replied.

156

"Spare me the back-in-my-day story," Bianca interrupted before Todd and Amell could get going. "I don't have time for this," she mumbled following the theater attendant.

Snatching his phone from his hand, Bianca repeated Todd's request for 108 tickets.

"We're here for a kiddie movie!," groaned a couple of older campers, expressing their desire to see an action movie that would probably give them nightmares.

"Start the popcorn machine too", Bianca demanded, still holding the kid's phone hostage.

"We don't have any," the kid sighed.

"Make. some.," Bianca demanded through gritted teeth. Seeing her with her hands on her hips and fire in her eyes, the attendant knew she meant business. He realized he wasn't going to win a battle with Bianca and relented.

"Are you the only one working?," Todd asked.

"Do you see..." the attendant started sarcastically, but stopped when he made eye contact with Bianca.

"Yes, sir, I am," he replied.

"Since there's a lot of us, I can assist you with our popcorn and drink orders," Todd offered.

157

"Not many people come to our theater," the attendant replied. "We haven't ordered soda in months. I wouldn't dare drink anything from here," he warned. "I don't even trust the water," he continued.

"Sorry kids!," Todd announced. "No snacks. Let's just go into the theater and find some seats."

As the volunteers and staff ushered the campers into the theater, Todd noticed the attendant wasn't the only one getting Bianca's evil glare. Derrick was feeling her wrath, too.
Since Derrick's interview, he and Bianca had become an official couple, but as Shakespeare once wrote, the course of true love never did run smooth. Todd assumed Bianca's current state of irritation was just the latest episode in their series of making up to break up. Mostly over petty teenage drama. Him forgetting to text her back or complimenting another woman in front of her. The coup de grâce was when she found out he'd made other plans after she'd spent an exorbitant amount of time getting ready. Todd only half listened to Bianca's relationship issues, which were many. He had relationship issues of his own, mostly for infractions similar to Derrick's. Unlike Sharon's style of revenge, Bianca ignored Derrick, shot him evil looks, and made him jealous. It doesn't get any better when you get older, Todd thought, just more extreme.

Expecting the theater to be frigid, Todd was shocked when he opened the door to find the air stuffy and humid.

"I'll turn on the fan!," the attendant yelled, darting to another room.

"Ewwww!," complained a camper. The stench of the theater made it clear that it hadn't

had air circulate through it for quite a while.

Squish…squish…crunch…crunch. The campers' feet stuck to the floor with each step. Dried fountain drinks and discarded slushies had dried on top of the cement, and dropped popcorn kernels and escaped Raisinets were everywhere.

The campers laughed uproariously as they took a seat. Pockets of air escaped from the splits in the seats, mimicking fart noises.

Suddenly, the screech of metal grinding against metal filled the air as the cooling system turned on. A stale, musty odor and blowing dust spilled down from the vents, further proof the system had been off for quite a while.

When the screen came to life, dark splotches covered it. Todd could only assume these were stains from someone using it as target practice for their discarded beverages. Old previews began to play, trailers of movies Todd had already seen or had someone spoil for him.

This was the first movie he'd seen since he married Sharon. Because he was always working, he never had the time for the luxury of going to the theater. Ironic, he thought: the only reason he had time for a movie now was because he was there for work.

Sitting in the very last row, Todd could look out and observe all the campers. So far, the contents on the screen held most of their attention. As expected, the volunteers and older campers were engaged in small side conversations.

Placing his hand on the armrest to support his head, Todd was ready to take advantage of the real reason why he'd chosen to sit away from the rest of the group. A nap. With no disturbance.

As he nestled his head onto the palm of his hand, he saw his phone light up. Another text from Sharon, one he planned to ignore. It was the usual "What are you doing? – Why haven't you texted me? – Call me back." kind of texts. The thirteen texts and four calls he'd missed since he last texted Sharon were about average for her. Trying to set a good example for the staff by not being on his phone constantly, Todd generally only sent the occasional message to check in.

"Hi, Sharon," he whispered, deciding to call her back.

"Why the fuck are you whispering?," Sharon asked aggressively. Todd realized calling Sharon back at this exact moment probably wasn't the greatest idea.

"I'm on a field trip with the camp," Todd replied quietly.

"That is a boldface lie," Sharon snapped. "You cannot be at the pool; it's storming," she said.

Excusing himself to the lobby, Todd knew he was in for a long conversation. "I know it's raining, honey," he replied. "We brought them to the movies as our contingency plan."

Todd thought calling Sharon a pet name would warm her heart a little and settle her down. Wrong!, he realized.

160

"You call me by my NAME around your mistress," Sharon barked.

Glancing up, Todd saw Bianca and the attendant were also in the lobby…making out. Another ploy to catch Derrick's attention or to make him jealous, Todd thought. He couldn't believe she still hadn't learned her lesson about making out with someone while she was on the clock. Furthermore, he could not believe she was making out with this rude kid. Either way, he didn't care. Bianca and her new fling's lip smacking was grotesquely sickening. She was kissing him as if she was putting on a show for Derrick if he happened upon them. Unfortunately, it was Todd who had that pleasure. It wasn't a show he wanted to see, and yet he couldn't stop looking. He watched, horrified, as she stuck her tongue out for the attendant to suck. That was too much. Todd could only imagine the amount of germs being exchanged. The added moaning and rubbing was another dramatic way to show a current ex-boyfriend what he was missing. It was almost comical, he thought.

Todd cleared his throat to try and catch their attention, but Bianca and the attendant ignored him. Todd tried to look away, but froze. He hadn't been fast enough. Bianca had seen him. She took a break from kissing the attendant, wiped the wetness from her mouth, and shot Todd an agitated glance.

"Ummm, sicko!," she began. "Are you watching us?!" Todd didn't respond. "Take a picture. It'll last longer!" Still no response from Todd. "Creep," she muttered.

"I hear your bitch talking," Sharon hollered through the phone. Todd just stood frozen; he'd completely forgotten she was still on the phone.

161

"What is your problem?!," Bianca asked, irritated. "We already caught you staring at us; there's no need to try to play it off."

Todd continued tuning everyone out. Bianca, Sharon, the attendant, the camp, his bills…. they all seemed trivial at this point.

"Cut it out!," Bianca demanded. "I'm not going to look," she continued.

The attendant began pulling on her shirt emphatically. "Beth, look!" he said.

Ready to slap him for calling her the wrong name, Bianca froze. Why did the attendant's face hold the same expression of horror as Todd's? Then she saw it, too. A man in a hoodie had a gun pointed at another man with a gun.

> *Try to look unimportant, they may be low on ammo.*
> *-Murphy's Law of Combat*

To say the scene was tense would be the understatement of the century. The two gunmen began shouting expletives at one another. They dared each other to pull the trigger and became louder and louder as they walked circles around each other. Around and around and around. They flung hateful insults at each other. Minimizing each other's manhood, comparing the other's mother to a female dog, claiming their gang, or their neighborhood, was the better one.

"Riverside, Bitch!" yelled one of them, flashing gang signs with his unarmed hand.

"Mead Street, Mother Fucker!," cried the other gunman.

"We eat Mead Street Bitches for breakfast," shouted the first gunman.

"Your mom eats Mead Street dick for breakfast, Bitch!," the other one retorted, grabbing his genitals.

"After I deal with you I'm gonna bury your kid and turn your baby mama out," the first gunman barked.

Suddenly, they stopped moving. They were directly in front of the theater entrance, mere feet from where Todd was standing. One of the gunmen had his back to Todd. A stray bullet is all that separated Todd from life or death. He tried to remain calm and prayed he at least looked like he was, even though he was frozen with fear on the inside. His heart was pounding, his mind racing, his nerves tingling. The air was tense. Todd could feel the utter hate between the two gunmen.

In the movies, situations like these always appear manageable. The hero can dodge the bullet or dive behind a barricade. But in his present reality, Todd couldn't feel his feet to dive, catch his breath to run, or move his hands to fight. He was at the complete mercy of two men. Todd had felt fear many times in his life. This was different. Indescribable

With guns drawn, it was clear neither gunman cared about the safety of their aggressor or any innocent bystanders. They were animated with their movements: arms flailing with guns in their hands. Todd wanted to cry. He wasn't sad about the possibility of losing his life in the theater; he was sad for the life he'd wasted. Abusive spouse, abusive jobs, and living to work was not a life worth living. Something has to change, he thought. Life is too short, and it appeared it might be even shorter than he'd thought given his current situation.

Stay calm, he kept repeating to himself. He began to pray, making heartfelt promises to God about what he'd do if his life was spared. In the distance, Todd could hear Sharon still screaming expletives at him through the phone. She was going to be the first change in his life, Todd thought.

Mouthing "Let's go," to Bianca, Todd backed away slowly. Have to go, Sharon, call the police, Todd thought as he tried willing calls of help to Sharon telepathically. Fearing the gunmen could hear her, Todd calmly hit the "end call" button on his phone. He continued to back away from the two gunmen carefully, then *CRUNNCH!*, the slow loud sound of a plastic lid from a discarded slushie cup cracking underneath Todd's shoe.

164

"Die, Bitch!," shouted one of the gunmen as he opened fire on the other one. A cacophony of shots thundered through the air. They found their target, and the injured gunman returned fire as he crashed to the ground. It was a sickening sound. Todd could see the anguish on his face and he wanted to run, but his feet would only move in slow motion. Todd was confused. He couldn't see the bullets, but he could hear glass shattering and wood splintering as they missed their intended targets. The malodorous scent of gunpowder filled the air, choking him.

The movie theater attendant shoved Bianca out of his way and dove into a supply closet. Todd heard the door lock behind him. Bianca let out a blood curdling scream as she hit the floor violently. The gunman who'd been injured got up. He and the one who'd shot him ran, continuing to fire at one another. The sound of glass shattering could be heard as they fled. Innocent bystanders were screaming as chaos filled The Plaza. Todd could see a pool of blood left behind by the injured gunman. He began to wonder if he, too, was hit. Am I dead and not able to tell?, he wondered. Am I hit but not able to feel it because my adrenaline is pumping so hard?.

Todd moved toward the theater door. Opening it, Todd glanced back, looking for Bianca. He didn't see her. Breathing hard, Todd scanned the lobby urgently as the door was closing in front of him. Then it stopped. Is it a gunman?, he feared. The door flung back open. Todd held his breath, fearing this was the end.

Just then, Bianca hurtled herself inside. She was crying, but she was alive. Todd noticed she was bleeding. "You're hit!," he cried. Todd was First Aid certified and had excelled in the training seminar, but real life was proving to be completely different. Still in shock, Todd couldn't focus long enough to remember what to do.

165

"I'll find a Band-Aid," he said. The words came out but he knew they were wrong. Bianca didn't need a Band-Aid. She needed….. She… needed…. Todd couldn't think clearly.

"I'm not shot!," replied a frantic Bianca through her tears. "That asshole attendant shoved me down and I cut myself on a shard of metal," she continued.

Breathing hard, Bianca desperately tried to find something – anything – to barricade the door. Breathing equally hard, Todd made contact with Amell, motioning him to join them.

"What is going *on*?," he asked Amell, wondering why Todd and Bianca were out of breath.

"Help me with this trash can!," Bianca pleaded frantically.

"I think it's bolted into the wall," Amell responded, still calm, though obviously confused.

"Shit! Shit! Shit!" Todd cried desperately, jumping up and down.

"What's going on here?," he demanded.

"Can I go to the bathroom?," asked Lori.

"They're shooting out there!," Bianca replied.

"*WHAATTT?!*" Lori's scream was shrill, loud, and assaulted everyone's ear drums. "Bianca's shot! Bianca's shot!," she yelled.

Shaking violently, Amell Immediately covered her mouth. "Settle down!," he pleaded. "Breathe."

Lori wasn't listening and continued to scream from behind Amell's hand.

The police, Todd thought, reaching for his phone. Realizing he dropped it in the lobby, he wondered how many missed angry calls he would have from his wife.

"I'll call them," Bianca volunteered, dialing. "Hello? Yes. Police? There's been a shooting at The Plaza Theater," she said. "I don't know," she responded to the 911 operator. "Just hurry up and get here!," she pleaded. "I think someone's dead."

"We need to shelter in place," Amell said, still holding his hand over Lori's mouth as she continued to scream.

"We need to lay low and not make a sound," Todd added. "Alright kids!," he yelled as quietly as he could. He feared the shooters might still be lurking looking to eliminate witnesses. "There's an emergency outside,' he started. "I need you to get on the ground calmly and quietly and stay there until I tell you it's safe.

Already fearful since Lori's outburst, the campers immediately dropped to the sticky floor. Todd felt badly that the campers had to get down on the disgusting floor, but if that was the trade off to not getting gunned down, so be it. Todd realized it was up to him, Bianca, and Amell to protect the campers from any armed assailants who might be left.

167

Todd emptied his pockets, searching for a weapon. A set of keys, two sticks of gum, and three dollars. Maybe MacGyver could've done something with those items, but Todd was no MacGyver. Grabbing his keys, Todd tried to turn them into a weapon somehow. Wondering how he could get close enough to a gunman so he could stab him with them, Todd decided he'd be better off *throwing* the keys at the attackers.

It seemed like it took days for the police to get there, but it was really only an hour. Todd couldn't believe he was still unable to catch his breath. The door began to move. Fear coursed through Todd's body as he prepared to fight. Barricading the door closed with their body weight, Amell, Bianca, and Todd used all their might trying to keep it shut. Amell could only use his back against the door because his front was still covering Lori's mouth shut in case she started screaming again. For someone raised around gunfire she sure isn't handling herself well, Todd thought.

All their effort proved fruitless when the 6'7", 300 lb. sheriff's deputy flung the door open effortlessly. "Freeze!," he yelled. Todd threw his keys at the officer's face. Irritated that he'd just had a set of keys hurled at him, the officer took a deep breath.

"Is everyone in here alright? Any injuries/," he asked" "Did any of you witness the commotion in the mezzanine?," he probed.

"These two did!," Lori said excitedly, shoving Todd and Bianca in the officer's direction.

"How about you, young lady, did you witness anything?," he asked Lori.

168

"No, I stayed here and protected the campers," she answered with confidence. Todd was amazed by her metamorphosis from panicked volunteer to Wonder Woman and rolled his eyes.

"Follow me," the officer directed the group. "Wait here," he instructed Todd and Bianca, "someone will come and get your statements. I'll also have someone check that out," he said, looking at Bianca's arm.

Just then, another officer grabbed them and escorted them into the lobby. Once there, Bianca, and Todd chronicled the details of their encounter for the officer. What seemed like an eternity, covering every inch of every detail of the incident, was only mere moments. Follow me asked a paramedic grabbing Bianca to look at her injury. Todd was relieved the incident was over. He was amazed how a rundown area could look even more out of sorts after a shooting. In the distance,Todd noticed the EMT escorting Bianca past a sheet covering what he surmised was a body. Meanwhile, officers escorted the campers out an emergency exit at the back of the theater to shield them from seeing the destruction and carnage of the shootout. What happened Todd asked the officer as he finished writing down Todd's statement You can go, the officer instructed Todd, completely ignoring his question. if you can remember any other details no matter how insignificant you might think they are, give me a call, he asked Todd while handing him a card. Todd determined that he wasn't going to find out anything more about what had happened from the officers on scene. They'd have to do an investigation and that would take time. They weren't likely to be able to share any information with him, anyway. He quickly caught up with the group.

As they made their way to the bus, Todd observed an assailant in the back of a squad car as well as several ambulances with injured bystanders in them, including Bianca. As they approached the bus, the officer escorting them noticed a man's body slumped over the steering wheel.

Fearing the worst, one officer escorted the campers back inside to safety while a group of them cautiously made their way towards the bus. With guns drawn, one of the deputies opened the bus door. The body remained motionless. The officer felt for a pulse and then called for the EMT.

"We have a victim with a possible G.S.W.," he alerted over the radio. The crackle of the radio startled
the motionless body awake.

The startled officer yelped. "Freeze!," he demanded.

"What'd I miss?," asked a half-awake Sebastian, yawning.

Todd was completely drained. What a first day of camp!, he thought. Only 41 more days to go.

If you're feeling good, don't worry. You'll get over it.
-Yogi Berra

Amell breathed in the morning air, his arms outstretched toward the high blue sky.

"Today is going to be a great day," he declared.

Inhaling the tantalizing aroma from a nearby flowerbed, beautifully decorated with a colorful mixture of blue hydrangeas, and blue jacket hyacinth, the fragrance delighted his senses. Bursting with happiness, Amell suggested that he, Todd, and Bianca have their morning meeting outside in the quad.

Commonly used as a gathering spot for events such as graduation, concerts, and bonfires, Todd found the quad the only aesthetically appealing part of the campus. He, however, steered clear of the flowerbed. It tended to attract a plethora of bees, and caused allergy sufferers fits of sinus problems.

Todd and Bianca glanced at each other in horror and then at their boss. Slapping her hand over his mouth, Bianca shouted, "Don't curse us like that!"

"You just jinxed the whole camp!," Todd chided.

"What are you talking about?" Amell asked, his voice muffled by Bianca's hand.

171

With her arm still bandaged from the previous day's field trip, Bianca directed her attention to Todd. "Todd, what happens when someone says something about nice weather?," she asked.

"It rains," Todd responded

"Health?," Bianca asked.

"Someone gets sick," Todd replied.

"Money?," Bianca continued.

"They go broke," Todd answered.

The two worked back-and-forth as if they were competing for prizes on a game show.

"Get your hand away from my mouth!," Amell demanded, pretending to spit Bianca's germs away from his mouth. "I do not know which thug's hand you were holding last night," he joked. "I get it," he continued. "You're both crazy *and* superstitious. But I feel it in my bones today will be a great day," he proclaimed. "I decree today will be a great day!," he shouted

"Were fucked," Bianca sighed.

"You will be if any of these campers hear your potty mouth," Amell threatened her. "Seriously," he continued. "The sun's shining, the birds are singing, and Todd has planned a wonderful field trip to the Butterfly House. What could possibly go wrong?"

172

Turning his attention back to Bianca, Amell asked, "How's your arm?"

"Horrible," Bianca complained. "Sixty stitches and a tetanus shot. Worse yet, I'll probably have a scar. How is that going to look when I wear a sleeveless top?," she whined.

Todd marveled at how someone who could have lost their life in the middle of a gun battle would complain about a scar showing if she wore a sleeveless outfit this summer. He was, however, impressed that she'd been able to find a blue bandage that matched today's outfit and nails.

Amell was just about to respond when he observed Terri sprinting around the corner. Todd couldn't help but blush at how tightly Terri's work t-shirt hugged her breasts in place. It was becoming more and more apparent that undergarments were not a staple in her wardrobe. He couldn't help but wonder if her tight t-shirt was Terri's passive aggressive response to Amell's threat to ban her from wearing blouses. She'd done that during orientation and training. Each was form-fitting and revealing. Todd remembered that the only thing keeping her from exposing herself to others was a button that appeared to stay fastened with only a hope and a prayer.

As much attention as Terri focused on her breasts, she spent an equal amount of time ignoring her hair. Worn in a loose ponytail, Terri often had several strands of hair flying wildly around her face. Her hairstyle was reminiscent of a bouffant. The top of her ponytail puffed out in a rounded shape.

At the moment, her hair was even more disheveled as the result of her sprinting. The frantic look on her face combined with her tight shirt, half untucked, warned Amell, Bianca, and Todd that something was truly wrong.

173

Gasping for air, Terri cried, "Amell! Come quick!" She doubled over in pain after her sprint and tried to suck air in in giant gulps.

"Take your time," Amell soothed, patting Terri's back.

Waving his hand away as if it were more of a nuisance than an aide, Terri dropped to one knee as she continued to try and catch her breath. "Blood," Terri started. "It's bad," she continued.

At that moment, Bianca and Todd looked at each other and then at Amell as if to say "Told you so!"

Struggling for more oxygen, Terri arched her back as she sucked in all the air her lungs could handle. Todd couldn't stop looking at her. Am I gazing too hard?, he wondered. Yes. Most definitely yes, he decided, turning his gaze away from Terri. Todd had just taken a sexual harassment course at his weekend job. He remembered learning that when someone's eyes are fixated on another's body, their leering is likely to be treated as sexual harassment.

"Put your eyes back in their sockets!," Bianca teased.

Terri flashed a quirky smile at Todd. She'd seen him staring, too. She quickly tucked in her shirt, arranging her breasts in the process. Todd needed to tread lightly here. He was a married man and needed to conduct himself that way. Hell, Sharon had gone ballistic on him because of a *dream*. Imagine what she'd do if she knew he was flirting at work. In addition, albeit different, Todd flirting at work was no different than Bianca's public displays of affection. Both were unprofessional, and neither had any place at work.

174

"Blood. Who's bleeding?," Amell asked urgently.

"Follow me," Terri said as she walked briskly back to a scene of shocked campers on the softball field. They could see a couple of volunteers helping a camper up who had been lying flat on her back.

Several campers gasped, shocked, as they saw the camper's injury up close. Had anyone called 911?, Todd wondered. Had someone called her parent or guardian? Todd wanted to scold the volunteers for moving someone who was obviously injured. He silently prayed she hadn't suffered a head injury.

"Shit! No! No! NO!," Bianca screamed, jumping up and down with nervous excitement. "Fuuuucckkkkk!," she screamed, quickly covering her mouth as she realized the word that had just escaped her lips was definitely not appropriate.

What am I looking at?, Todd thought. At that moment, Amell shot an angry glance at both him and

Bianca. Oops, Todd thought. I guess I accidentally verbalized my thought, too.

"He didn't see her," Terri said, pointing to a little boy no older than 10. We were finishing up a game of softball when she ran across the field as he was swinging.

"You left a camper! An **INJURED** camper!," Amell shouted.

"To go get YOU," Terri responded. "Why didn't you send a volunteer?

Another camper? Lassie?!," Amell snapped.

Todd and Amell have spent many nights supervising adults at the warehouse; this was the first time Todd had ever witnessed Amell reprimanding another adult. Conversely, Todd couldn't remember Amell ever reprimanding a student. He'd usually coach the student and then apologize to them for coming off harsh.

Now, in front of volunteers, campers, and staff, Amell was laying into Terri. As a supervisor at the warehouse, Todd believed those in positions of power should never chastise an employee in front of an audience. He felt it brought down morale and diminished the level of authority and respect they had.

As Amell continued his rampage, Todd instructed the volunteers to herd the campers inside the cafeteria. He also suggested to Bianca that she fetch the injured little girl some ice. Bianca was watching Amell berate Terri as if it was a movie, though, and Todd had to repeat his request.

"Bianca!," Todd said sharply. "She needs some ice!"

"So get her some!," Bianca replied. "It's not like it's going to help."

"Izzz itt bwad?," the injured camper struggled to ask.

"Is what bad?," Todd answered, acting clueless in an attempt to distract the injured camper from her injuries.

He once again motioned for Bianca to get some ice and Bianca finally acquiesced.

"My fwace!," the camper exclaimed.

It wasn't bad, Todd thought. It's way worse. The imprint of the aluminum bat stretched from her eyebrow to the top of her lip. The entire left side of her face was so swollen it was difficult to distinguish its original contour. Her eyebrow, cheek and lips had swollen several inches. There was blood streaming from her brow, nose, and upper lip, Todd guessed, though it was hard to tell since the side of her face looked like one big bump. Every time she spoke, she spat blood.

"Will I need swtitches?," she spit.

Dodging the spurts of blood coming from her mouth, Todd tried to comfort her and change the subject.

"What's your name?," he asked.

"Cccceleste," she responded with a whistling sound. Looking down on the ground Todd realized why the pronunciation of her name sounded like a whistle. Pieces of her teeth glistened in the sun as they lay in the dirt. Choking back the urge to vomit, Todd guided the injured girl to a nearby bench to sit down.

Just then, Bianca returned with the ice. "Damn girl, you about to get paid!," she shouted as she looked at Celeste. "Todd! Take the ice!," she demanded, as she handed Todd a small cup of crushed ice.

"Where am I supposed to put *this*?," asked a frustrated Todd.

177

"You can shove it up your ass," Bianca retorted. "I don't work for you, asshole; I'm not here to fetch things for you. Just because I am a LOT younger than you doesn't mean you get to order me around. I'm just as responsible for this camp as you are. So stay in your lane!," she demanded.

Todd had no clue what the words she was saying meant. Another generational gap between the two of them. He was just as perplexed when she would text him acronyms and emojis. Mostly he just ignored her.

"What's up with the ice chips?," he asked. "I needed a *bag* of ice to reduce the swelling in her face.

"Her whole face is jacked," Bianca replied.

"I can put it on her swollen eyebrow," Todd said back.

"Freezing that area may damage her ocular cavity," Bianca responded.

"Well then I could put it over her nose," Todd argued.

"And what? Freeze her sinus cavity?," Bianca snapped. "And before you say it, cold ice on her warm lip might cause the ice to stick and cause more pain or damage when she tries to remove it. Clearly she has an injury inside her mouth so the ice chips will help soothe it."

Deflated by her unprofessionalism and knowledge, Todd encouraged Celeste to suck on the ice chips.

Scanning his surroundings Todd noticed Amell was still admonishing Terri. "I was hoping he'd be done by now," Todd started. "We need to call your mom

178

to let her know what happened so she can take you to the doctor.

"Nooo!," Celeste screamed at the top of her lungs. "I don't like the doctor!," she exclaimed. "I don't want a shot!" Crying frantically, Celeste jumped up to run away.

Suddenly, Todd heard a clinking sound, sharp and crisp like the noise an aluminum bat makes when it hits a ball. And then he saw it. Celeste on the ground again. Todd couldn't believe what he'd just witnessed. With one eye swollen shut and the other filled with tears, Celeste didn't see the light pole and rammed the good side of her face into it going full speed.

"Bwahhhhha ha ha!" Bianca was doubled over, roaring with laughter. If this was a movie Todd, too, would find Celeste's antics funny. The scene was reminiscent of a cartoon, only this was far more serious. The child was motionless on the ground, her arms and legs outstretched.

Nervously, Todd dashed over to Celeste to check the extent of her new injuries. On his heels,
Amell, who'd finally stopped his verbal assault on Terri, also sprinted towards Celeste. Seeing the seriousness on her coworkers' faces, Bianca's tears from laughter quickly turned to tears of fear and worry. Terri followed cautiously, as she was overly concerned at seeing Celeste lying motionless for several moments. She feared for the worst.

"Celeste! Celeste! Are you okay? Can you hear me?," Todd cried out.

"Are you ok?," asked a concerned Amell as he stood over Todd

Gently grabbing her hand, trying not to disturb the rest of her body, Todd called out, "Celeste. Celeste! Are you all right?"

"No I'm not," Celeste replied softly. "What happened?," she asked.

Relieved that she was conscious, Amell knelt down beside Celeste and Todd and told her everything was going to be okay.

No it won't, Todd thought as he looked at Celeste's new injury. The skin from her right eyebrow to her cheek was flayed open. Hopping to his feet, Todd turned to Bianca to ask her to fetch some more ice but thought better of it.

"I'm on my way," Bianca replied calmly as if she could read Todd's thoughts.

Celeste was trying to sit up but Todd urged her to stay still. "I'm not okay," she repeated.

"Neither am I," Terri declared as she stood over Amell. "It's my turn now," she continued, looking down at her boss with her left hand on her hip and her right hand pointed directly at him.

This can't be good, Todd thought Todd. He remembered Sharon striking this pose many times before.

"If your bald, fat ass let me speak earlier, you would have known that all this happened under Gerri's watchful eye. I only came to get you because these cheap walkie-talkies don't work outdoors," Terri yelled, slamming her walkie-talkie violently to the ground and stomping on it. "When I came to get you, Gerri was still here. I haven't a clue where she is now," she continued.

180

"Oh. She's in the bathroom puking," Bianca answered, returning with a bag of ice. "Here, sweetie; find a spot to put this," she continued, handing Celeste the ice.

Dumbfounded, Amell searched for words to express his apology. Just as they began to form, Terri interrupted.

"Save it!," she snapped. "I don't need this shit! I have a degree in education. You need someone with a Master's in babysitting. Amell, since *you're* in charge of this shit show, I hope you're held solely responsible for this little girl's injuries."

Collecting herself, Terri took a deep breath, wiped the perspiration away from her brow, stood up straight, and calmly looked in Todd and Bianca's direction. With a huge smile on her face, Terri wished them a wonderful day. As she turned back to Amell, the smile disappeared.

"F you," she shouted. "How was my language **that** time, Todd?," she sneered as she walked off.

Since he was still kneeling on the ground reeling from Terri's tirade, Todd hesitated in reminding Amell that a parent or guardian had to be notified of Celeste's injury.

"Go get me Gerri. Now!," he demanded, rising to his feet.

"Maybe we should focus on the severe head injury staring us in the face right now," Todd suggested calmly. He knew Amell talking to Gerri when he was angry wouldn't work out well. It would probably go the same way it had when he just did it with Terri.

181

"You're right," Amell agreed, trying to gather his composure. "Bianca, go find Gerri and ask her to fill out an incident report. Please," he added.

Pulling out his phone, Amell took a deep breath as he prepared to inform a parent that the camp he was in charge of failed to protect their child.

Todd listened to Amell while he was on the phone with Celeste's mom. He listed all the visible and suspected injuries that Celeste had sustained. He *also* exaggerated the care his staff had provided her daughter.

After he ended the call, Amell asked Bianca to find some more ice, some towels, and some bandages. "Celeste's mom is leaving work to come get her and take her to the doctor."

The threat of the doctor did not rouse a reaction from Celeste this time. Maybe the blows to the head had finally knocked some sense into her, Todd thought.

"Maybe we can get her swelling down and her bleeding stopped and covered before her mom arrives," suggested an extremely worried Amell.

His plan to treat the child's injuries as though they'd magically disappear didn't work. Her deep red, purple, black, brown, and yellow skin discoloration was too pronounced to hide. The swelling alone made her look like she had a Quasimodo-sized bump on her face.

"What did you do to my precious angel?!" a woman hollered. Todd turned to see Celeste's mom standing in the doorway. The look of heartache, fear, and anger were all over her face as she inspected her daughter's injuries.

Todd was amazed that she'd arrived less than thirty minutes after getting off the phone with Amell.

"Ma'am, I understand how upset you are, but could you keep your voice down?," Amell asked, trying not to draw the attention of other parents as they arrived to drop off their campers.

"Keep my voice down?!," Celeste's mom roared. "I am about to whoop. some. ASS," she declared. "Who did this to my baby?!"

"Ma'am, this is still a religious institution," Amell began, trying to shush the concerned parent. "*Please* be respectful of the other children," he pleaded.

"You're seriously telling me to be respectful when my daughter looks like the monster from *Goonies*?!"

"His name was Sloth," Bianca chimed in. "See, Todd! I know things from your precious decade."

Amell shot Bianca a sideways glance as if to say "you are definitely not helping."

"What did you say to me?," Celeste's mom asked as she began removing her earrings and necklace.

Amell stepped in front of Bianca in an effort to subdue her sass.

"Oh, I get it," professed Celeste's mom, reaching inside of her purse. Todd began to back away cautiously, fearing she was going to pull out a gun. "I am going to beat **some**body's ass," she said again, pulling a belt from deep inside her purse.

Stepping toward Amell, she swiftly swung the belt, striking Amell on the buttocks. "I will beat the Holy *Spirit* out of everyone here for what y'all did to my baby!"

The stinging noise the belt made as it connected with Amell's backside was extremely comical, but also concerning.

"Ma'am, stop!," Amell pleaded as he danced out of the way of the mother's repeated strikes. "If we could please go in here to discuss what happened I'm sure we can work something out," he continued.

"If I don't like what I hear I'm calling all THREE of my babies' daddies to whoop your asses," she threatened, pointing at Amell and looking at Todd.

"Bitch, I will *saaaavor* the ass whooping I'm going to give you," she avowed to Bianca, shoving her out of her way as Amell escorted her into an empty classroom and shut the door behind him. Before the door closed, Todd heard Celeste's mom ask if her daughter had been jumped by a gang armed with baseball bats.

"No, ma'am," he heard Amell answer. "Half of her injuries she did to herself."

CRACK! Another lash of the belt connected with Amell's leg.

"Jinxed!," Bianca said, thinking back to the way Amell had said that morning that it was going to be a great day.

"This is a little more than tempting fate," Todd replied. "I guess we should get the remaining campers ready for our field trip. If this is the worst thing that happens then we're doing good," he said.

"Dammit, Todd! Haven't you learned yet? You can't make comments like that!," Bianca cautioned.

"I don't believe in curses, superstitions, bad luck, or anything of that nature," Todd said. "It was fun and games earlier when we gave Amell a hard time, but playtime is over. We need to get to work, and I am the master of my own fate, not some rabbit's foot, four leaf clover, or silly sayings," he concluded.

"Well, Captain Todd of the Titanic," Bianca retorted, "a baseball bat to the face is as big an iceberg as *I've* ever seen."

With Terri's sudden departure, Todd was forced to take her place on the field trip to The Butterfly House. Maybe there *is* something to Bianca's cursed theory, he thought. Nah! It couldn't be *that* bad. Beautiful scenery, peaceful butterflies… This should be an easy, therapeutic outing.

Mother nature is a bitch.

-Greg Bear

"Stay still, and don't swat at the butterflies!," instructed the Butterfly House attendant. "If one approaches you, just admire them with your eyes," she directed. "Scan the entire area in front of you so you DO NOT step on a butterfly," he continued dully, as if she gives this speech a hundred times a day. Robotically raising her arm and pointing to an area without turning her head, she continued, "Do not
disturb their feeding area. Do not touch the butterflies," she continued slowly. It seemed clear to Todd that she wanted to be anywhere but giving instructions to a group of campers.

"Did you know butterflies can fly up to 12 miles per hour?" the attendant asked. It was supposed to be an exciting fact, and yet Todd could tell the campers had never been more bored in their entire lives. Neither had he. He was worried about the outing's success of the outing. The sauna-like conditions of the solarium made him feel uneasy and irritable, and the attendant's lackluster presentation made standing there unbearable.

"That's not fast at all," replied an unimpressed camper. Timidly, the attendant replied, "But look at their size! That *is* fast for something as small as they are," she rebutted, as if she was personally offended by the camper's statement.

"*I'm* faster for my size," said another camper.

"No you're not," another camper argued.

"Yes I am!," the first camper replied.

Ignoring the campers' lack of enthusiasm for her butterfly facts, the attendant continued with her spiel. Did you know that after bees, butterflies are the second largest group of pollinators?

"I thought they were caterpillars," a younger camper asked innocently.

"What's a pollinator?," asked another.

"Good question!," the attendant replied, excited that there was interest in butterfly behavior. "A pollinator is anything that helps carry pollen from the male part of the flower to the female part of the same or another flower."

"Butterflies have *sex* with flowers?," Lori shouted. The whole group of campers started snickering.

The now-embarrassed attendant walked off. Usually, Amell would tell his students to settle down when they started to get a little rowdy, but he hadn't said a word since his closed-door meeting with Celeste's mom. Todd remembered how after he received a spanking as a youth he would keep his mouth shut.

As the campers began exploring the solarium Todd noticed they ignored every single rule. The two campers who'd been arguing over who was fastest raced down the aisles.

"Told you I was fast!," one of them yelled.

"I'm STILL faster than the butterfly!," yelled the other.

Another group of campers went from observing the butterflies to playing "let's catch one." A group of young girls tried in vain to take a selfie with a vibrant purple butterfly. It flew higher to try and escape, and the girls, determined to capture the perfect picture, stomped into an array of beautiful white, yellow, pink, orange, red, and purple wildflowers, crushing several feeding butterflies in the process.

"Are you crazy?!," Todd yelled. "Get out of there!," he demanded.

Unfazed by their annihilation of the gentle insects, the giggling girls scurried away, only to be distracted by a bigger, more photogenic butterfly that seemed ready for its close-up with them.

CLAP!

"I got him!," yelled a camper, smashing a butterfly between his hands.

STOMP!

"I got one, too!," cried another one as he jumped on top of an unsuspecting victim.

"I want one!," whined a camper, hurtling herself into a meticulously-manicured landscape.

Todd stared in disbelief as this once tranquil greenhouse full of vibrantly-colored insects became a crime scene. What is *wrong* with these future psychopathic serial killers?, he thought. Butterfly carcasses, dirt, and pieces of plants and flowers were strewn about. Artistically arranged flower

188

beds had become disheveled fits of chaos. Campers were chasing butterflies with no regard for their surroundings, and volunteers were chasing campers, also with little regard to their surroundings.

Bianca was yelling at whoever ran past her, demanding that they slow down. Gerri was ignoring everyone and talking to Sebastian on the phone. Amell was deep in thought from the dreadful events of earlier in the day.

"Get out! GET OUT! **GET OUT!!**," the once-timid attendant yelled furiously. She pointed at the once-pristine butterfly oasis, now reduced to nothing more than a shambles. "How?," she asked.

As embarrassed as Todd was about his campers' behavior, he was thrilled to get out of the hot solarium.
Whose dumb ass idea was it to plan a field trip to a sauna, during the summer, to look at butterflies, he wondered. Oh yeah. It was mine. This trip *would* have been enjoyable if the staff had been trained well enough to handle the campers, he thought angrily. One unseen benefit, though; I get to go home early! Once the bus arrives back on campus I can leave; spend some time with Sharon, which will make her happy; and, of course, take a nap before work at the warehouse tonight.

Packing the campers onto the bus was more of a chore now than it had been earlier. The heat of the day had warmed the seats, making it painful to sit down. Todd considered it instant gratification, the perfect punishment for what they'd done to The Butterfly House.

As the bus began its trek back to the school, Todd tried to will the hunk of junk to pick up speed. He hoped the bus could generate enough wind to cool them down. Todd had always hated riding on school buses in warmer weather. They were never air-conditioned so the hot faux leather always burned exposed skin. It felt like they were constantly going over speed bumps as the bus' shocks never seemed to work properly. They always smelled of exhaust, and, worst of all, urban legend had it the square windows didn't slide all the way down since some student somewhere had stuck his arm all the way out and gotten it ripped off.

Why does his stupidity mean I have to sit and simmer on a broiling bus, Todd fumed. Despite the fact that the mercury level inside the bus continued to rise rapidly, the bus started a leisurely slow down, eventually stopping on the side of the road.

The campers instantly started voicing their theories as to why the bus had stopped. Straining to hear what was going on from his seat, Todd relented and made his way to the front of the bus.

"What seems to be the problem?," Todd asked Gerri as she turned on the bus' hazard lights.

"You want to tell me why we're sitting on the highway with 80 loud, hot, sweaty campers?," an annoyed Amell chimed in. Todd noticed there was a tone of disdain directed at the driver. These were the first words he'd uttered since his encounter with Celeste's mom. The driver, Gerri, had escaped Amell's persecution because of the baseball bat incident out of necessity. Gerri and Sebastian were the camp's only registered bus drivers. Sebastian, who usually drove for field trips, had failed to let Amell know that poker was more important than his job. He always felt he was one or two good hands away from winning the jackpot.

"Ummm," Gerri stammered. "I ummm...."

190

"Spit it out!," demanded a frustrated Amell.

"I ummm," Gerri replied.

"QUIET!!!!!!!!!!," Amell screamed at the rowdy campers behind him. The fury in his voice shook the bus, or at least it appeared to. Silence settled in eerily. The only audible sound was the sound of traffic speeding past the stationary bus.

Without saying a word, Amell's eyes burned into Gerri's very soul. He very slowly and deliberately asked his question again, "Tell me why we are stopped on the side of the highway."

Gulping hard, Gerri stuttered, "I-I-I-I got sick when Celeste was injured. I spent time in the restroom and didn't inspect the bus. I-I-I-I forgot to get gas."

Still staring at her intently, Amell's breathing became more forceful. Todd likened it to a bull about to
charge. Am I going to have to tackle Amell before he strangles the life out of Gerri?, he wondered. And do I *really* want to stop him?

Sweat was pouring down his forehead and into his eyes. Todd started contemplating what the best move was for the safety of the campers. If we keep them on the hot bus it could become fatal. He could see the headlines now: "Eighty campers broil to death inside a school bus. Story at ten." If they waited
outside the bus, though, one of the campers might get hit by a passing car.

Just as Todd was about to discuss their options with Amell, Amell threw his hands up in the air as if to say he was giving up. Darting down the steps toward the door, Amell attempted to exit the bus dramatically. It didn't work. He couldn't get the door open and was struggling with it as if he were a bird trying to escape its cage.

"Do you want me to open the door?," Gerri asked.

Amell didn't respond and finally wiggled himself free.

Gerri started to cry. "Do you think he's going to be angry with me?" Todd wanted to respond with "Bitch, what do *you* think?," but his consoling side took over instead.

"It'll be okay if we can work together to figure out a solution," he said.

Todd felt encouraged when he saw Gerri reach for her phone to make a call. Opening the doors of the bus, Todd walked over to an extremely upset Amell who was trying to calm himself down.

"I blame *you*," he started as Todd approached him.

"Me?!," Todd replied, shocked.

"Yes," Amell replied. "I could be in the A/C somewhere with my fiancé planning a wedding, but instead I'm out here with eighty campers, in the heat, on the side of the road."

Todd knew he needed to strap in as Amell was going to take him on one of his rambling rides. "The school's about to be sued for Celeste's injuries; and

192

The Butterfly House will probably sue us, too, for the way we destroyed the place," he continued. "There's no *way* I'm going to make my appointment with our wedding planner," he sighed. "My fiancé is going to have my butt."

"I got spanked, Todd," he went on. "Do you know what it's like to be spanked?, he asked.

"Yes, I do," Todd said.

"At FORTY!," Amell snapped. "I was spanked like a child in front of children. That woman not only spanked me with a belt, she threatened me and called me names. Names I never even heard before! I wanted to take notes to use on my employees at the warehouse when they yell and curse at me but I was afraid she'd spank me again if I tried. Todd, she even spanked me for answering a question! I understand now why Celeste is so well-behaved. Her mom is very heavy-handed. I'd almost rather get jumped by her babies' daddies. That belt **hurt**; I probably have welts on my skin. My fiancé and I have talked about spicing up our love life, about using chains, whips, and candle wax. After today there is no way in heck that I'm going to want to try being spanked for pleasure. There is no pleasure in that! What sick person thinks getting beaten up during sex is fun?!"

He's obviously never met Sharon, Todd thought.

"I wish she were here right now," Amell continued. "She could use her belt to spank some sense into Gerri. Why didn't you stop me from hiring her?," he asked.

Todd just stood there biting his tongue. He didn't want to add any fodder that would allow Amell to continue his rant.

"She and her husband are FIRED!," Amell finished.

"Gerri has a plan," Todd said, trying to diffuse the situation. "She's making calls now."

After fifteen more minutes listening to Amell ramble on about how Celeste's mom called him every name in the book and how she wants charges pressed against the kid that hit her daughter with the bat they were interrupted by a minivan pulling up behind the bus.

"Who is that?," Todd asked.

"Probably a Good Samaritan," Amell said.

As the two stood on the side of the road gazing into the minivan trying to figure out who the driver was and what they were doing there, Gerri rushed past them.

"I can't do this job anymore!," she yelled. "It's too stressful." She got into the van and waved pleasantly as it drove away. Todd turned to Amell

"Not. right. now, Todd," he barked. He marched off, grabbed his phone, and made a call.

About an hour later, the camp's savior arrived. Unfortunately, it was Amanda. Amell had had no choice but to call her. In addition to all the other things she did, Amanda was also a licensed bus driver who also knew how to get things to work. That didn't mean she knew how to fix things. Her expertise and the school's directive (based on its budget) was get it to work for now and when they could afford to repair it the right way or replace it they'd do it then. But replacing was never in the budget.

Amanda was also the reason for half the wrinkles on Mr. Franklin's face. She was the school's resident snitch, Franklin's eyes and ears. Like Mr. Frank, Amanda hated everyone and wanted to see them fail. The summer camp was her biggest target at the moment.

Years ago, she'd been placed in charge of starting a summer camp. It failed. No one signed up. The reason for its failure? The price. Or at least that was the excuse the school board gave. The real reason, Todd's guess, was that people viewed it as a cult. The camp had advertised a particular week in which they were going to 'pray away the gay' in campers. No wonder it failed! Parents wanted to send their kids to an environment to have fun, not be a part of a controversial event.

Todd wanted to walk to the gas station, or even push the bus to the gas station uphill and barefoot and then drive it – albeit illegally – back to the school. Anything that didn't include Amanda getting involved. The last thing the camp needed was the superintendent hearing about the camp's hiccups, especially since they were happening so frequently. But Amanda was there now, so they had no choice but to let her take over. Arriving with two five-gallon gas canisters, she was their knight in shining armor. It was just enough to allow the bus to coast onto campus on fumes. But they make it back safely, and that's all that mattered.

As Amanda had been driving, Todd listed the minor mishaps she'd witnessed in his head. Unfortunately, there were many. They ranged from campers using scissors as weapons, to turning a hallway into a slip 'n slide during a severe thunderstorm. There were food fights with the free breakfast (though Todd used the term food loosely); and the volunteers were constantly on their phones, ignoring trash that littered the hallways. There was the occasional fight that usually just consisted of name calling and shoving (the volunteers ignored that, too), but no matter what, Amanda was always there to witness it all.

When they arrived, there was a group of parents waiting to pick up their campers. Amell had sent an email from his phone alerting them to the incident and now the angry mob was swarming. Mr. Franklin was also among the crowd. Todd could only assume Amanda had told him what happened. I'll let Amell and Bianca handle this one, thought Todd. He was ready to clock out and head home

> *Anything good in life is either illegal, immoral, or*
> *fattening!*
> *-Alexander Woollcott*

"Stop checking the forecast; you're going to make it rain!," Amell joked.

Todd was desperate to make today's field trip to the pool a success. Their previous attempt had been washed away in a tumultuous thunderstorm. And though he would never admit it, Todd was just as excited. He knew this was the one activity they looked forward to, and Todd was pleased when they were pleased.

It was more than the fact that he was an Activities Director pleasing his customers. The campers' innocence and their unbridled excitement brought joy to his life. Their smiles transported Todd back to a time in his life when he was truly happy. A time before stress from Sharon, bills, and work. Todd knew his activities would one day be described by the campers as the good ol' days, so he thought of himself as less an Activities Director and more a Memory Maker.

After checking the forecast on his phone, Todd glanced up to inspect the clouds in the sky. There were none. It was a high, bright blue sky. The temperature was forecast to be in the mid-nineties, the air quality was yellow. It was supposed to be sunny with zero chance of precipitation. Todd still didn't trust it. This was going to be one of many checks of the forecast. Even when they got to the pool he wouldn't be satisfied. He needed today to be perfect. He was determined to have a day free of mishaps. He wanted to restore faith in the camp, and in him as its Activities Director among both the parents and the school board. He'd planned for every contingency;

nothing bad was going to happen.

"You can never be too sure," Todd replied. The two were taking their daily walk around campus. They were pleased by what they had seen so far. The majority of the campers were smiling and laughing in anticipation of today's field trip.

"I don't trust that one," a woman's voice said. Someone was approaching them rapidly. It was Amanda, but Todd refused to acknowledge her presence. What the hell is this bitch about to complain about?, he wondered.

"Good morning, Amanda!," Amell said. His usually chipper tone had a slight hint of agitation to it.

"That one. Right there," Amanda said, pointing – and not inconspicuously – at the subject of her disdain. Derrick. "I think he's dealing drugs on campus," she added.

Todd stopped in his tracks. Were her accusations based on facts? He'd had the same suspicions in the past, but if this was still the case then they had a major issue. His customers would be campers. **Young** campers.

Todd glanced across the playground in the direction of their suspect. He felt as if he and Amell were Starsky and Hutch and Amanda was their informant Huggy Bear. They were on a stakeout. Derrick was conversing with a couple of campers. Judging by their body language, Derrick was reliving his basketball glory days. That is, if you can call winning playoff games during your senior season by forfeit's glory days. The crowd of boys were obviously enamored by his tales.

"I assure you," Amell started, "Derrick is an outstanding young man. He has been nothing short of a beacon of a role model."

"Look, look!" Amanda interrupted, completely ignoring Amell's character reference.

The trio observed Derrick mimicking a jump shot with a bunch of onlookers staring in amazement. He stopped suddenly as a young camper approached. The two exchange a couple of words. Derrick looked around as if to make sure no one could see them and then flashed two fingers to the camper. The camper reached into his pocket and pulled out some cash. The two looked around again before mimicking a handshake exchange. The camper walked off while Derrick continued his basketball story.

"I knew it. I knew it!," Amanda boasted, pulling out her phone. "I'm calling S.W.A.T. to have him removed from the property," she threatened.

"Wait!," Amell pleaded. "Let Todd and I do some investigating before you have the school raided," he added, trying to lighten the mood a bit.

"This is a serious matter," Amanda said. "I will not have my daddy's legacy tarnished by a drug dealer."

"I know," Amell said, "And Todd and I will get to the bottom of it," he promised.

"Go!," Amanda urged. "I'll wait here."

Sighing heavily, Amell walked toward Derrick. Todd followed quickly.

199

"How are we going to handle this?," Todd asked. "Good cop bad cop?"

"Nope," Amell said. "I'm going to ask him point blank what that exchange was."

"Seriously?!," Todd said, amazed.

Amell stopped walking and looked at him. "We have too much riding on this camp. You heard Amanda. We can't let the camp's – or the school's – legacy be brought down by a drug dealer."

"Amell," Todd began. "He's *way* too smart to admit something to us. We also can't just walk up to him and start accusing him of something we don't have concrete proof of. I think we should go shake down his customer first."

"Good plan," Amell agreed.

The two tracked down the camper they'd seen with Derrick. "Good cop bad cop?," Todd asked as they approached.

"Which one am I?," Amell asked. But it was too late. Todd was already standing next to the camper. He stepped in front of him, bent down, and keenly made uncomfortable eye contact with the boy.

"What's your name?," Todd asked. The kid smelled of chocolate.

"Cody," he said in an endearing voice.

"Wipe that smile off your face!," Todd snapped. "The way I see it, you have

200

two options. Come clean, or feel my wrath."

Todd was *way* too into his bad cop routine. "Now tell me what you did," he demanded.

Cody started crying. "Don't tell my mom! I'm sorry!! I won't ever do it again. I promise I won't!," he sobbed.

"Tell us what happened," Amell said in his best good cop voice.

"I knew it was wrong," Cody started, "but I couldn't help it. I didn't think anyone would find out. I thought I was being careful!"

Todd was disgusted that a kid no older than nine was beginning to make such major life mistakes.

"Go on," Amell encouraged.

Sniffing heavily and then wiping his snotty nose on his arm, Cody continued his confession. "I snuck into my dad's room and found it."

Completely confused by the turn Cody's story had taken, Todd could only glance at Amell with a 'let's see where this leads' look.

"I opened my dad's secret drawer and found it. A DVD. I put it in the DVD player and watched."

"Watched what?," asked Amell, intrigued.

"Boobies!," exclaimed the excited pre-teen.

Todd bit his tongue to hold in his laughter. He couldn't comprehend how they'd wound up on this subject.

"No, kid. Not that," he said. "We're talking about your nefarious dealings with Derrick."

"My what?," Cody asked. "I don't know what that is."

"Don't play dumb with me!," Todd snapped.

"I'm not!," Cody whined. "I don't know what that word means."

Sensing the conversation was jumping off track again, Amell went back to playing good cop.

"Son," he started, "What were you doing with Derrick earlier?"

Cody's face went blank. Then he became agitated, nervous. He began to shake. "I-I-I-I d-d-d-don't w-w-w-want to get in trouble," he began. "My mother told me I need to stay away from the stuff but I'm addicted. Derrick has the best product at the best prices."

Todd became enraged. Their camp was in jeopardy. But he wasn't mad at Derrick; his anger was directed at Amell. Derrick had been a questionable candidate but Amell wanted to give everyone a chance. His mercy may have led to a death sentence for the camp.

"Do you realize how much trouble you're in?," Todd asked. "This is serious business."

"Don't tell anyone I snitched!," Cody cried. "Please!" Cody put his hands in his face and began sobbing. "I'm weak. I couldn't help myself! My mom won't let me have candy at home."

"Just because you can't have candy at home doesn't mean you start taking drugs!," Amell yelled. "Drugs lead to lifelong problems," he continued. "Son, they can cause you to lose your teeth, cause you to smell, make you lose control of your mind and body. You can go broke, become homeless, and live a life of despair. People on drugs can wind up in jail or dead!," he concluded.

Though what Amell was saying was factual and needed to be heard, Todd felt Amell's preachy delivery lessened its impact of message. It sounded like one of those cheesy public service announcements he'd heard as a kid. Todd never seriously compared his brain on drugs to a frying egg or the D.A.R.E. to say no to drugs messages.

Cody, now crying hysterically, emptied his pockets. "I will never eat another candy bar again. I don't want to go to jail or die because of a Snickers bar."

Huh?? Todd was confused. Where are the drugs?, he wondered. "Cody," Todd started. "What exactly did you buy from Derrick?"

"Some chocolate," Cody confessed. "My mom won't let me have candy because of my ADHD and childhood obesity," he continued. "I didn't know chocolate was a gateway to drugs. I'll never touch the stuff again."

Embarrassed by their candy shakedown, Todd scanned the playground, eager to confront Amanda. Too late. She was already gone. Todd felt terribly.

He'd misjudged a young black male based on a racist societal construct that said Derrick doing what he was doing with Cody meant he was selling him drugs. This was a thing Todd himself had been a victim of, he himself had perpetrated. He'd not only profiled Derrick, but Cody, too.

"Cody, we're sorry. We thought something worse had occurred. We were just trying to keep you safe." Todd's bad cop antics had completely disappeared. He wasn't a good cop, either. As much as Todd detested the way Amanda was always judging people, he let her suck him into the exact same behavior. By not giving Derrick the benefit of the doubt and seeing only the bad in others he was training himself to *find* only the bad in others. He'd been a young African American boy once, too. He knew society often ignores, or defines them negatively. And far too narrowly. He'd done to another what he'd spent the majority of his life trying to escape. He couldn't apologize to Cody enough, but he tried. He felt compelled to apologize to Derrick, too.

Walking towards the group of boys Derrick was standing with, Todd could overhear their discussion about girls. As was typical for adolescents, they were bragging about their various experiences. Todd slowed his pace, contemplating how to broach the topic of appearance creating judgment.

Just then, a young man ran up to Derrick. The same exchange he'd seen take place between Derrick and Cody happened again. This is my opening!, Todd thought.

"Hey boys!," he greeted them.

No one said anything.

"I couldn't help but notice your little exchange a second ago," he continued. "What are you selling?," he asked.

"I don't know what you're talking about," Derrick lied. His entourage of campers was just as tight-lipped.

"Your exchange was sloppy," Todd fibbed, not wanting to give Cody away as his informant. "Honestly, I don't care that you're selling candy, I just wish you'd approached Amell or myself first. The problem I *do* have," he continued, "is you imitating a drug dealer to complete your sale."

"I guess it's in my nature to do it that way," Derrick joked. The group of boys chuckled. Todd remembered looking at Derrick's resume during his interview and thinking it looked like one a drug dealer might have.

"You're **bragging** about that?," Todd asked, incredulous. "Can any one of you tell me why a person in their right mind would want to sell drugs?"

"**MONEY!**," the group of boys exclaimed in unison.

"Money.," Todd responded. "Hm. Well, unless you plan to be a kingpin, you'd make far more money working at McDonald's."

The looks on the group's face let Todd know they weren't believing him.

"Whatever," Derrick responded. "The boys on my block clock much paper."

Todd shook his head at Derrick's vernacular. He wanted to address that issue, too, but one battle at a time.

"How many of your peeps have been locked up?," Todd asked, mocking Derrick's street mentality. "How many of your 'boys' can walk freely up and down the street without being worried about being robbed, killed, or arrested? How many drug dealers do you know personally who will be able to retire with enough money to afford a house, car, and support a family? Do you actually *believe* the rappers that boast the money they make from selling drugs? If they actually sold drugs, their songs would incriminate them and they'd be locked up in a heartbeat. If you *do* believe that," Todd continued sarcastically, "then I guess you also believe the story of the little girl who wound up in the Land of Oz after a tornado. Or the one about the boy who defeated an evil empire in space with nothing more than a beam of light and The Force."

"How do **you** know what goes on in my 'hood?," Derrick asked. "I've seen your car and your clothes. If *anyone* needs to sell drugs it would be you. You could probably benefit a great deal if you worked my old block." The group of boys erupted in laughter again.

Feeling a little embarrassed about his perceived socio-economic status, Todd was even more motivated to change the kids' perception of street life.

"The block that your boys work. Is it in a great neighborhood?," he asked. The boys erupted in laughter again.

"Nah!," Derrick replied. "It's in the 'hood."

"They *work* in the hood," Todd began, but they live in a great neighborhood, right?"

Less enthused now, Derrick responded, "Nah, they live there, too."

206

"So they make all this money but they continue to live in the 'hood. How honorable," Todd mocked. "They have a better car than me but live in a worse neighborhood than I do. There isn't any crime in my neighborhood, but there's crime all the time in the 'hood. Oh, but they're 'stacking much paper,'" he laughed. "I bet they work all the time."

"Sun up to sun down!," Derrick bragged.

This time, it was Todd who laughed. "A fast food worker typically works forty hours a week. That's eight hours a day, five days a week. That's sun up, and they typically get off while the sun is still up. So they make about fifteen grand a year?," he asked.

The boys gasped at the that figure.

"That's big bank!," one of Derrick's entourage said.

"Yeah that's about five bucks an hour," Todd laughed. "Minimum wage in the state of Missouri is $6.68 right now. Drug dealers in the hood make over a dollar less per hour than someone working at McDonald's does. Plus they don't get free fries. Instead, drug dealers have to deal with police, thieves, and self-consumption. But don't think it's that easy to get rid of the drugs," he continued. "You need to have good customers. Do you boys think of a person buying drugs on a street corner as a good customer? You also need lots of customers. How do you advertise to a customer base that you're selling drugs when you don't want a lot of people knowing you're selling drugs?," he asked. "It's not like you can put it on a billboard!," he laughed. "Maybe it's just me, but it sounds like too much of a risk to me. Not everything that glitters is gold. So, Derrick, you can sell candy all you want.

But if some nefarious person thinks you're selling drugs since you feel the need to emulate that lifestyle, don't be surprised if that fake lifestyle brings real world problems." Mouths agape, the campers looked disappointed. They seemed sorry for the life choices Derrick was making. Then, like most kids do at that age, they ran off to pursue another, more interesting activity.

And just like that Todd, too, walked off. He felt a euphoric feeling of satisfaction. I really think I got through to those boys!, he thought. Being able to make a difference in another's life makes life worth living. I'm glad I came up with this summer camp.

"Line up campers!," he yelled. "It's field trip time!"

208

If it's green or it wriggles, it's biology. If it stinks, it's chemistry.
If it doesn't work, it's physics.
-Magnus Pyke

The glare of the sun reflecting off the pool was blinding. Todd regretted not bringing his sunglasses. He hadn't planned on attending any field trips this summer. His plan was to stay on campus and work on lesson plans for the academic preparedness portion of the camp. He also wanted to take it easy during the day. Avoiding field trips would definitely ensure a relaxed day. He'd had to force himself to attend today's outing. He'd have felt guilty bailing, especially after begging Terri to come back to work. It's a good thing she came back; they'd have been down to one female staff member older than eighteen otherwise, and they needed more than one for trips like these.

True to form, Bianca was going to be fashionably late. If she showed up at all. Todd had even tried to recruit some parental volunteers. No one responded. Todd felt this was unusual. When he was growing up it had seemed like parents were tripping over themselves to be part of school functions. Different era, presumed Todd.

Todd did not feel comfortable assisting any of the female campers as they changed into their swimwear so he was even more grateful that Terri had come back. And though he was there to assist, he was not going to participate. He'd enjoyed swimming as a child, but his experiences had shaped his reluctance to swim in public pools as an adult. The strong smell of chlorine sparked painful memories of being blinded by the chemicals. Growing up in the eighties, he wasn't sure what burned more: the chlorine in the pool or the chemicals kids used in their hair? Aquanet and Jheri Curl Juice were both popular substances used back then, and both were really powerful. One product put a hole in the ozone layer and the other left stains everywhere. No wonder so many of his friends were bald and gray!, he thought.

He remembered visiting the pools and seeing an oil sheen floating on top of the water, as if an oil tanker had had a spill. Regardless, he always left the pool with red, burning eyes. Accompanying the scent of chlorine was the smell of coconut from the sunscreen. He didn't mind that one, though it did make him long for a tropical vacation.

"Ladies, please follow Teresa and Terri, and gentlemen follow Derrick into the locker room," Amell said.

Todd followed Amell to the ticket counter to pay for their admission. Walking along the deck, Todd saw several parents turning up their noses at the group. Many began to gather their belongings to exit. Todd didn't blame them; they were about to have their peace transformed into chaos. Over 100 campers under age 12 tend to be excitable. And loud.

At least the pool staff seemed excited that they were there. A huge summer camp in attendance meant they were going to be paid a premium rate. The concession workers were especially giddy. There's just something about a hot day and the thought of cooling off with a snow cone. What camper *wouldn't* be motivated to spend their allowance on the sweet treat?

"What's taking them so long?," Amell asked.

Todd hadn't been paying attention; he was still focusing on all the evil looks

210

the guests had given his group. He tried to dismiss it as it being because there were so many of them there, but in the back of his mind couldn't help but wonder if the reason for the looks was because the majority of the campers were African American.

Amell's question made Todd wonder why not a single camper had made it to the pool yet. He'd assumed the staff would have had to block an onslaught of children racing to see who was going to be the first in the water.

"I'll go check on the boys," Todd volunteered. On his way to the locker room, he checked the forecast on his phone one last time, still pessimistic that a pop-up thunderstorm might interfere with their day.

As he approached the locker room he could hear the boys doing what boys tend to do. Compete.

"Mine is bigger," yelled one camper.

"No mine is!," said another.

"No, I think *mine* is," argued a third.

"No. MINE is," declared an older voice.

As he entered the locker bay area, Todd was dismayed by the scene in front of him.

"What in the fuck?," he said. Todd had done well keeping his warehouse persona separate from his Christian school identity. Today they met.

211

The campers were shocked by Todd's outburst, Todd was shocked by the scene. They were all standing there stunned by each other, with their privates in their hands (Todd figuratively, the campers and Derrick literally).

"What is going on here?!," Todd demanded. He knew the answer, and he didn't want an explanation, but he still needed to hear one. He understood boys' inquisitive nature as well as their need for competition. He did **not** understand why several staff members, including Lori and Derrick, were either observing or, in Derrick's case, taking part.

"Timmy said his was bigger than mine," a camper explained.

"Mine can grow bigger but it's not working today," another one said.

"Stop! Stop! Stop!," Todd yelled. He didn't have the patience to hear the large group of half-naked boys give color commentary on their little…. pageant.

"Campers, put your suits on and go to the pool," Todd instructed. "You two," he started, frustrated and disappointed by the two camp employees, "Here. Now." He meant business. The two were frozen in fear.

Todd began to massage the area around his nose; he could feel the start of a stress headache. There were so many issues to tackle with this one that Todd didn't know where to begin. He wanted to get Amell and let *him* deal with it. Unfortunately, Amell was too lenient with his punishments.

Todd wanted to fire them on the spot, but they were needed to observe the campers while they were in the pool. He also needed to ensure the camp maintained a ratio of one staff member for every ten campers. This really

212

should be Bianca's problem, he concluded. **She's** in charge of staffing. I'll listen to their explanation first, Todd decided, though he couldn't fathom any reason to validate their involvement in the boys' display.

"Someone had better say something!," he said in his sternest voice. "Someone had better explain to me why a grown man–"

"I'm only 18," Derrick interrupted.

"Eighteen is a legal adult," Todd barked as his nostrils flared and spit inadvertently flew out of his mouth. His blood boiled.

"What aspect of what has occurred here today isn't child endangerment?," he asked. "What aspect of this event isn't considered child pornography?"

"Waaaaiit a minute," Derrick interjected.

"No *you* wait a minute!," Todd yelled. "You brought another person – a *female*, no less – in here to watch a bunch of minors exposing themselves! How exactly would *you* define it?!," he snapped.

"Well," Lori started…

Todd didn't want to hear her explanation. She tended to over-embellish her side of events so she would appear to be the victim. She also tended to ramble, and to talk without thinking.

"Why are you in the boy's locker room?," Todd interrupted Todd.

"The guys needed a judge," Lori explained.

213

"Why you?," Todd asked. He couldn't believe he even asked that question. "What part of this made you think it was okay?," he continued.

"I've never seen one before," Lori explained, "So I'm the perfect judge. I can be impartial.

"Why do they look like those wrinkly dogs?," she asked.

"Get out NOW!," Todd hollered.

"That will be all," Todd sighed, furious with her responses. "I'll deal with you later," he added.

"Wait!," Lori said. Todd couldn't believe that his demand was being met with even an ounce of resistance. "I thought boys had two balls. Do they stay in the same sack? Or does each ball have its own? Is the sack filled with liquid, or do the balls bounce around like dice in a Yahtzee cup? How does it grow? Does it, like, hulk out? Does it hurt when it grows? Does it have its own type of stretchy skin? How does pee come out of that small hole? Why does the ball sack look like the skin on my elbow? Why do some of them curve? Why is there hair above it and hair below it but not on it?"

"Lori!," Todd interrupted. "Stop!," he yelled. "Get out!," he demanded, pointing toward the door.

Ignoring him completely, Lori continued her line of questioning. "Why are they different sizes? Why doesn't the skin color down there match the rest of their skin color? Why are some innies and some outies?"

214

"Lori, get the hell out of here **right. now**," Todd bellowed.

"Derrick!," Todd started as an angry Lori marched out the door. "I expected more from you."

"It's no big deal," Derrick replied nonchalantly. "They wanted to see who had the biggest dick and I asked Lori to be the judge."

Todd couldn't believe that Derrick was completely dismissing the problem with this incident. "You are an ADULT!," he screamed. "You're in here circle jerking with a bunch of minors!" His warehouse demeanor continued to invade his Christian school persona. "These campers don't know any better. You. do," he snarled. "**Plus**, you introduced a member of the opposite sex to this outrage! Your actions may have been illegal. You are suspended effective immediately."

"Why is Lori asking me penis questions?," Amell shouted as he entered the locker room. "Why is she saying you two showed her a bunch of privates?!"

"I walked into it," Todd said, holding his hands up as if to say 'I had no part of it.' "I was in the process of suspending Derrick since he decided to join in the fun and whip his privates out in front of a bunch of minors before holding a show and tell beauty pageant with another minor, a female, as the judge." Todd purposely made his description as crude as possible. He wanted Amell to understand the seriousness of the situation. He wanted Derrick to contemplate the seriousness of all his actions in the future. Even if it *had* been an innocent act, they carried serious weight.

"I'll take it from here," Amell said. Todd was irritated. In the past, Amell tended to be passive as a disciplinarian. What had happened today was too serious an infraction to show mercy, Todd thought.

"We have a bigger problem with our female staffers," Amell warned.

"How could anything be a bigger problem than this?!," Todd said, stupified

"Oh, you'll see," Amell said. "You'll see."

216

*If you view a problem closely enough, you will recognize
yourself as part of the problem.*
-Ducharme's Axiom

"What seems to be the problem?," Todd yelled into the women's locker room.

"I'm not coming out!," yelled Terri and Teresa in unison.

This is why I hate field trips, Todd thought: too many problems.

"Why aren't you coming out?," he asked. He really couldn't have cared less about their excuses; he just wanted them to come out and monitor the female campers who were ready to jump in the pool. If they would just reveal the problem he was confident he could solve it, they could hurry up and get the field trip over with, and he could go home and nap.

"I'm faaaatt!," Terri whined.

"If she thinks *she's* fat, then I am **defin**itely fat," Teresa added.

Todd didn't know what to say. He didn't want to appear insensitive, but he also didn't want to sound condescending. He wanted to go back to the men's locker room and curse Amell out for setting him up.

"No, you guys aren't!," he said. Todd knew his response wasn't reassuring to either party. Ignoring their issues, he decided to be practical. "Please come out," he continued. "The campers need you."

No response.

Todd decided to take another approach. "You both are more than your image. No matter how you feel you look today, it's hard for anyone to focus on anything besides the wonderful women you are."

"Okay," they said. Todd was shocked that that worked.

Damn!, Todd thought when Terri exited the locker bay. Her sensuous curves were divinely appealing. Her well-proportioned and developed body was radiantly inviting, but Todd couldn't focus on anything except the hair under Terri's arms and on her legs. It was overwhelming for someone who didn't expect it.

"You look nice," Todd said, trying to downplay her choice to be natural.

"You look nice, too," he added as Teresa came out. She was standing next to Terri so Todd only noticed her because he was trying not to look at Terri's underarms and legs.

"I look fat," Terri replied. "Look at this pooch," she added, pointing toward her navel. Todd tried not to. The area she was pointing to revealed that she didn't shave *any* of the hair on her body.

Terri was wearing a dental-floss-thin bikini. Like everything else she wore, it was too revealing. Todd worried that it might be too risqué for a public pool. It might've been too revealing for a nude beach.

"Me, too," Teresa said. Unlike Terri's, Teresa's swimsuit was perfect for her: a one-piece with a Wonder Woman print on it that read 'Girl Power.'

Todd was confused. How could a woman like Terri, who's constantly being warned about wearing midriff shirts that accentuate her breasts, be shy about her swimsuit? And how could a woman like Teresa, who is extremely confident in every task she engages in, be humbled by her image? I'll never understand women, he sighed to himself.

"It's not working!," Todd heard a boy yell.

"Derrick lied to us!," shouted another.

The mention of Derrick's name prompted Todd to focus his attention on the campers.

"What are you doing *now*?," Todd called from across the pool. Todd was not the only person interested in their answer. Several other guests seemed intrigued as to what the boys were up to.

"Derrick told us when you pee in the pool the water turns blue. It hasn't worked for any of us."

The screams of other guests filled the air as droves of adults exited the pool. Countless parents shot looks of disgust at Todd as they headed for the ticket counter and demanded a refund. Todd himself was disgusted by the thought of fifteen boys urinating in the pool to make the water turn a different color.

"Everybody out of the pool," yelled the facility's manager. The happiness she'd shown when they arrived was replaced now by anger as she kicked them out. The loss of revenue and cleaning fee was going to be substantial, Todd thought.

219

"No running!," Todd heard one lifeguard yell. "Slow down!"

Todd was confused about who they were talking to; the pee party participants were still in the pool.

"Slow! down!," the lifeguard demanded again.

Is she talking to me?, Todd wondered. They were looking in his direction.

"Watch out!," someone behind him yelled. Todd turned around just in time to see three campers rushing toward the pool with what looked like a hawk flying behind them. It was too late for Todd to react as they plowed into him. As he flew through the air, Todd could only think of how he was still dressed in his slacks, shoes, and camp t-shirt.

SPLASH!

Todd had had the wind knocked out of him and began to swallow the water that entered his mouth. The deeper he sank, the more observant he became. He saw the hawk fly overhead, and then he saw the circle of boys who had just filled the pool with urine.

He quickly swam to the surface and tried to clear his mind. It would be alright if he didn't think about it. Stop thinking! he told himself. But it was too late. His involuntary reflexes took over. The that he'd just swallowed water that fifteen boys just urinated in sickened him.

Poor Timmy's face was in the line of fire as Todd threw up. It started a chain reaction. First John, who'd been triggered by Todd's regurgitation, vomited

220

on Todd's back. It was warm and chunky and cascaded from Todd's head down his neck. After that, every camper in the pool got sick as, one by one, they were exposed to another's vomit.

Todd's diaphragm began convulsing. He was going to vomit again. Several involuntary heaves, and then he opened his mouth, just enough, and for just long enough to catch one of the campers' vomit. The realization that the camper had had bologna for lunch sickened him even more. Todd hated bologna, and it was even worse coming from someone else's mouth. After just two minutes Todd was floating in a soup of urine and bile. He regretted scheduling the field trip immediately after a lunch of Sloppy Joes. He was surprised at how well Sloppy Joes were able to maintain their color after digestion. The smell alerted him to which end it had exited the body.

Todd wanted to end it all now. He wanted to drown, to flush his life and body through the pool's filter. As he swam through the cesspool, he desperately tried to keep his mouth and eyes closed. He was mad. He wanted answers. He didn't wait until the trio left the pool.

"Why did you tackle me?," he demanded. He wanted to stay mad but couldn't. As he watched the boys struggling to exit the pool he'd just escaped he got queasy again. He was going to get sick again. Covered in shit, puke, urine, and Sloppy Joe left Todd feeling a little more than uneasy.

"We saw a bird attack a rabbit," one of the boys answered. "We tried to save it." Todd had forgotten he'd even asked the question. He just wanted to go to the locker room and shower. With his clothes on. He felt like a human Port-a-Potty.

"We threw rocks at the bird and it started to attack us. So we ran," the boy continued.

"What in the world did I miss?," asked Bianca, arriving – as always – after everything had exploded. She was sporting a black Dolce & Gabbanna one-piece swimsuit and expensive DKNY sunglasses. Todd only knew the brands because he'd once told her he thought the initials DKNY stood for Dee King of New York. D&G read 'dog.'

Todd tried to answer her. Unfortunately, the scent from her Quelques Fleurs L' Original perfume made him vomit all over her.

You never know how soon is too late.-
Ralph Waldo Emerson

Dripping wet, tired, smelly, and nauseated, Todd was thrilled when the bus arrived back on campus. The fully-clothed shower he'd taken at the pool had done little to wash away the fact that he felt disgusting. His plan was to get off the bus, drive home, burn his clothes, and take a REAL shower.

Amell had forced Todd and all the boys who'd gone swimming in the cesspool to sit at the back of the bus. Todd sat closest to the window; he feared the smell of one of the campers may cause him to lose his proverbial lunch. Again.

As the campers started to exit the bus, Todd noticed Mr. Franklin and Amanda, rushing in their direction. Todd would be shocked if they'd heard about their accident and were coming to check on his or the campers' wellbeing. He stood up quickly, eager to make his way to the front of the line to see what all the commotion was. His haste was blocked by a bus full of slow campers with zero sense of urgency.

Ten minutes later, Todd finally made it off the bus just in time to see two squad cars pull into the campus parking lot.

"I'll handle this," Mr. Franklin said as he walked in the patrolmen's direction.

"See?," Amanda needled, "Just one example why we don't accept kids from outside our covenant."

Todd was angered and confused by her statement. She made the school sound like a breeding ground for a cult. Though at times he *did* feel like that was the case, he was angered by her assumption that a little horseplay and an act of animal kindness could be considered a criminal act. He wondered how a religious institution could refuse to accept everyone.

"Amell," Todd said. "All this because the camp soiled a pool? Or was it because of Derrick's actions?," he continued in a whisper.

"I wish," Amell said. "Someone from the pool is accusing one of our campers of stealing their cell phone."

"Line them up!," Mr. Franklin yelled. He had two officers behind him already, and just then, another squad car pulled into the parking lot.

"Is all this really necessary?," Todd asked. "Did they *see* one of our campers take the phone?" Six officers to find a missing phone. But his questions fell on deaf ears. Todd was pissed that the campers were being treated like criminals. Unfortunately, that made him feel like a hypocrite. He himself had been ready to persecute a camper for allegedly engaging in a drug deal.

Todd was angry and scared. At that moment he felt his words carried no weight, not because of *who* he was but because of **what** he was. No one listened to an educated black man, they only saw a black man, or possible suspect.

Todd had led a sheltered life. He grew up in an area in which affluent African Americans lived. Everyone he knew had families with both parents in the home. Both parents worked and were themselves highly educated. Growing up, he was surrounded by teachers, lawyers, engineers, scientists, and entrepreneurs. He would occasionally be told that he sounded white, or that he didn't sound black. He was also told on many occasions that he was one of the 'good' ones. Occasionally, someone would ask if he knew his dad, or if they could touch his hair, but most of the time they didn't ask, they just touched. He always looked like he was taking it as a compliment, but internally it caused pain and anger.

Todd hated being seen as a color, rather than as a man. No one took the time to get to know him, they just assumed he fit most inaccurate stereotypes. He hated telling people about his educational background, most commented that he must've filled a diversity candidate quota, or said that he must be able to run fast or catch a ball. And being in an interracial relationship was *extremely* difficult. Sharon never understood or cared why Todd wouldn't return an item he'd bought that was broken or didn't fit. Even with a receipt. She didn't understand the accusing mannerisms of store staff or the passive comments they'd make like, "he must've stolen it or bought it just for one night." She didn't understand what it felt like to receive the piercing, hateful looks he endured being out in public with a caucasian woman. Most probably assumed they were together because she had money or good credit.

Seeing all the boys lined up along the bus with their book bags opened made Todd wonder when African American boys stopped being seen as cute and being labeled a threat to society.

"Where's the phone?!," screamed an officer at the first camper. The boy remained stoic and silent. His calm demeanor was evidence that he'd grown accustomed to being lined up and interrogated.

"I'm talking to you, boy!," the officer yelled, grabbing his bag. He emptied its contents on the ground. A phone fell out. "What type of phone was it

225

again?," he asked his partner.

"That's *my* phone," the camper said.

"Shut up!," the officer barked.

"It's a Nokia," his partner said.

Realizing this camper didn't have the stolen phone, the officer began to move on to the next one. "Pick this shit up," he demanded of the first camper.

Todd had seen enough. "Hey!," he yelled to the group of officers now rifling through several campers' belongings. "Is what you're doing even legal?," he cried. "These are a bunch of minors. Don't you need parental consent to search?," he asked.

"Step back," an officer demanded, reaching for his pepper spray.

Todd didn't have a chance to react before he was tackled to the ground by another officer. "Put your hands behind your back!," he yelled. Before he could comply, the officer hammer-locked Todd's left arm behind his back. A sharp pain radiated down his arm. Todd cried out and tried to wriggle free in an effort to ease the pain.

"Stop resisting!," the officer shouted as his partner rushed over to further subdue Todd. He pinned Todd's head to the ground, applying an excessive amount of force. Todd gritted his teeth as the scorching blacktop seared the side of his face.

226

"Get up!," yelled the first officer as he finished applying the cuffs to Todd's wrists. They were tight, but the pain in his wrist was a comfort compared to the pain in his face and left arm. Scared to move, Todd was lifted by the cuffs and spun around to face the officers. He felt humiliated and was so angry at the way he and the campers were being treated that he wanted to cry. He fought back valiantly by refusing to display any form of emotion. He wanted to show the officers they weren't bothering him. He wanted to show the campers that you have to stand up for yourself and others when you're doing right, but are wronged anyway. The officers were all white; Todd and many of the campers were black. He tried not to make this a race issue, but he couldn't think of any other reason why he – why *they* – were all being treated this way.

"Alright, let's go!," yelled one of the last-arriving officers. Apparently, the 'victim' had left her phone at home.

Grabbing Todd's shirt, the officer who'd tackled him pulled him in close, violating any personal space he might have had. The officer's nose brushed up against his. Todd tried pulling his head back when he smelled the mint-flavored Skoal in the officer's mouth, but the officer pulled him closer. "I could run you in right now BOY," he began. "I have at least five witnesses who heard you obstruct justice and saw you resisting arrest."

Todd winced with every 's' the officer spoke as particles from his chewing tobacco landed on his face. Spinning him around violently, the officer hissed, "I'm going to let you go, but only because I know your wife, Sharon. Tell her Rick the dick misses her," he said, laughing heartily. "She was my best customer," he added. As he undid Todd's cuffs, Rick added, "I'll be seeing you!"

227

Todd wasn't sure if that was a threat or not. He wasn't a violent person, but Todd contemplated hitting him, not only because of the way he'd treated Todd, but also because Sharon had once bragged about the size of a former police officer boyfriend's penis. Sharon had told him how Rick was the one she'd once threatened to have dispose of an ex-boyfriend's body and make it look like an accident. Todd had always thought she was joking. Still, in the moment, he wanted to knock Rick the dick out. He knew the other officers would ground and pound him immediately after if he did, though. Hell, they might even shoot him.

"Alright, everyone! Back inside!," Mr. Franklin directed. "Todd, next time try not to make a peaceful situation worse," he advised.

Maybe he's the one who needs to be knocked out, Todd thought. Not looking back at him, Todd couldn't fathom how the superintendent could justify the officers' actions toward the campers. Todd felt he should be viewed as a hero for standing up to the victims' brush with tyranny. Unfortunately, he was just seen as another angry black man.

Todd walked to his car. He got in and just sat there. He still wanted to cry as he gently caressed his left arm and inspected his face in the rear-view mirror. Good. No scarring, he thought. He couldn't wait to get home and shower, but he didn't leave. He was scared to. What if the officers were waiting for him? Now there wouldn't be any witnesses. No one to save him. How did all this go so badly? He was just standing up for his campers' rights. Was he wrong to do that?, he pondered seriously. Mr. Franklin apparently thought so. Todd continued sitting in his car in silence, scared to move. Scared to make a sound.

Finally, after thirty minutes, Todd felt safe enough to go home.

228

The first myth of management is that it exists.
--Robert Heller

Entering the warehouse is what Todd imagined what it would be like visiting a maximum-security prison. A sign read "No electronics, no cell phones, no weapons beyond this point" as he passed through the guard shack on his way in.

He had to walk through a metal detector every time, and no matter what he wore, the detector would go off since employees were required to wear steel-toed boots. That rule is what helped Todd and every other employee sneak their phones in, and, unfortunately for some, weapons.

In a half-ditch effort to make the employees feel safe, the security guards would then use their handheld
metal detectors to check the employees. Paying the guards no mind, employees arriving to work never
broke stride as they strolled through the detector.

On the opposite side of the guard shack, employees ending their shifts were doing the same thing. The metal detector would go off as some employees stuffed their pockets with stolen products. Todd often wondered what would happen if security actually did their job and thoroughly searched everyone who set the alarms off. The fact that guards were armed with only a notepad and a pen meant they were at the mercy of those employees willing to cooperate, which weren't many. Like Todd, many of the employees were running late to work and viewed these security measures as a means of slowing them down.

230

Once through the guard shack, the prison experience continued. The warehouse was surrounded by a stainless-steel fence with razor-sharp barbed wire running along its top. Immediately behind the fence was a twelve-foot-high concrete barrier meant to keep people from seeing into the property. Todd often wondered if this was made to keep people out or to keep employees in.

The pathway leading into the warehouse was brightly lit. Todd had noticed it wasn't for employee safety but rather to provide a better visual for the security cameras. He often had to look down to keep from being blinded. The closer he got to the building, the more anxious he became. His body tensed with each step: first his shoulders, then down his back and continuing to his legs. Todd's fists would clench as though he were holding on to a rope to keep him from falling into an unseen abyss. His heart rate increased and he began breathing rapidly. The closer he got to the door, the slower he found himself walking.

Nightly, Todd was met with an array of unnecessary drama. Because he was a member of middle management, Todd was sandwiched between abuses by upper management and by the teamsters who worked for him or both. He also had to contend with sabotage from coworkers in his same position jockeying for a position in upper management.

Todd had no ambition of promotion within this company. Everyone above him, although well-compensated, were dependent on drugs and alcohol in an effort to cope with the constant demand the company had on its management's time. Todd had heard countless stories of how his superiors made six- and seven-figure salaries but missed their kids' birthdays, graduations, family vacations, and countless milestones. When retirement finally came and they could enjoy their lives, they would drop dead on day one. And though Todd wanted to enjoy his life, at this point, he was too broke and miserable to criticize his superiors' decision to sell out happiness for money.

As he reached for the door to enter the warehouse, Todd would always say a little prayer to minimize that day's stress. His prayers were never answered, though. The company encouraged, no, demanded that middle management manage by intimidation. They encouraged getting in employees' faces and loved to hear middle management celebrate how they would yell at, berate, and embarrass their subordinates. This only happened with the new hires since they were under probationary status. Seasoned employees would strike back with a vengeance and have the teamsters union protect them.

Todd himself had been a victim of this abuse when he was first promoted to mid-management. Looking at the scar on his hand as he reached for the door handle, Todd remembered when his superior once hurled a clipboard at him for failing to fill out his paperwork properly. He'd apparently written too small. The result of this assault was a busted knuckle and five stitches. When he'd filed a grievance with the warehouse's night manager he'd been told he needed to grow thicker skin. He was then handed a rag and was told to clean his blood off the warehouse floor and not to dare miss a day due to an injury.

As Todd pulled the door to the warehouse open, a blast of searing heat caused him to gasp. Todd would joke that this sensation was the building sucking the soul out of his body. It reminded Todd of preheating an oven and opening the door when it reached the set temperature. The searing heat of the day would roast the interior of the building, and the night sort employees were the recipients of the sweltering environment.

232

Todd had learned long ago not to touch any metal objects, as they were known to cause burns. As Todd walked through the warehouse, it took a while for his eyes to adjust to the dimly-lit interior. Many of the bulbs were either burnt out or the casing that housed the bulb was so covered in heavy dust that the light couldn't break through.

Above his head, Todd could hear the ear-piercing sounds of the conveyor belt as it struggled to transport products through the warehouse. Todd peered into the trailers that were stationed at the dock doors. He could see employees drenched with sweat and covered in dust. They resembled chimney sweeps covered in soot. The majority of the dust came from the fans marooned at every dock door. They did little to cool down a trailer but were noisy enough to distract employees from how hot the warehouse was.

As Todd reached the night sort office, he was greeted with an arctic blast of air-conditioning. Ahhh! Instant relief, he thought.

A person who can't lead and won't follow makes a dandy roadblock.
-Murphy's law

Every night before the sort began all middle management were required to congregate for a meeting. Todd and his co-workers spent this time being browbeat and berated about how poorly the previous evening's production had been. They were constantly being told that they were indolent and that none of them deserved to work there.

Todd tried to fly under the radar, trying desperately to not have his name called.

"Listen up!," bellowed Damion Fisk, the night sort manager. Todd had detested this man ever since he told Todd his busted knuckle was his own fault and that he needed tougher skin. "We will be having an impromptu inspection tonight," Damion continued. His news was met by a chorus of moans and groans. "I want all of you pissants to make sure you're working if they come by your area," he demanded. "But don't work too hard because I can't afford to have the teamsters giving us grief for working too hard."

Todd hated the threat of grievances from the teamsters. If anyone who was not union was ever caught touching the product, the teamster who reported it could receive an hour of compensation. Their argument was if the company hired more employees then management would never have to touch the products.

The teamsters felt management touching the product took money away from the union. In theory, this

234

made sense. If Todd touched the product, there was a need for more union workers. More union workers meant more union dues to pay. What Todd didn't like was that he could be grieved against if he touched the product due to safety concerns.

"The warehouse's internal temperature is 116 degrees tonight, so make sure your employees have plenty of water breaks. But not too many," Damion continued. "I don't want people coming in here because they fell out from heat stroke. Lastly, last week's production report has Todd leading the district again," he said, making a jerking-off gesture that minimized Todd's achievements. "That's six weeks in a row, Todd. I still think it's luck. But to show our gratitude, here's a $10 McDonald's Bucks book."

Damion nonchalantly tossed the prize away from Todd's outstretched hand. As the room gave a chorus of half-hearted applause, Todd was disappointed to see that there were only three bucks left in his ten bucks award.

"Congratulations!," Amell said, patting Todd on the back.

"Thanks," Todd said sarcastically, tossing his award in the trash right in front of Damion.

Todd's passive-aggressive pettiness was another reason why he would never get promoted. Not only did he not play the kiss-up-to-your-superior game, he used every opportunity he could to show his disdain for them.

"Amell, what in the hell are you doing in your area? How is it that you lead the sort in grievances? If you're going to help out and work, at least make sure it adds to your production," Damion barked. "You're also near the bottom in production almost every time. You're a teacher, right?," Damion said. "How about teaching your workers to do their jobs?"

"Bottom line? Don't you mother fuckers *dare* embarrass me tonight!," Damion threatened. "Now get the
fuck out. You're sucking up all my A/C."

After a tumultuous day at camp and an even more torrid evening with Sharon, Todd was not in the mood to put on a dog-and-pony show tonight. He often referred to the corporate audits this way since his superiors would parade the upper brass through the warehouse, showing them how they kept their subordinates in line and productive.

Tired and hungry after his traumatizing day at camp, Todd would often sacrifice a meal in exchange for extra sleep. That had been the plan again this evening, but Sharon had ruined things by keeping her t.v.'s volume at an obnoxiously-loud level. Todd wished they had doors to separate the rooms, but those had been knocked off their hinges during one of Sharon's tirades.

Finally arriving at his work area, Todd was displeased by the condition in which the previous manager had left it. Not only did it leave his crew behind the eight ball because they had to clean it up before they could start their work, it was too hot for any extra work tonight.

"Get this shit cleaned up!," Damion yelled as he walked past Todd, aggressively bumping him
in the process.

Calling his crew of eight employees over for a meeting, Todd humbled himself in an effort to raise morale.

236

"Hey guys," he started. "Thank you all for the thankless effort you all continue to give. Once again, we rose to the top. Not only are we the best team in this warehouse, we are the best in the district, and the region. You all are amazing," he praised them. "Unfortunately, we're being audited tonight," he cautioned. "You know that when you're the best, people want to see the best, so that means we're going to be fish-bowled."

"Fish what?," asked a portly man wearing a t-shirt that only came down to his belly button.

"Fish-bowled, Alan," Todd said. "You know, like in an aquarium when people come to look at the fish they stop, observe, and tap on the glass before moving on?" Laughing at his reference, Todd's employees clapped at his comparison. "If anyone asks why I just stand here, tell them if I have to work then I don't need y'all. Then reassure them that it's working because we're the best in the country," Todd said.

"Sounds like a devilish plan," said a tall, dark-skinned man named Demond.

"You have no idea," Todd responded.

As the evening went on, Todd's energy continued to disappear. He wasn't sure if it was because of his long day or because of the heat. Todd's uniform consisted of khakis and a shirt made from non-breathable material so he was sweating profusely. Just then, Todd heard a commotion coming from the dock next to his: Amell's dock.

"This mother fucker is trying to write me up!," an angry woman yelled. "Get me a shop steward!"

237

Like a child trying to calm his sibling down after he'd caused an injury he didn't want to get in trouble for, Amell pleaded for the woman to calm down.

"Calm down? Calm DOWN?!," she screamed. "*You* don't tell me what to do."

Karen, the woman Amell was arguing with, was a management nightmare. She knew the policy book front to back and was always using it to get out of work. Sneaking ever so close to Amell's dock so he could hear what was happening, Todd also made it appear as though he was observing his own.

Pleading with her, Amell asked what would keep her from getting further upset.

"I'm hot!," she cried. "I should be able to take my shirt off and work in just my bra," she snapped.

"That would be inappropriate," Amell said.

"So!," Karen started, "These guys can strip down to their wife-beaters but I can't work in just my bra.

Todd would love to see a lot of women in the warehouse work in just their bra, including the wife he'd met working there, but not Karen. At 5'3", Karen was close to 300 unflattering pounds. Most of her weight appeared to come from her saggy breasts.

"What if I put you in a slower trailer?," Amell asked.

"I'm still working in the heat," Karen responded.

238

"How about if I let you walk around and help anyone who needs it?," Amell offered.

"Okay... For now," she snapped.

"What was *that* all about?," Todd asked.

"I went in there to tell her she wasn't meeting production goals and I was going to give her a verbal warning and she threatened to complain to her union rep about me," Amell told him.

Shaking his head in disbelief, Todd cautioned Amell about being a pushover with his employees.

"Heads up!," Alan warned. "The masters are coming!"

Masters was the term Alan used to refer to upper management, inferring that they treated their employees like slaves. Just then, Amell ran into a trailer to pretend he was too busy to acknowledge their presence. Still a dock away, Todd lazily walked towards its middle. At that moment, Damion approached him to warn him of the upper brass' proximity.

"Look busy, Todd," Damion warned.

"Aye aye, Captain," Todd mocked. Damion just glared at him.

Moments later, a group of five men dressed in suits approached Todd's work area. Todd was amazed
at their attire, especially with it being so hot inside the warehouse. They

must be incredibly uncomfortable, he thought.

"Why aren't *you* working?," the man leading the pack asked Todd. The other four men were hanging on his every word.

And…*ACTION!*, Todd said to himself. Keeping a calm, cool demeanor, Todd kept his left hand in his pocket and his clipboard in his right.

Staring past the leader of the pack, Todd responded with "I *am* working."

"You could've fooled me!," the leader said.

Before Todd could answer, Damion squeezed his way past the yes men and introduced them.

"Mr. Kimble, this is Todd. His area leads production for our warehouse."

"District," Todd corrected arrogantly.

"It must be by luck," Mr. Kimble retorted.

Todd glanced quickly toward Mr. Kimble, made eye contact with him, then turned his attention past him as if to suggest Mr. Kimble wasn't worth his time.

"Alan!," Todd yelled.

"Yes, sir," Alan replied.

"Come here, please," Todd said.

Alan hurried to stand next to Todd. Looking away from him as if something more important was going
on in his work area, Todd asked "Why do I keep my hand in my pocket?"

Standing at attention as though he was in the military, Alan responded, "Because if you have to take your hand out of your pocket, to work, then you don't need us."

"Why do I stand here, Alan?," Todd asked, pointing to his spot on the floor.

"Because you can see everything on YOUR dock and can direct the work to make us more productive, sir," Alan responded. Todd had to bite his tongue to keep from laughing at Alan's over-the-top militaristic
responses.

"That is all, Alan," Todd replied.

"Demond!," Todd yelled.

"Yes, sir!," Demond shouted, drenched in sweat.

"Can you please come here?," he asked.

"Yes, sir!," Demond replied.

"Why do I stand here?," Todd asked.

"So, you can observe us and make us productive," replied Demond, unimpressed with this interaction.

241

"And does it work?," Todd asked.

"Damn fucking right, it does!," Demond replied. "We the best in this district, Bitch!" he shouted in the direction of Mr. Kimble and his yes men.

"Now if you would please excuse me," Todd started, "my dock does not run itself, and we have numbers to achieve."

And...*SCENE!* Now that is Best in Show, Todd thought as he sauntered away, privately applauding his dog-and-pony show performance.

"Damion!," Mr. Kimble shouted, "***That*** is upper-management potential," he said, pointing at Todd. "All your employees should have his confidence instead of running away when we approach their work area. Todd!," yelled Mr. Kimble. "Good job. I see great things for you," he continued as he walked over to the next dock, Amell's dock.

Todd wanted to say "fuck you" in response. He knew this wasn't a career he wanted to be trapped in. Like his marriage, the thought of continuing to be employed here was choking the life out of him. He felt locked up with no means of escape.

He wasn't happy here or in his life; he needed a change. Then it hit him, the perfect event for the summer camp.

"Your nose is bleeding," Alan interrupted.

"Oh, shit," Todd responded, touching his upper lip and feeling blood trickling out of his nose. Rushing for the restroom, Todd shouted to Alan to let Doug

242

know where he was. Doug was Todd's immediate supervisor. Todd had a lot of respect for him because he was fair, but he didn't trust him because he became a kiss ass when the upper brass came around.

As soon as Todd entered the restroom, he rushed directly toward the mirror. Though he suspected his nose bleed was a result of the heat, he wanted to make sure it wasn't from an injury. Not seeing
anything out of the ordinary besides the stream of blood trickling down his face, Todd grabbed a handful of brown paper towels, turned on the cold-water, dampened the paper towels, and splashed the cold water on his face. He then stuck a damp paper towel up his nose. He thought dampening the rough paper towels would soften them enough that they wouldn't make matters worse when he stuck them up his nose.

As if he were in the front row of a show, Todd glanced in the mirror, hoping to see his nose stop bleeding. It didn't.

Back to the sink to grab more paper towels, Todd thought. Repeating this process for over twenty minutes, Todd was beginning to wonder how much blood he'd lost. Glancing over at the trash can, the pile of discarded paper towels now soaked in water and blood was evidence that it had been a lot. Looking around the bathroom floor, Todd began to feel disgusted at the realization that if he passed out from blood loss, collapsing on this putrid-smelling floor would be less than ideal.

Todd made his way over to a stall. I'll sit on the toilet, he thought. So if I pass out, hopefully the stall walls will keep me from laying out on the floor. Wrong again!, he realized as he saw the repugnant shit-and-urine packed toilet completely full from failed flushing attempts. Even with one nostril stuffed with a soaked paper towel, Todd could still smell the stench.

243

"Todd? Are you in here?," yelled a voice Todd recognized as Doug's. Seeing the trash can packed with blood-soaked paper towels and a trail of blood droplets arranged on the ground, Doug feared the worst.

"I am in here," Todd responded, still assessing the explosion of human waste in front of him.

"What's going on with you?," Doug asked, looking at the disgusting toilet.

"That was *not* me," Todd argued as he turned to face Doug. Seeing yet another bloody paper towel, Doug was truly concerned about Todd's well-being.

"I have to ask," Doug started. "Are you using nose candy?"

Insulted, Todd snorted back, "If I did drugs and worked here I would probably be on something stronger. My nose is probably bleeding because I can smell this shit from my work area."

Todd often used jokes to mask his anger, and Todd was both angry and scared. His nose had been bleeding for half an hour. What could the cause possibly be? Having his boss ask if he was on drugs wasn't how he wanted him to address the situation. He wanted Doug to offer a ride to the hospital or at least call 911 to ask what to do.

"I'm sorry," Doug said now. "You know we have to ask."

"I know," Todd responded. But he didn't. With all the procedures this company makes us memorize, I don't ever remember reading that I had to ask an employee if they were taking drugs.

"What the hell is going on in here?," asked an angry voice standing at the doorway of the bathroom. "I don't pay you two to play tickle booty on my dime," Damion inappropriately yelled.

Surveying the condition of the bathroom, Damion looked at Todd and then at Doug. "I hope his nose is busted because you socked him for the shit he pulled during the audit."

Todd could tell Doug was confused about what was going on and wanted to ask for clarification but decided against it.

"No, sir," Doug started.

Sir, Todd thought. Damion doesn't deserve the respect of being called sir.

"I was attending to Todd's nose, sir."

Turning on his heels, Damion left as abruptly as he entered. Confused by his exit, Todd and Doug looked at each other before they attended to Todd's nose.

"WebMD says that you shouldn't lay your head back," Doug said, reading the contents off his phone.

Tilting his head forward, Todd asked, "What about leaning forward?"

Before Doug had a chance to answer, the door opened violently, and there stood Damion. "Doug!," he exclaimed. Can you give this to your employee

245

with the bloody nose?"

Why is he acting like I'm not here?, Todd wondered. Grabbing whatever it was Damion had, Doug walked over to Todd and placed the object in his hand. Looking down, Todd was perturbed to find a tampon.

"Doug," Damion said, "Tell your employee to shove that up his nose and to get back to work. Now!," he demanded.

Todd thought about his options. He dreaded the reaction he'd get if he had a feminine product hanging from his nose.

"I said now," Damion repeated, agitated. Todd couldn't swear to it, but as Damion exited, Todd thought he saw a wide smile creep across Damion's face. This amazed Todd. He'd never seen Damion smile, nor did he imagine that he had teeth. Maybe just fangs, Todd imagined.

The tampon he'd been given had a yellow floral design on it. The prospect of having a citrusy fragrance in his nose excited Todd. Anything was better than the smell of shit emanating from the stall behind him. He flipped the tampon over and was dismayed to find it didn't come with instructions.

Todd removed the wrapper and wondered how a woman bled into the plastic shell. What in the hell, he thought. No wonder women are agitated during their cycle; I would be, too, if I had to shove all these parts inside me every month.

What's this string all about, he wondered. Do I pull this to get it to work? Todd turned to Doug and started to ask a question, but Doug shrugged, "Google just confused me, too."

246

"Here goes nothing," Todd said, shoving the applicator up his nose, plastic and all. "Let's get this
night over with," he sighed.

He was met with a chorus of laughter as he exited the restroom. Damion led the cacophony, followed by Mr. Kimble and his yes men.

"I guess he *could*n't handle the pressure of having corporate's eyes on him," Damion said. "I guess his wife really does have his balls in her purse."

Embarrassed, Todd walked past the group from upper management thinking his morale had hit rock
bottom. Karen ran up to him as he reached his work area.

"Hey dumb ass," she called.

Todd stopped and turned to her. He fixed his posture, raised his head, and prepared for a fight. He refused to let Karen walk all over him the way she did to Amell.

"Men," she snorted as she removed the plastic applicator from his nose and walked off.

Whew! That feels so much better!, Todd thought.

"I need to quit this place," Amell said, walking over to Todd. "Those suits reamed me during this audit," he continued. "We need to make this camp successful; we need to turn A.S.A.P. into a conglomerate. I don't want to continue to work for other people," he complained.

"I have an idea," Todd said.

If your project doesn't work, look for the part you didn't think was important.

-Arthur Bloch

Amell's words echoed in Todd's mind all night. He was tired of working himself ragged just to live paycheck to paycheck. None of his jobs was going to make him rich. Hell, I'd settle for just living comfortably, he thought. Neither were possible in either job. The school was hemorrhaging. The warehouse's path to success was covered in indignation and its environment reminded him too much of his home life. He desperately needed out of both.

The only saving grace with his jobs was he felt he had a purpose. He was succeeding at the warehouse, though he was not reaping the benefits of that success. At the school he felt he was bestowing wisdom and words of advice to the campers and volunteers. It made him feel fulfilled.

As he lay in bed next to Sharon he strained to remember the woman he initially thought he'd married. Gazing at her as she slept, Todd was amazed at the permanent scowl she wore. Her arms were folded across her chest as if she was always angry. If resting bitch face could be a pose, Sharon was nailing it in her sleep.

Planning, organizing, and running the camp had been a stressful ordeal, he thought. Not once had Sharon asked about it or empathized with his plight. Whenever he *did* discuss his life's pitfalls, Sharon always made the conversation about her. The last loving thing she'd done came only after she'd tried to kill him. Even when he'd told her about the incident at the mall, how the police determined a stray bullet was mere inches from striking him in the head, her only concern was that his life insurance premium was current.

In the past, Todd had suggested they see a marriage counselor but Sharon shot it down immediately. They didn't have enough money. She *did* recognize her anger issues, and even though she promised she would get better at managing her emotions, she also said she didn't need a counselor telling her she was crazy or angry. Todd envisioned his wife sitting on someone's couch, blaming her mother for all her problems. "My diagnosis," Todd imagined the counselor saying, "is that you're crazy." Would Sharon jump up and attack the counselor, too?

Todd himself couldn't complain about his wife's refusal to get help from a stranger. Men, especially those in the African American community, had spent generations telling the generation following them not to talk about their issues to anyone outside the family. They always viewed someone seeking counseling as weak or crazy. Hell, even discussing mental health issues within the family, no matter how crippling the illness, was viewed as inappropriate and forbidden. Years of distrust and mistreatment both within and outside the community had always left African Americans wondering who they could trust to help. Would what they shared be used against them?

Todd questioned sharing his marital problems with his parents; it was just better to keep it bottled up inside. They would definitely call him crazy for staying married to Sharon and weak for allowing her to get away with the abuse she did.

Todd couldn't stop thinking about the way Sharon had chosen to get help: an illegal prescription from a street pharmacist with a sip of tequila to wash

250

it down. Todd worried for her health. How can she trust a drug dealer?, he wondered. How does she know she's getting the right drug? The correct dose? How does she know the drug isn't laced with something?

Todd's mind was racing frantically. He needed to calm his thoughts. He needed to put down his phone and rest. Putting a few of Sharon's behaviors into an Internet search revealed she was depressed. Well *that*'s an understatement, Todd thought. There were several other possibilities, but Todd only focused on the one. Depression. Maybe, he thought, depression was something he could fix. Deep down, Todd knew there was no easy fix when someone was broken and needed help. But he was clueless about mental illnesses. He wondered which of Sharon's tequila-drinking friends prescribed her Xanax. They're probably just as clueless as he is, Todd thought.

He had voiced his vehement displeasure with her drunken self-medication. He tried desperately to convince her that doctors spend years practicing the diagnosis of their patients, and prescribing the correct doses of the correct medication. He tried explaining that what works for one person doesn't necessarily work for another. He worried about the side effects of the medication she was taking. Sharon always met his concerns with intense exasperation. I'm trying to get better for you, Todd remembers her saying. I don't want you to get hurt, he recalled her telling him sarcastically.

Todd had worried about his wife's behavior for some time,so much so that it was keeping him up now when he so desperately needed to rest. Her mood shifted violently from one extreme to another. Todd had noticed that when his wife is medicated she acts like a zombie. She shows zero emotion. She's just....there, Todd thought. When the medicine was out of her system, the littlest things set her off.

251

Earlier in the day, Sharon had lashed out at him for getting the floor wet when he got out of the shower. Though he'd made sure to step on the faux fur bathroom rug, Sharon became livid when she stepped on it in her dry socks. Infuriated, Sharon had run into the kitchen, her pants still down after using the bathroom, to use her finger as a weapon. As she berated him, Sharon thrust her index finger into the middle of Todd's forehead, hurtling insults and threats.

Todd was still haunted by finding Sharon in the fetal position crying hysterically because she was out of drugs and her supplier was out of town. Seeing his wife in that state had brought tears to Todd's eyes. How do you help someone when they're broken? How can you guide someone to get the help they need? He'd vowed to love his wife in sickness and in health. She's sick, but she refuses to get help. This infuriated Todd. How do you help someone who knows there's a problem but refuses to do anything about it?

He began to look inside himself. How can I continue to love someone who constantly hurts me? He was tired of being the only one in this relationship. He needed a queen to support him in his quest for greatness, not a woman who treated him as a pawn. He needed his wife to sense his pain when he was hurting, to mend his spirit when it was broken, and to support him mentally when the weight on his shoulders became too much to bear. As a black man, he needed her to truly understand how the world was against him and their relationship. There's still love in her heart, he thought. Just not for me.

Every time he turned around Sharon had adopted another cat. She'd started with two when they exchanged their vows. Now there were thirteen. She showed them unconditional love. All Todd got was grief and sinus infections

252

caused by his allergy to cats. He couldn't sit down anywhere without getting cat hair everywhere, including in his food. How can she love these fur balls more than me?, he fumed.

Todd was reeling. He felt trapped. Trapped in several dead-end jobs, and trapped in a bad marriage. I need to find a new job, he strategized, but how? Working all day as well as through the night severely limited his ability to go job hunting. And even if he *did* find a new opportunity, he couldn't afford to take off to go on an interview. If he doesn't work, he doesn't get paid.

Glancing in his wife's direction, Todd fumed over the financial situation she'd put them in. Sharon was completely able to work but refused to get a job. Whenever the subject came up, she either became withdrawn or aggressive. To make matters worse, she purposely overdrafted their account so she could have spending money. What she spends it on has plagued Todd. She doesn't pay bills or buy him gifts. Her son's video games can't be that expensive. How much does she spend on her illegally-prescribed medication?, Todd wondered.

Whatever it was, Todd is always financially behind. Every paycheck was used to cover their overdraft fees. Todd was in a constant state of wonder as to which bill collector would be calling? What utility was on the verge of being shut off?

Should he drop everything and leave his unloving wife? Did it really matter that he honor his vows
if she didn't honor hers? Todd wanted to break down. He'd been stepping up and powering through
their struggles for months. I shouldn't have to live the rest of my life without

the support of my spouse.

The more he focused on his situation, the more he found himself hating his wife. And could he even really call her his wife? She was more of a bully than a wife.

Then it dawned on him. Was he an abused spouse? Laughing at the notion that his tiny 4'11" spouse was a bully, Todd began a web search on spousal abuse. The evidence glowed brightly in the pitch-black room. As Sharon tossed and turned, Todd dashed into the bathroom, closing the door behind him. Anxiety filled him as he read the various signs of abuse that he'd experienced. Sure, she hit him. Sure, she threw things at him. But that's not abuse, Todd thought. Yet there it was in black and white, abuses he constantly experienced at the hands of his wife. Making unfounded accusations of infidelity. She made accusations about everything she didn't understand. If he experienced something different from what she expected she thought he was doing something nefarious. She was constantly monitoring calls and texts. If he wasn't able to call her back right away, she went back to the accusations that he was cheating.

The next example Todd read stung even more. Exerting financial control and manipulating or overspending. Sharon gave Todd $20 a week for allowance, in cash. Though she had the bankcard and asked Todd for money, she only did it as a courtesy. Todd often felt Sharon would ask for money so that he could plan how many more hours he needed to work to help her afford whatever she wanted.

His revelation shook Todd to the core. What do I do? Too embarrassed to tell anyone, too nervous to confront Sharon, Todd decided to keep it all inside. How would it look? He, being a man, asking for protection from his wife. The

254

police, judge, and society would laugh at him. He turned off the light in the bathroom and headed back into the bedroom.

He felt her presence before he could see her. Her presence scared Todd; he wasn't expecting her to be standing in the bathroom doorway. He delayed speaking to her because he didn't want Sharon to know about his research. How would she respond if she found out? Confronting her about the Xanax hadn't gone well. Todd imagined this would be disastrous, too.

"Who the fuck is she?," Sharon said. Her question was deliberate. As his eyes adjusted to the dark, Todd could see the rage in her face.

"I was just using the bathroom," Todd replied.

"Then why don't I hear the sound of the toilet flushing?," she asked.

Caught, Todd thought. "I actually came in here to think," he confessed. "I need to come up with an event to help the camp end on a positive note." Good comeback, he thought.

Sharon snatched Todd's phone out of his hand. Meticulously, Sharon checked Todd's call log, text messages, and email. Knowing he had nothing to hide, Todd stood confident that she was finally going to end her inconsonant badgering of there being another woman. Slowly turning around, Sharon revealed his search history.

"Why you little bitch," she snapped. "You think you're being abused?," she asked. "You're not being abused. I was abused! My dad used to punch me in the face," she revealed. "He hit me so hard he chipped a tooth. My ex-husband would choke me until I would black out," she recalled.

255

Shoving Todd into the wall, Sharon continued her revelation. "I was burned, choked, beat, raped, and insulted. *That* is abuse, motherfucker. Me calling you a name here and there is not abuse. So wipe your tears and man up, you little bitch."

Climbing into bed, Sharon chucked Todd's phone in his direction. "You need to sleep on the couch," she said. Todd felt it best to oblige. He'd had a rough, bloody night at work and an even longer day at camp. The stress from his jobs were weighing heavily on him. His marriage and home life were causing him to sink. He was tired. He didn't want to fight with Sharon. Todd walked toward the bed to grab a pillow.

Hopping off the bed, Sharon grabbed Todd's arm, swung him around, and squared up in front of him. "Listen you big, dumb, Nigger," she sneered. "I refuse to share my bed with another Bitch. Nigger!"

Shocked and angry, Todd was taken aback. How could his wife call him such a hateful word? Although Todd had experienced racism, he'd never expected it from his wife. This was the first time someone had ever called him that word face-to-face. He should be livid, he thought. He should call her something back. But he was too devastated to react. The woman he'd vowed to love for the rest of his life had just deliberately attacked him in the most hurtful way. She'd labeled him a term African Americans had been fighting for generations to shed. That term cut his legs right from under him. Sharon wanted a fight; Todd did not.

"We need to talk," she demanded. At that moment, Todd couldn't have cared less about what she had to say.

"Can we talk in the morning?," he asked. Her talk needed to include the words 'I'm sorry' and 'please forgive me,' but Sharon had never said those words to Todd.

"No. We need to talk now," she replied. Sharon was a communication bully. She knew Todd was tired, but she didn't care. This was about her, not him. She didn't care about compromising or about Todd's feelings; she only cared about winning a fight.

Todd never wanted to fight. He always hoped things would blow over. He unrealistically believed their issues would resolve themselves. But now he knew they wouldn't. The more tired he grew, the more irritated he would become. He tried desperately to keep his composure, but it was hard and was getting harder.

Sharon continued to insist that Todd stay up and talk to her. The more she pressed, the more silent, frustrated, and non-communicative he became. Not saying anything is the only way Todd felt he could survive Sharon's fights.

Still belittling her husband at the top of her lungs, Sharon hurled insult after insult. Finally, Todd just walked away, heading for the couch. He placed his pillow down, but Sharon was right there to pick it up and fling it on the floor. Todd stepped around her and lay on the couch, completely ignoring her. Even if she stopped, Todd's hopes of sleeping were dashed. His nerves were wrecked, his adrenalin pumping. He was mad. Not just at her, but at himself. He couldn't believe Sharon had so much control over his emotions and it pissed him off. He was furious that his well-being depended on having a conversation with Sharon. He hadn't walked out of her life after being called a nigger. Maybe he should have.

Sharon kicked the edge of the couch, disrupting his opportunity for peace and quiet. She was behaving like a child.

"Leave me the fuck alone," Todd said, finally erupting with furor and fire. His outburst startled Sharon. Had the bullied scared the bully? The outburst felt good. He was tired of holding his anger inside. He didn't care about the repercussions of his outburst, he just wanted to get some sleep.

What should have been three hours of rest dwindled down to just ninety minutes.

"Sleep with one eye open," Sharon threatened as she stormed off.

Fuming, any chance of rest evaporated out of fear. Todd's best bet was to focus on an epic summer camp finale.

> *Friendly fire isn't.*
> *– Murphy's law of combat*

"Surprise, motherfucker!," Sharon sang sweetly and sarcastically.

Todd opened his eyes slowly, and there she was with a smile on her face. She was standing next to the couch. Todd wasn't surprised by her curiously gleeful nature or the fact that she was standing over him. He'd woken up like this many times: his wife standing over or laying next to him, just staring at him. But this time was different. This time she had a Colt .38 Special pressed against his temple. Todd was flooded by a range of emotions. He was full of fear, but not like before at The Plaza. There, he was at the mercy of total strangers. Now, in front of someone who'd vowed to love him, he could sense that Sharon was using this opportunity to get back in control of their relationship.

Last night had been the first time Todd had snapped back at her. He'd seen Sharon startle at his reaction. It had been a turning point for him. He was tired of putting up with the bullshit in his life. Work, marriage, more work, the summer camp, and even more work were all going to have to take a back seat. He had finally come to the realization that he can't be someone else's savior if he can't even save himself.

Todd tried to play it cool with his wife now. As much as he wanted to believe that she wouldn't really shoot him, he couldn't help but wonder what would happen if he was wrong. What if she accidently pulled the trigger? What if the gun has a hairpin trigger? Accidents happen, and he didn't want to be a statistic.

259

Dying by gunshot was one of Todd's greatest fears. He'd always assumed it would hurt and would be messy. He didn't ever want to be in a position to test that theory. His biggest fear now was not being in control of the situation. Sharon appeared to be suffering from the same fear. She tried desperately to hide it, repeating actions that had given her control when she'd attacked Todd with the knife in their bedroom. It wasn't working this time.

"Tell me," she started, "Is this what it felt like at The Plaza?" She was trying hard to make her voice sound menacing and dark, but it crackled and sounded weak.

"Listen," Todd said. "I'm tired of the way you treat me. If we're going to make this work you need to treat me as if you love me and want to be with me. If not, I'm out of here." Todd was positive he was going to leave his wife no matter what she said or did. "Now if you don't mind, I have twenty minutes left before I have to get up."

Sharon's jaw dropped, she was flabbergasted. Todd closed his eyes and pretended he was actually going to go to sleep. Sharon lept on top of him, moving the barrel of the gun from his temple to the middle of his forehead.

"Do you think this is how murder suicides happen?," she sneered. "One person loves the other so much they can't imagine themselves without them? I *have* shown how much I love you," she said. "I take pills to bury the rage brewing inside of me because I don't want to hurt you. Do you care?," she asked. "No you don't. I reached out to you and expressed the deep, soul-crushing pain inside of me and you offered me fucking ice!" Sharon was sobbing now. "I need comfort at night, or during the day, but I'm placed on hold until you get off of work. I'm *always* put on hold in your life and I'm

260

tired of it," she cried.

"I could pull the trigger right now and end your pain, then turn the gun on me and end my suffering, too. You say you want this to work out, but you have to be **home** to work on it," she snapped. "You may not like the means I use to get your attention, but it's what I know to do. You asked *me* to marry *you*, remember, not the other way around. We promised to love each other until death do we part. I'm willing to part with you right now."

Todd's heart started to pound out of his chest. His wife's perspective, though heartfelt, was frightening. Terrifying. How does her definition of love make any sense? Todd thought long and hard about what he wanted to say. What he *needed* to say. He did not want to say something that would give him a hole in his head, nor did he want to commit to something that meant these things kept occurring.

Sharon pulled back on the hammer of the gun. Times up!, Todd thought. Tears welled up in her eyes and she began to tremble. Todd was frozen in fear, unable to speak.

"I...," he started. His voice trembled as he struggled to find the right words. "I....," he began again. He couldn't decide what to say. Do I say I love you? Do I say I'm sorry. Time was ticking.

"I will try harder to be the man I need to be for you," he said.

"Promise?," Sharon asked with a slight grin on her face. Had Todd just been duped into being Sharon's puppet on a string? Again?

Sharon leaned in and placed a tiny kiss on his lips as she hopped off of him.

261

"We're going to have a wonderful life together," she said with a giggle. Todd was convinced she was truly the devil, or insane. Maybe both.

"Why are you looking so serious?," Sharon asked. "I wasn't going to shoot you. The gun's not even loaded." She aimed the gun and pulled the trigger. "See? Nothing happened," she laughed. "Next time I don't want to do the dishes I'll just bring my little friend here and make you do it," she joked, aiming the gun in Todd's direction.

BOOM! Sound filled the air as a bullet escaped from inside the gun. Todd saw a spark fly from the barrel, but all he could do was close his eyes. A piercing whistling buzzed past his ear as the bullet tore first through his pillow and then the cushion on the couch. Fibers from both filled the air and slowly rained down as the bullet obliterated them.

Stunned, Sharon dropped the gun in disbelief. The painful ringing in his ears made Todd wonder if he'd been shot. Gingerly touching his ear, he was shocked to find no blood present. Disoriented, Todd struggled to get his bearings. He couldn't comprehend what had just happened.

"You shot me!," he said, his voice wavering.

"I-i-i-t was an a-a-a-accident," Sharon stuttered. "I'm sorry! I'm so, so sorry!"

Todd couldn't hear whatever it was she was saying. All he heard was a high-pitched ringing in his ears. Sharon ran off crying. Sitting up, Todd realized he'd wet himself. Soiled pants and hearing loss was a win in his eyes considering the alternative.

For the second time this summer Todd had experienced a bullet whizzing past his head. He silently prayed that it wouldn't happen a third time. Examining his pillow and couch Todd shuddered to think what could have been. A rush of oxygen escaped his lips and he realized he hadn't exhaled in quite some time.

Tense, and incredibly stressed, Todd began taking deep breaths. He had escaped death once again. Was she trying to kill him and claim it was an accident? No marriage was worth this trauma, Todd thought. As if she could hear his thoughts, Sharon came running back in the room. She threw her arms around his neck, kissing him and apologizing repeatedly, saying 'I love you' over and over again. Todd wasn't buying it. He could barely hear it.

"Things will be different," she professed. Doubt filled Todd's heart. He could taste and smell the tequila on her breath.

"I have to go," he said, pushing his wife off of him.

"Already?!," she whined.

"I have to earn money to replace our furniture. Look at our couch, it's been killed."

You never find a lost article until you replace it.
– Murphy's law

"Kidnapped!," Amell yelled. "Someone tell me how one of our campers managed to be kidnapped!," he barked, slamming his hand on the desk.

Todd could tell Amell was pissed, seething. The saliva gathered around the corners of his mouth was foaming. Beads of sweat pooled on the top of his head. His speech cracked as he choked back the four-letter explicative he wanted to say.

"Kidnapped," he repeated emphatically, continuing to bang his hand on the desk.

Amell had demanded the staff arrive early this morning for an emergency meeting. Todd was stunned that Amell had gotten there earlier than he did. This had to be serious, he thought. For his part, Todd was pissed off knowing he was missing an hour of sleep in order to be here for a meeting. He suspected it was going to be another of Amell's pep talks designed to motivate the staff and volunteers to work hard. Amell's meetings were usually rah-rah, kumbaya sessions and Todd didn't have the energy for it. The last thing Todd wanted was to waste the tiny bit of energy he had left faking excitement of being at work.

264

Todd's exhaustion was on full display once again. When he arrived in the classroom he sat in a quiet corner and wished he could master the art of sleeping with his eyes open. His eyes were heavy; his *eyelashes* hurt. And thanks to his wife, his ear did, too. Todd wondered what he looked like to others, his eyes crossing as he strained to keep them open. Every blink was euphoric, but when he heard the word 'kidnapped' he was suddenly wide awake.

Adrenaline took over. His mind began to race. Which camper was kidnapped? Was there a ransom? Who are the suspects? Todd became a Hardy Boy. He scanned the room looking for clues. Then his thoughts became darker. Was the camper dead? Had they been targeted? Are more campers at risk? Where are the police, the FBI, the CIA?

Todd was anxious for answers. He became irritated by Amell's critique of the staff and volunteers. He's wasting time!, Todd thought. He needed details. As he continued to scan the room, he noticed a look of concern plastered on everyone's face. Some of the staffers appeared to be having the same dark thoughts Todd was. Several were weeping. Everyone except for Bianca. Where is she?, Todd thought. Bianca's attendance this summer had been erratic to say the least. So much so that she'd been issued several 'final warnings.'

"This camp's environment and the attitude of its workers and volunteers needs a drastic change," Amell said. "Effective immediately, I'm instituting Todd as the new director of staffing!," Amell announced. "Todd, they're all yours," he avowed. Amell stormed off, emphatically swinging open the spring-loaded door. It didn't match his vigor. Once again, an attempt at a dramatic exit thwarted by a door. Under any other circumstance this would have been comical. Not today. Not after the day's news.

Taken aback by the situation and by Amell's declaration, Todd was still reeling from the news of a camper's kidnapping. Amell's bulletin was incredibly vague. Todd now had the room's attention and the position he felt he deserved. He didn't want it anymore, though. His fury began to swell as he pondered what could have been. Would there have been a kidnapping if he'd been in charge? Would there have been injuries if he'd been in charge? Would the staffing be running as a skeletal crew if he'd been in charge? Was it too late to change the behavior the staffers and volunteers had become accustomed to?

Formulating a plan in his head, Todd felt he had to match Amell's intensity. He needed to grab and hold the staff's attention. To make a lasting impression. Without saying a word, Todd slowly walked the room. peering deeply into the eyes of each person there. As he slowly made his way back to the front, Todd took a long, deep breath.

He pointed at everyone in his audience. "You are failing this camp," he barked. "You have not only put this camp at risk, but someone's **life** is in jeopardy." He paused to let his statement sink in. He could sense that everyone felt responsible for the kidnapping. "It's time for you all to realize that you're responsible not only for *your* actions but the actions of everyone here. From now on, every action has to have a reaction. If a camper falls and scrapes their knee, I want an incident report done. In the report, I need details of what happened, how it happened, and how we addressed it. I need follow-up for at least a week, maybe longer depending on the severity of the injury. I want attendance checks done every ten minutes. If someone is unaccounted for we go on lockdown. We all report to the cafeteria and stay there until everyone is there. If someone appears sad or despondent, it's up to you to attend to them and try to put a smile on their face. I want everyone to feel included," he said. "Is that understood?"

A chorus of yesses filled the room. "Lori, what does 'despondent' mean?," Todd asked.

"I don't know," she replied.

"Chad? John? Any of my volunteers? What does despondent mean?" Silence filled the room. "Are you kidding me?!," Todd bellowed. "Don't lie and say you understand something when you don't," he yelled. "You all need to start taking this job seriously. Some of you are getting paid for working here. It's time to earn your paycheck," he continued. "Others are receiving much-needed community service hours toward their graduation requirement, and I'm not signing off on anything that isn't earned," he declared.

Todd had always prided himself on being able to keep his warehouse demeanor at the warehouse and his school demeanor on campus. Today was different. His warehouse personality was spilling over into his school temperament. Spilling was an understatement. This was a flood.

Todd was losing sight of who he thought he was. He had to play a role at all his jobs, in his home life, even within himself. Fake forty is how he described his jobs. He would fake how he really felt about his jobs for forty hours a week. He didn't like who he was becoming. He did not like the warehouse demanding he manage by intimidation, turning him into a bully. Todd wasn't a bully. He hated coddling everyone at the school, or 'showing mercy' to use the school's terminology. Life doesn't work that way. His home was a warzone; there was no love there.

Todd felt his entire life was simply him going through the motions. He wasn't happy, and this wasn't a life worth living. He wanted to explore the world but couldn't see past his small bubble. He had zero ambition anymore. Sharon was sucking the life out of him, and he didn't have just one dead-end job, he had three. Even his weekend job offered no refuge. He was living the life of a prisoner. But even that wasn't entirely accurate. Most prisoners have parole to look forward to. Todd had nothing.

"I don't know the particulars of the kidnapping," Todd continued, "but it's our responsibility to be held
accountable for every single camper's safety and well-being. You've failed one of them," he snapped. His statements continued to upset everyone in the room. Mission accomplished, Todd thought.

"Now let's go out there and have a productive day. Dismissed," he said.

The adrenaline began to wear off and Todd sat down immediately. He knew he needed to walk the campus and check to see how well his words had sunk in with his crew, but he just didn't have the energy.

"Did you make everyone cry?," asked a voice from behind Todd. It was Amell's. Todd turned around and began bombarding him with questions:

"Who got kidnapped?," he started. "Are they still alive? Is there a ransom? Where are the FBI and amber alerts?"

"There was never a real kidnapping," Amell confessed. A mother drove by, picked up her child, then came back and asked where her child was. We searched for a good forty-five minutes before she came clean that she'd had him the whole time. Do you know how embarrassing an ordeal this was? I

268

never should've put Bianca in charge of staffing," he admitted. "I thought if I put you both in areas you weren't best suited for it would help you grow and become more well-rounded."

That actually makes sense, Todd thought, but not when we're trying to make money. "Lessons like those should be left for the classroom," he said.

Amell stared at Todd with a look that said he'd overstepped his boundary a bit, so Todd immediately changed the subject.

"By the way, Amell. Where *is* Bianca?"

"She left early yesterday but didn't tell anyone she was leaving. We spent fifteen minutes looking for her, too. Can you imagine wondering if she'd been the one who kidnapped the kid we were looking for because she wound up missing, too? So, I suspended her for two days."

Look around the table; if you don't see a sucker, get up,
because you're the sucker.

"What is a lockout?," Amell asked.

"Lockout with your cock out," Bianca blurted.

"Don't make me muzzle you, Amell threatened. His words were calculated. Todd sensed Amell was getting tired of her antics.

Todd had put a lot of energy and thought on how to salvage the camp's first year with an epic finale.

"We all know what a lock-in party is, correct?," Todd asked rhetorically. "It's pretty much like a big slumber party, only everyone is "locked inside" until morning."

"Yeahh….," Bianca and Amell said in unison.

"Since we're a summer day camp," Todd continued, "We lock ourselves out of all the buildings on campus. We camp out beneath the stars," he said. "We'll have all the fun and games of a lock-in, just outdoors," he concluded.

"I can see it," Amell started Amell. "Carnival games, food, a bonfire…."

"Exactly!," Todd replied, excited. "Hamburgers, hot dogs, slushies…," he added.

"I can't be there," Bianca stated matter-of-factly.

"I haven't even set a date," Todd replied.

"That's a stupid idea," Bianca argued.

"I like it!," Amell said, defending Todd's idea.

"Why don't you like it? Todd asked Bianca.

"Bugs. And the heat," she answered. "Mosquitoes. Especially mosquitos. Those flying assholes spread West Nile, malaria, Zika and Dengue. They're little assassins responsible for around 1 million deaths per year! Plus," she continued, "I don't work on the weekend."

You barely work during the week, Todd thought. Her attendance and work ethic had been on a steady decline, ever since she and Derrick broke up again. After Amell fired him for his antics at the pool, her work performance had become horrid, like a personal vendetta against the camp.

"This would be on a Friday," Todd responded Todd.

"Are you *serious*?!," Bianca cried. "Friday is the definition of a weekend! After we clock out, it is literally the end of the week," she argued defiantly. "Are we pulling in doubles now?," she asked. "Look guys. You may think this is a great idea, but I think I'm done." Bianca's once vibrant spirit now seemed deflated. "This camp has caused me to reach my breaking point," she explained. "Between being a magnet for a wart-carrying beast, Todd's lunch covering me at the pool, bratty kids, racist cops, horrible field trips, and witnessing a murder, I don't have the energy to carry on."

Bianca's head slumped, and her shoulders dropped. She was exhausted. Todd wondered how much of her resignation had to do with Derrick no longer working with the camp.

"I wish you two the best, but my heart isn't in it anymore." Her eyes filled with tears. "Todd," she started, "Go talk to someone about your situation at home. You deserve to be happy." Then she turned and walked away slowly.

"And then there were two," Todd said. He'd known it was only a matter of time before Bianca quit. Having been placed in charge of an inexperienced staff had proved too much for her. Hell, it's even caused *Todd* to question his commitment to the camp that he himself started! Bianca had increasingly exhibited the traits of a burnt-out employee. She never made it in on time, but her arrival had gotten later and later, if she came in at all. She began ignoring the incompetence of her employees. Todd wanted to blame her behavior on the trauma she experienced at the theater, but he suspected there was more to it than that. Todd was curious about what was going on in her life but didn't have enough to find out. He had his own problems to tend to.

Now, it was his turn to pick up the slack left by her departure, to plan an epic lockout. Todd had plenty of ideas in his head as to what he wanted to include, but he, too, was burned out. His marriage to Sharon had taken its toll. He was filled with nervous energy. It came from everywhere, not just his wife. His jobs, his financial situation were all straws that were breaking his back. He had nowhere to turn and felt he couldn't breathe. The walls were closing in on him, and now another responsibility added to his plate.

"Todd!," Teresa called. "I heard you talking about the lockout. Can I help plan it?"

272

Todd wasn't really a fan of working with a teenager when so much was at stake, but with the camp's success on the line, he felt he had no choice. Maybe I can keep her busy doing all the mundane tasks.

"Sure," he said. "I'll give you a list of everything I need done." His list included buying the meat they'd be grilling, renting an inflatable, organizing a bonfire, and advertising the event. Busy work, but mundane tasks.

"Todd? Come in," Terri's voice crackled over the walkie-talkie. Time to put out the fires!, Todd thought before responding. "We have an...umm...situation near the back of the softball fields," Terri continued.

"The back of the softballs fields?," Todd repeated out loud. There's nothing out there but trees, he thought. "I'm on my way," he said.

"Teresa!," he yelled. "Can you please take the younger campers to the gym? This is usually the time Bianca would let them have their free time in there to burn off their extra energy."

"I'm on it!," Teresa responded, excited by her new tasks.

Arriving behind the softball fields moments later, Todd was greeted by a bunch of campers and Terri looking up into a tree.

"What's going on here?," Todd asked. The group pointed up. Todd expected to find a ball stuck between some branches. Nope. Two campers had climbed high enough that they were now too afraid to come down.

"How did this happen?," Todd asked, pulling out his phone.

273

"They were debating who was the fastest tree-climber," Terri said. "I never thought they would climb as high as they did, nor did I think they would be too scared to come down."

Todd tried to judge how high the campers were. No more than fifteen feet. I can rescue them, he thought, reminiscing about his own days climbing trees as a kid. He jumped to the first branch he could reach then swung his legs upward, latching them onto the branch. He hung there like a sloth for a second as he debated what his next move should be.

CRACK! The branch snapped, and down he went with the branch. It was so much easier when he was younger and lighter! Landing on his back, Todd felt the wind get knocked out of him. The campers loved his effort, even the boys who were stuck in the tree.

Todd had managed to make it only seven feet off the ground. As entertaining as his failure had been, Todd's snafu erased any chance of the boys climbing back down themselves, even if they found the courage to. The nearest branch to the ground was now nine feet away. Todd contemplated asking Amanda for a ladder, but he didn't want to get her involved. His only other option was to call the fire department.

"Hold on tight," he cautioned the boys. "Help is on the way. Who won the race?," he asked, trying to keep the boys calm. His distraction technique worked as the two began arguing the results of the race. When the firefighters arrived, they were not surprised by the scene.

"Contrary to the myth that we rescue cats from trees," one firefighter said, "We usually rescue more kids and parents who've gotten stuck climbing or

274

rescuing. We're getting a ladder!," he yelled up to the trapped boys.

"A *ladder*?!," yelled one of the boys, disappointed by the rescuers' method.

"Where's the giant trampoline they use on TV?," hollered the other one

"You can't believe everything you see on television," the firefighter cautioned. "Jumping from that height onto a trampoline would cause more issues than it would solve," he warned.

"Awww, man!," the boys cried in unison as they both started climbing down from the tree.

"What in the world?!," Todd said.

"Stop!," the firefighters yelled as the boys expertly made their way down the tree. When they arrived at the area where Todd had destroyed the branch, they jumped down effortlessly. Todd was speechless and angry. But before he could scold the boys, his cell phone began to ring. It was Amell.

"Todd, why aren't you answering your walkie-talkie?"

Todd began to remind Amell that the cheap product he'd purchased for the camp didn't work outside, but decided not to pick that battle, especially since Amell sounded frantic.

"Todd are the firefighters still here?," Amell asked in a panicky tone.

"They are," Todd said. "They seem to be a little preoccupied at the moment, but I can send them your way if you'd like."

The firefighters weren't doing anything incredibly important. They were just gathered around Terri, perplexed as to why she was trying to put the fallen branches and tree limbs from his failed rescue attempt back on the tree. As he re-joined the group, Todd saw Terri not only planting the casualties from the tree, but also the sticks that lay around it.

"I give them back to you, Earth Mother," she said.

"Is this lady serious?," one of the firefighters asked.

"What type of institution is this?," asked another.

"She's, ummm, different," Todd explained. "It seems as though we have another emergency for you."

Sometimes the light at the end of the tunnel is a train.

"She said she took a whole bottle of pills," Amell said, panicked. "Hold on, Erica, help is here," he pleaded.

Erica lay still on a stretcher, her eyes closed, her breathing calm. A volunteer for the camp, she'd been a fifteen-year-old sophomore at the school that year. She was a diminutive young woman who was usually brash and loud. The students called her extra. Erica always made sure to be the loudest person in the room, just so she could be heard or get her point across, even if she was wrong. Her classmates at this ultra conservative institution didn't dare debate her for fear of the extra attention she'd draw. Looking at her now, though, Todd would describe her as frail. Quiet. Peaceful. The growing crowd of volunteers and campers were shaken, somber, subdued by her state.

"Why would she do this to herself?," asked one camper.

"Will she survive?," probed a volunteer.

"Erica! Erica!! No, no, **NO**!," cried a young man who appeared to be the same age as Erica.

"Stay back," an EMT cautioned.

"Let us do our job," another one said.

The fire department had called the paramedics when they saw an empty pill bottle laying on the ground next to a passed-out Erica.

"I am so, so sorry," sobbed the young man who'd screamed Erica's name earlier. "She meant nothing to me," he declared.

"I can't believe you chose that bitch over me!," screamed a now-conscious and very excited Erica. "I've been nothing but good to you!," she yelled, sitting upright on the stretcher.

"She's talking to me," the young man confessed.

"I can't...," Erica started, placing her arm over her head and appearing to faint.

Crying, the young man begged the paramedics to do something. "I love her!," he declared.

"First we have to call her parent or guardian and ask which hospital to transport her to."

"Call my mom," Erica said. "No. Don't call my mom," she said as she hopped up off the stretcher. "I'm fine. I think the pills have passed through my system," she continued.

"Ma'am," a paramedic cautioned, "Faking a suicide attempt is serious offense. Your mom will still need to be contacted."

"What if there'd been a serious emergency elsewhere?," he scolded. "A person who needed medical attention might have died because you decided to use us as a prop in your little drama to upset your boyfriend over there."

278

"He's not my boyfriend anymore," Erica said. "I dumped him when I saw him talking to Janice in the quad," she added.

"I don't care who was talking to whom," the EMT added. "All I know is I will be talking to your mom, and that the city charges $500 for a wasted trip."

"$500?," Erica repeated. "$500!," she said again before her eyes rolled in the back of her head and she hit the floor.

Thump! The sickening sound of her head smacking the linoleum floor made Todd's stomach churn. The paramedics recognized the seriousness of the incident immediately and sprang into action. Erica remained motionless. Once again, everyone was shocked by her condition. Half the crowd that was still gathered expected Erica to pop up and rant and rave about the cost of an ambulance call. But she remained motionless. The emergency crew quickly secured her head and neck before placing her back onto the gurney. They told Amell where they were taking her and asked him to call her guardian.

Everyone stood in silence as they loaded her into the back of the ambulance. The roller coaster of emotions had drained all the spectators. The silence was broken by the Imperial Death March, Todd's ringtone. Todd knew instantly that it was Sharon.

"Hello?," he whispered.

"Why the fuck are you whispering?," Sharon screamed. "I knew you weren't working at the school. It's summer time! Who are you with?," she demanded.

"There was an incident at the school," Todd started.

"I don't care," Sharon interrupted. "I need money."

"For what?," Todd asked.

"They just shut off our electricity," Sharon replied.

"Shut off our electricity?!," Todd repeated, confused. "You said you paid it!

"I was going to, but my son needed a video game to practice his skills," Sharon said.

"What are you talking about?," Todd asked. He could feel his blood start to boil. He was tired of going around and round with Sharon financially. He'd mistakenly given her the only debit card for their joint bank account. It had seemed like a good idea at the time. Since he was always working it would be easier for her to stay on top of the bills.

"I told you he's going to be a game blogger. He needs games to review and learn cheats and tips for so he has something to write about."

Todd walked away from the crowd of campers, getting angrier and angrier with each step. This was ridiculous. Every step he takes forward Sharon knocks him back three steps. "Sharon," he started in a condescending tone, "Can you please explain how he's going to play a video game without any way of powering it on?"

"Do you have any money on you?," Sharon asked.

280

"You're joking, right?," Todd laughed sarcastically. "*You* are in control of our finances," Todd reminded her. "You barely give me money to put gas in my car, so no I don't have any money," he added.

"What good are you?," Sharon snapped. "If you can't help with our bills, why do I keep you around?"

"I think it's the other way around," Todd retorted. He was at his boiling point.

"That's fine," Sharon snapped. "I withdrew $460 from our account to pay the bill. I was just letting you know as a courtesy."

"That's fine," Todd replied.

Wait what? Todd got excited and confused all at once. He was excited that his account had $460 in it, but he was confused as to where in the hell that kind of money had come from. Was it a banking error? Did one of his jobs give him a raise and forget to tell him about it?

"How did the money get in our account?," Todd asked. Maybe it was a premonition, maybe it was logic. Either way, Todd felt queasy. He knew he didn't want to hear the truth of where the money came from.

"I overdrew the account," Sharon said nonchalantly. "We have that overdraft protection. I can withdraw up to $500," she continued. "I should've done that, but I didn't want to be greedy."

Todd doubled over. He hadn't felt this sick since the swimming incident. He couldn't breathe. Dropping to one knee, Todd gasped for air. "How are we going to pay the bank back?," he asked.

"You get paid again on Friday," Sharon answered Sharon. Todd's illness intensified. Once the bank was paid back they would barely have enough for other bills. He wouldn't be able to afford gas to put in his car to get to work. How were they going to eat? Todd fought to hold back his tears of frustration and stress. He needed to figure out a solution to this problem. He'd fought the good fight up to this point, he just needed to keep on fighting.

"Sharon," Todd said, his voice cracking with emotion, "It's only Tuesday."

"So what?," she answered.

"Honey!" Calling Sharon that burned his tongue. She was anything but his honey at this point. "The bank charges a $35 dollar overdraft fee for every two days we don't pay them back," he said.

"Oh," Sharon said. "Well, can you pick up an extra shift somewhere to pay for it? What about a work-today-get-paid-today day labor place?," she suggested.

"I have to go," Todd said, quickly hanging up and turning off the phone.

"Todd!," Amell called, placing his arm on Todd's shoulder. "Are you ok?," he asked.

Blinking hard, Todd tried sucking back the tears that threatened to escape. He cleared his throat and gathered himself before he said, "Yeah yeah, I'm good. I thought I saw something on the ground," he lied.

"Just checking," Amell replied. "We have another problem."

Virginity can be cured.

"Dare I ask?," Todd began as he and Amell walked down the hall. He marveled at how eerily different the halls were in the summer compared to during the school year. Without students, the pair's footsteps echoed throughout the hallway, bouncing off the walls that were usually covered with posters telling students to read and achieve. Poster putty and sticky tack were left in their place. The floors, barely visible with students' foot traffic during the year, revealed the scuff marks they'd left behind. Todd felt bad for Amanda and her staff. Normally they would spend the summer stripping, buffing, and waxing the floors and painting the walls. But not this summer thanks to the summer camp.

"Some of the campers heard moaning coming from a janitor's closet down the hall," Amell answered. "The two of us are going to investigate," he continued.

As the pair approached the closet a handful of campers had their ears pressed up against the door and were giggling.

"Out of here!," Amell directed the campers.

Though they dispersed, the campers didn't go far. Peering around a corner, they eagerly awaited the fallout from what they all assumed was happening.

Amell motioned to Todd to stay silent as the two pressed their ears against the door.

"It's so stiff!," they heard a female say.

284

"Keep kissing it," a male responded.

"My jaw hurts," the girl complained. "And my lips are dry," she continued. Amell had heard enough. Reaching for the door, he found it had been locked. Banging on it, he demanded whomever was inside to open up. Silence. The closet's occupants didn't say a word. They didn't have to. Their clumsy, erratic movements alerted everyone in the hallway to their presence.

Todd, who *had* been wondering if he wanted to have kids one day, decided at that moment that he did not. He'd admit that he'd done a lot of dumb things growing up, but some of the things he'd seen campers do this summer went beyond dumb. Would his parents agree that he'd been just as dumb at the campers' age? Did he block out important details of events that had skewed his beliefs that he was a well-behaved adolescent capable of thinking critically?

Knocking on the door himself, Todd repeated Amell's request that the occupants open the door.

"In a second!," the female voice said. "I'm looking for some window cleaner," she added.

Todd took a step back and inspected the space between the door and floor. "How are you looking for something in the dark?," he asked. "Open up now," he demanded.

The sounds of fumbling around, belt buckles clanging, and bodies bumping into each other filled the janitor's closet. Todd could hear someone feeling around in the dark for the door latch. When it finally opened, Todd was shocked to see Lori.

"Get out here," Amell demanded. With her head hung low, Lori slowly obeyed.

"Who's in there with you?," Amell asked.

"No one," Lori answered.

Todd reached into the closet and flipped the light switch on. The space was a cramped 36" wide by 72" high by 18" deep. Directly across from the door was a portable plastic sink with a garden hose attached to the faucet. The hose was used to fill up a mop bucket directly in front of the sink. Gray wire shelves flanked both sides of the closet and held cleaning supplies, toilet paper, and paper towels. To the right of the sink, a broom and mop holder was drilled into the wall. Hiding poorly behind the mop was the male voice Todd and Amell had heard talking to Lori.

"We can all see you," Amell said to the boy. The young man didn't move.

Hanging from the wall, the mop was only five feet off the ground. The boy, who appeared to be about 5'9", had to crouch down, to hide his face behind the mop.

"Does he know he's visible?," Amell asked aloud. Still the boy didn't move. Todd wondered how long this idiot was going to pretend he was invisible, even though he clearly wasn't. He became more and more impatient with every passing moment.

"My cholesterol level is too high to be playing games with you," he snapped, marching into the closet.

Still annoyed by his conversation with Sharon, Todd snatched the mop off the wall and threw it down. Making eye contact with the young man, Todd could see it was the same kid who just twenty minutes ago was mourning his girlfriend Erica's fake suicide attempt.

"Get out of here!," Todd commanded. The young man closed his eyes and held his breath as if it would make him invisible. "That's it.," Todd said. He kicked the mop bucket out of his way, grabbed the young man by his shirt, and yanked him out of the closet.

"What was going on in there?," Todd demanded to know.

"How did you see me in there?," the young man asked, believing he had had the perfect hiding spot.

Todd turned away from the young man and focused his attention on Lori. "Do you want to tell me what's going on or do we need to call your parents for answers?" Out of the corner of his eye Todd could see the young man gesture for Lori to be quiet. For the first time since Todd had met Lori she abided by the young man's request and stayed silent.

"So," Todd began, "Is this is how we're going to play it?" He could once again feel one aspect of his life spilling over into another. His mounting frustration with Sharon was going to erupt on the two kids standing in front of him. Todd tried reminding himself they were just kids, but at this moment he didn't care. He felt he'd lost control over everything in his life and it was time he got it back, starting with some damn respect from these two volunteers.

"I don't have time to play your little games," Todd said. "Hey, Lori!," he continued, "how about I call your dad and tell him you won't be receiving your community service hours because you were locked in a closet with a boy? How would you like it if I added what Amell and I heard the two of you say while you were in there?

"Sir," the young man started. "It's not like that. We were playing hide and seek with some campers."

"Hide and *seek*?," Todd repeated, incredulously. "Don't piss on my head and tell me it's raining," he shouted. "Campers. Is **that** what you call your little friend in your pants? Because it looks like he's pitching a tent?"

"Amell placed his hand on Todd's arm to calm him down, but Todd stepped away from Amell's grasp. "No, Amell. I'm not going to be played for a fool," Todd exclaimed. "We are **responsible** for everyone here," he continued. "I'm not going to be lied to and told it's innocent when this young man's baby boner is sticking out of his unzipped pants next to a wet spot," he said.

Lori burst into tears. "Do you want to explain to Lori's father that this young man's pecker was playing hide and seek with his daughter!?"

"Todd!," Amell yelled. "That is quite enough."

Amell's words were stern. Todd knew he'd crossed the line with his hide-and-seek comment, but he didn't care. He was still fuming over his wife's "management of" their shared checking account. He was at the end of his rope. Short of winning the lottery or trying to find ten extra hours in a

288

day to work another job and get zero sleep, Todd was defeated financially. His treatment of the volunteers was him throwing in the towel of life. Misery loves company, he thought. Might as well ruin their day, too.

"Todd," Amell said. "I will handle this situation. How about you check on the younger campers? I think they're with Teresa in the gym.

Todd turned and walked away without saying a word. He felt betrayed by Amell. Amell was probably the only person in the entire school who believed in mercy. No matter what someone did, Amell felt they deserved a second chance. Todd thought everyone took advantage of his kindness. His second chances turned into third, fourth, and fifth chances. Todd assumed the same thing would happen here. Amell's passive-aggressive mentality is what angered Todd most. Sometimes mercy wasn't enough, Todd thought. It took making a statement to make a difference.

Todd knew his own line of thinking was hypocritical. He was embarrassed to admit that he was a doormat to others: to his wife, to his bosses at the warehouse, to Amell and the staff at the school. He knew his bark was silent, and he had no bite. He would roll his ears back, let life hit him as if it were a rolled-up newspaper, and still act like a loyal, lost puppy.

As Todd entered the lobby of the gym, something seemed off. On the wall to his right was the school's trophy case. There were only four trophies in it. Three of them were from a dominant women's soccer team old enough that the members of that team probably had children old enough to play varsity for the school. The fourth was from this year's championship basketball team, led by Derrick. Todd sneered at the term 'championship team.' It was true, the team had been crowned champions, but playing in a small, private Christian league meant there were only ten teams in the state. Each school in the league got to compete for the championship, regardless of its record. Though the school's team would have been slaughtered by any of the state's public schools, they got lucky in the state tournament. Four schools couldn't afford to travel to the state tournament's location. The first team the school faced had had a rash of injuries, was playing with a skeleton crew, and *still* almost won. The second and the championship games were won by forfeit. Those two teams were favored to win and went to a buffet dinner together. Both were struck down by food poisoning.

Bringing his thoughts back to the present, Todd was put off by the eerie silence. As he approached the gymnasium doors he heard the sound of a basketball hitting the floor twice, a chorus of gasps, and Teresa yelling for them to be silent. Todd flung the doors open and was astonished by what he saw. The girls were playing hopscotch on tippy toe. The boys were playing basketball, or some semblance of it. Apparently in their version they couldn't dribble or pass the ball.

"Teresa!," Todd yelled. His voice bounced off the walls, startling all the campers. Their faces brightened when they saw Todd.

"Yes, sir?," Teresa answered.

"Do I even have to ask the question?," he asked.

"They were way too loud," Teresa said.

"It's summer break!," Todd exclaimed. "They're here to have fun, blow off steam, and enjoy themselves. Maybe you should try it!," he added. "Hey kids! Are you having fun playing in silence?," he asked.

290

Nervously, they all looked at Teresa, too frightened to answer.

"It's okay," Todd encouraged them. Still no one made a sound. "Arrrrrgggggghhhh!," Todd bellowed. All the campers flinched. The roar bounced off the floors and walls and was deafening.

Whoa!, Todd thought. The release was exhilarating. He wanted to do it again. He *needed* to do it again.

"It's summer, kids! Let it alllll out. Let's make some noise! Arrrgggghhh!," he screamed. This time, several campers joined in. "We can do better than that," Todd cheered. "Let's have some FUN!," he shouted. "Get on your feet! Stomp! Scream! Yell," he hollered.

Todd put his all into making a commotion. Finally all the campers joined him. "Arrrggghhh!," Todd screamed as he jumped and stomped around the gym. He was cleansing himself. He felt invigorated. He felt as if he were being purged of all his pent up frustration. Fuck his wife, fuck his jobs, fuck his bills, he thought as he yelled. Tears began to flow unexpectedly and Todd quickly exited the gym. "Have fun!," he shouted on his way out.

What the hell is wrong with me?, Todd thought as he wiped the tears from his eyes. He couldn't remember the last time he'd cried openly. He didn't cry at relatives' funerals or when a pet passed away. The only time he could remember crying was when he'd watched *The Fox and The Hound*. The scene when the old lady told the fox he couldn't be friends with the hound brought on the waterworks. Thinking of it now, Todd began shedding more tears to replace the ones he'd just wiped away.

Fixing his face, he decided to find a place to work quietly on plans for the

291

lockout. He needed to immerse himself in some sort of activity before any more embarrassing outbursts of tears struck.

"Todd! Hold up!," Amell shouted, walking toward him at a steady pace so he could catch up.

Todd faked a yawn in an effort to make Amell think that that's why his eyes were moist. It didn't work.

"You good?," asked a concerned Amell.

"I'm good," Todd lied. "Just a little tired."

"It's me," Amell responded. "I'm here for you," he said.

"Seriously, I'm good," Todd said again.

"You need to take care of yourself," Amell started. "Your outburst back there wasn't like you at all. Those are kids," he continued. "They're bound to make mistakes."

Todd could not hold back his disdain for Amell's assessment any longer. He was tired of students being coddled and their actions dismissed. The 'they're just kids' excuse was wearing thin. Todd had watched all summer and all the previous school year that students were behaving the way they were because they could get away with it.

"Back in my day," he started, "we had respect for our elders, for property, and for the rules." He knew he sounded like a grumpy old man, but he didn't care. "This generation doesn't respect or care for anything or anyone, and

292

there aren't any repercussions for their actions," he concluded.

"That's a discussion for another time," Amell replied. "I know your tirade back there wasn't because of our volunteers' behavior, no matter how egregious it was. What's really going on?," he asked, his face full of concern.

Todd stayed silent and stoic. He refused to discuss the problems in his life with Amell. "I'm fine," he maintained.

"Okay," Amell relented. "If you need someone to vent to you can come to me. If not me then a pastor or a counselor," he suggested.

Todd became angered. None of those suggestions was an option in his mind.

Amell has used Todd's marriage as a punchline in the past. Besides, he knew that when you tell a friend or relative something personal, no matter how many times you urge them to keep it secret, it leaks out bit by bit. And although he works at a religious institution, Todd doesn't believe in a particular system of faith and worship. He believes in God, but he's not sure he believed in a man of the cloth. Too many church scandals throughout the world have led him not to trust men in positions of religious authority. He also felt that if a pastor helped him he would be expected to attend their church every Sunday, paying a tithe he couldn't afford. Plus he worked on Sundays.

A counselor would be his complete last resort. And he couldn't afford one, anyway.

"A counselor?," Todd asked cynically. "Black people don't go to therapy."

293

"I know, I know," Amell responded, "but maybe we should."

Todd laughed at the suggestion. "There are four things black people don't do," Todd replied. "We don't split up in scary situations, we don't get our hair wet when we're swimming, we don't open up to other black people, and we don't tell our problems to white people. You know all this just as well as I do," he concluded.

"Todd, you're married to a white woman. How can you still have that mentality?"

Todd didn't have to think about his response; his only thought was whether to share his response with Amell or not. Both their parents had grown up in the midst of the Civil Rights Movement, and before that segregation. Only one generation removed from this hateful, hurtful time, Todd had been naïve to think times had changed. Sharon's calling him a nigger had opened his eyes that times may change, but people do not. If his wife didn't have his best interest at heart, how could he trust a stranger? It didn't matter if they were a counselor, doctor, or dentist. Todd kept his response to himself.

"Brother," Amell began, "so many young black men never make it to 18. We're among the lucky few. We have to live fulfilled lives. For them if not for ourselves. I know the stresses of violence, oppression, racial profiling, and egregious stereotypes can take their toll on every black male. Hell, we have to damn near have split personalities around certain groups. We have to sound 'white' in professional settings, but we have to sound 'hood' around our people. We risk not fitting in in both situations. It's exhausting. Plus a black man has to put on a damn near Oscar-worthy performance so others feel safe around him. One hint of agitation and we're labeled an angry black man and thought of as an animal. On top of that," he continued, "you have

294

to contend with the masculinity perception bestowed on every male. Any sign of weakness means you're not a man, you're a failure. Trust me, it takes a toll on one's psyche. You need an outlet In order to cope. Not having one can lead to mental health problems such as depression, anxiety, and personality disorders."

"There are physical symptoms, too," Amell added. "Cardiovascular disease, including heart disease, high blood pressure, abnormal heart rhythms, heart attacks, and strokes. It wasn't easy for me, either" Amell confessed. "But I had to relent, trust someone, and seek help. Keeping everything inside was taking its toll on my health. I *had* to make myself a priority. It was the best decision I ever made," he said. "I stopped trying to impress others, stopped caring about what people think of me. My father once told me a life isn't yours if you always care what others think."

"Okay," Todd replied dismissively.

"Just remember this," Amell added. "If you don't value your own life, start smoking. You'll die ten years early. Drink excessively. You'll die fifteen years early. Or if you continue to fight to love someone who doesn't love you back, you will die **every** day." And he walked off.

Standing by himself, Todd remembered something *his* dad once told him: God delivers messages through people. Pay attention. Message received, Todd thought.

There will always be edits when your schedule is already packed

Over the next couple of weeks, Todd made the camp's lockout a priority. The finish line was in sight and Todd was prepared to finish strong. The camp's day-to-day operation ran on autopilot even though it was on life support. On Mondays, the campers went swimming. On Tuesdays, they stayed busy with games and activities on campus. On Wednesdays, they'd have an on-campus field trip: a guest arriving to show the campers fun and interesting stuff, and then leaving.

For the most part, this has been the most successful aspect of the camp. There haven't been many mishaps. One week, clowns came to the camp to show their circus performance. Todd was amazed to find out that kids actually have a fear of clowns. Lesson learned, he thought.

Another week they had a balloon artist show the campers how to make several different types of balloon animals. Outside of a few hundred popped balloons, this, too, was successful.

The only real Wednesday-on-Campus mishap happened last week with the exotic animal show. When the guest passed around spiders, lizards, and reptiles, one camper freaked out when the tarantula was passed her direction. She dropped it and another camper stepped on it, killing it. And a lizard ran away so the company won't want to deal with the summer camp ever again.

On Thursdays the campers went bowling. And Friday was a free day. The routine had become manageable.

296

Todd opened the lockout invitation to family and friends. It was going double as an open house for the

school. It was a chance to show families that despite all the pitfalls, the summer camp really is run with the utmost care. In addition, we know how to have fun.

"Todd, I need to speak with you," said a female voice from behind him. Turning around, he saw Amanda with her arms crossed and her permanent scowl tattooed across her face. Todd didn't have time for whatever complaint she was about to present him.

The lockout had to go off without a hitch. I only have two hours before everything begins, he thought.

He'd even invited Sharon to tonight's event. It was an opportunity for Sharon to see all the hard work he's done this summer. Maybe she'll start to respect him. Maybe she will see him as a leader, he hoped. Part of him wanted to try to create a spark, rekindle what they once had for one another. She's my wife, he'd tell himself. I need to honor the vow I made to her.

That was his irrational, unreasonable side, though. The side that needed to wake up and move on. On the other side, the rational side, Todd was tired of the abuse. Tired of the ultimatums, tired

of walking on eggshells, tired of her making everything about her. Todd was on his last leg. He was

beginning to realize there was no reward for sticking around. He wanted emotional equality in their

marriage, but Sharon seemed incapable of that. Fuck that. He needed out. He was drowning himself by swimming around in the turbulent sea she'd made of her life.

"Yes, Amanda? What can I do for you," Todd asked in his most sarcastic tone. Todd was tired of her, too. How is she going to make my life a living hell now?, he wondered.

"Are you planning to use the soccer and softball fields tonight?," she asked. Todd was annoyed by her question. Looking in the direction of the soccer field, Todd could see a company inflating a giant bounce house. Gazing in the direction of the softball field, he could see several carnival rides being assembled. Todd knew she could see them, too. He knew she was setting him up with her line of questions.

Taking a deep breath, hoping to absorb the bad news Amanda was sure to deliver, Todd said, "Yes we are." Todd looked down as if focusing on a list of duties in his hand. He didn't want her to see his face as she delivered her bad news. Todd assumed she got off on the reaction she got from people when she ruined their plans.

"You can't use those areas," she declared with a slight grin on her face.

Todd lowered his clipboard slowly and sighed deeply. "Why not?," he asked, trying to stay calm.

"We need to keep the grass on the field looking presentable for the soccer season," Amanda replied.

Looking out onto the field, Todd questioned her definition of presentable. The field was barren. There were just as many dry spots of dirt as there were on the softball field.

298

"Where do you suggest I put the bounce house then?," he asked. He desperately wanted to give Amanda a piece of his mind. Why would she stand around watching the inflatable crew assemble and inflate the enormous bounce house before saying anything?

"I do not care what you do with it!," she snapped. "You could put it in the gym," she suggested, matching Todd's annoyance with the conversation.

Todd assumed her aggravation came from his lack of emotion at her news.

"Do you mean inside the hot gymnasium?," he asked. "The gymnasium that's been waiting for its air conditioning to be fixed by your crew for weeks?"

The question hit Amanda below the belt. Todd knew she and her crew had worked tirelessly to prepare the campus for the first day of school. He also knew time working on the school had been lost when she'd had to rescue the camp when they were stranded on the side of the road and when repairs had been needed from damage caused by his campers.

The gym had been off limits to the camp for the past two weeks for cooling maintenance. But Todd had overheard the maintenance project had been placed on hold due to a missing part. He'd also overheard that the school was short on paying the HVAC company and were going to try to repair the unit themselves. Without HVAC experience, Todd was unfairly matching Amanda's pettiness with his
own.

"What's wrong with using the softball field," he asked.

299

"You can't have the field lights on past 9 PM," Amanda informed him. The look on her face said this was something he should have known.

This was a legitimate excuse, Todd thought. He was truly mad at himself for not thinking of that problem.

"Excuse me, Amanda," Todd started. "I need to go tell the inflatable crew to deflate the bounce house and set it up in the scorching gym."

"And the softball field?," Amanda asked.

"You said it yourself. We'll keep it running until 9 PM." Todd scurried off before Amanda could object to his suggestion. He didn't want to be around her as she celebrated her small victory.

After receiving looks of irritation from the inflatable crew, Todd decided to check on the food.

At Amell's insistence, Todd had reluctantly placed Teresa in charge of food. He envisioned her doling
out the food as if it were a prison chow line. He could see her rationing out the portions. As long as campers kept the line moving in an orderly fashion, the food shouldn't be a problem. Hot dogs, chips, and s'mores. Simple!

Heading for the quad, Todd wondered why he couldn't smell the smoke from the grill. Nothing was more intoxicating to him than the smell of hot dogs grilling over an open flame. The crunch from one that was slightly charred was nothing short of incredible. Maybe a little relish or mustard on his dog, but no ketchup. Never ketchup on a hot dog. A burger yes, but on a

hot dog? That's sacrilegious. Todd had even gone so far as to argue –
vehemently argue – against even offering ketchup at the lockout. He'd
shown Amell and Teresa articles proving his point. They hadn't been
convinced.

Todd had specifically instructed Teresa to have the food already prepared for
guests as they arrived. With parents arriving shortly after getting off work he
felt a meal was the least the camp could
do to show appreciation for their attendance and support. They were lucky
to still *have* parental support after everything that had happened over the
summer.

I guess as long as the campers had fun and survived, parents didn't mind the
trials and tribulations, Todd thought.

A conclusion is simply the place where you got tired of thinking.

"Teresa!," Todd called out. Teresa was standing ten feet in front of him, adamantly scolding a
man in front of her. Clearly it was a personal matter, Todd thought. The passion in Teresa's gesturing
indicated this was a matter of the heart. Geez, he thought; we don't have time for this tonight.

"Teresa!" he called out again, ignoring whatever was going on. "What's happening with the food?," he asked impatiently.

Startled, Teresa turned around to face Todd. She looked as if she had just seen a ghost. "H-h-hi, sir," she stuttered. In all the time Todd had known Teresa, this was the first time her confidence seemed shaky. "I would like you to meet my father," she said, presenting Todd to the man she'd been arguing with.

Todd was taken aback. He'd seen Teresa's mother at every school event, but never her father. He'd just assumed she didn't have one.

"Hi," the man said. Todd was knocked back by his vigorous welcome. The overpowering smell of
alcohol nearly choked him. Todd ventured to guess that drinking was a full-time job for Teresa's dad. His
tattered, wrinkled clothes had absorbed the stale odor of old alcohol and cigarettes. He looked like he hadn't shaved in weeks, and Todd wasn't sure when he'd last bathed. The evening's warm breeze did not provide Todd

302

with any favors as it blew the man's body odor directly in Todd's path.

"Teresa," Todd started again, "What's going on with the food?" He didn't waste any time waiting for a response. "Campers and their families are going to start arriving shortly. We want them to be able to eat something when they get here," he said. "Or at least smell the food cooking," he added. "You haven't even started the grill!," he exclaimed

"I, sir, am your chef, reporting for duty," declared Teresa's dad, saluting Todd drunkenly.

Wide-eyed in disbelief, Todd looked displeasingly at Teresa. He scanned her father up and down and shook his head in disappointment. I don't have time for this, he thought. So many other areas needed his attention.

Todd suddenly felt dizzy. He needed to find somewhere to sit down. He broke out in a cold sweat. He hadn't felt well for a while, but he had to shake it off. People were depending on him. There was far too much for him to do to grab a seat.

"Get the fire lit and the food on the grill," he said. "Teresa, he is *your* responsibility," he cautioned.

"I'm on it, Captain!," her father said with another salute.

Todd wanted to salute him back with only one of his fingers but decided not to. Instead, he snuck inside the school to prepare his classroom.

Sharon had never been to the school. She rarely even asks about any of his jobs. The only conversations

they had about his work started with "call off" or "can you work overtime?" Todd wanted desperately to
impress her tonight. He began to clean the way a young child might if he was preparing to show off his desk and his work at Open House. He wanted to repay Sharon for surprising him with a home-cooked meal earlier in the day. It had been a while since she'd cooked, though; the chili she made tasted off somehow. It had a sugary sweet yet somehow still bitter taste.

The last time Sharon had even used the oven was to protect a delivered pizza from the cats until Todd got home from work. Maybe she's turning the corner and wants to make our marriage successful, Todd thought gleefully.

Let me call her, he thought. I need to make sure she knows where she's going. That was the excuse he gave himself, anyway. In truth, Todd fully expected Sharon to give him an excuse as to why she couldn't come.

"What, Todd?," Sharon said as she answered the phone. She sounded disappointed that it was him. Nothing new, Todd thought.

"I was just calling to tell you to meet me at the front of the school," he replied.

"I thought the flier said the events were in the back," Sharon said.

"They are," Todd told her, "I just want to show you around the campus."

"Todd! We have a problem!," called Lori from the hall.

"Who the fuck is that bitch?," Sharon yelled

304

"It's just one of the volunteers," Todd answered. "Can you be here in an hour? I unlocked the main entrance to the school."

"Todd! Todd we have an emergency," Lori repeated.

"I have to go, Sharon, I'm sorry."

"Are you fucking kidding me?!," Sharon started, but Todd had already hit the end button.

Following Lori down the hallway, Todd glanced at his watch. Not realizing he had spent so much time prepping his room, he was glad there was an emergency. He needed to greet the campers and their families.

As he made his way toward the grill, Todd heard a cacophony of complaints. "This is burnt." "Mine is cold." "The soda is hot." A bunch of parents and campers had assembled, and in the middle of all the commotion was Teresa's inebriated father.

"What's going on?," Amell asked, arriving on the scene.

Todd was upset that Amell hadn't been around during the preparation of tonight's events. Like he had for most of the camp, Todd was doing everything by himself.

"This drunk found a way to burn frozen hot dogs," complained one parent.

"Why are the hot dogs still frozen?" asked another.

"Wait what?," asked a very confused Amell.

"I accidently put them in the freezer," Teresa admitted. "My dad thought he could thaw them out on the grill."

"The grill's not even ready, " observed a parent. "The fire's barely been lit!"

"Let me take care of that," Teresa's dad volunteered. Emptying a bottle of lighter fluid over half-warmed coal briquettes, he lit a match and tossed it onto the grill. "Bon appetit!," he yelled as an explosion filled the sky.

"Well, shit," he said.

"You dumb fuck," cursed a parent. "That wasn't lighter fluid!"

The parent was right. Clearly marked on the canister was a label that read 'gas for bonfire.' It was too late. Another disaster had befallen the camp. Campers were scared and crying. Parents were mad and cursing. Todd just stood there, wondering how his great idea had turned to shit.

"Don't you dare yell at me!," Todd heard Teresa's dad yell. He'd become enraged. Shoving Teresa out of the way, he went after the parent who'd called him a dumb fuck. The two men began pushing and shoving each other, showing no regard for the safety of the children standing just feet away. Was there going to be a fight? Todd didn't even care anymore.

Dejected, he started walking to the front of the school to meet his wife. He was feeling nauseous again. If only I could grab a seat, he thought. He couldn't see. Everything in front of him was silhouetted in a purple haze.

306

"Ahhhhhhhhhhhhh!" A blood-curdling scream filled the air. Panicked shrieks for water followed. In a trance, Todd didn't bother turning around. Horrid screams of people in pain echoed throughout the campus. Todd assumed someone fell into the fire from the grill. Todd guessed it was Teresa's father. He didn't care.

"Call the fire department!," he heard Amell yell. "The quad's on fire!"

"It's spreading!" Todd could hear a parent yell.

Todd suddenly remembered Mr. Franklin's haunting premonition that the camp would cause the school to burn down. He couldn't care less. He'd done the best he could, and no one could fault him for that.

For the first time in a long time, Todd put his own well-being above others'. He entered the school and walked blindly through the deserted hallway. He finally felt some peace. He didn't have a care in the world. It was pleasant. It was silent. There was calm.

Reaching to open the door and hoping to see his wife on the other side, Todd felt a sharp pain radiate from his chest down his left arm. The intense pain made Todd feel light-headed. He broke out in a cold sweat. He felt sick to his stomach and couldn't catch his breath. He dropped to the ground violently, agony coursing through his entire body.

His phone fell out of his hand and slid a few feet in front of him. Unable to move, he felt nauseous. He started to wheeze as his body began convulsing. He vomited. He could taste the horrible meal Sharon had prepared for him earlier. It actually tasted better coming up than it had going down. Reaching in vain for his phone, Todd could see his fingertips had turned blue. He could

307

only hope Sharon was on her way and would find him, but he knew better. Experience had taught Todd that Sharon couldn't care less about him.

Todd began to hope his wife *wouldn't* come. He didn't want to be found this way. He had hoped they would grow old together and would say their goodbyes from hospital beds, reminiscing about the wonderful life they'd shared. He knew now that this was a pipe dream. Life with Sharon was a nightmare. Her face was not the face he envisioned having a long, loving life with. That person was long gone. An old fling. Another wasted opportunity in a long line of regrets.

Todd could sense the end was near. Even though he was in excruciating pain, Todd was finally at peace. He could rest. No more anxiety, no more queasy feelings in the pit of his stomach. No more worries about others' feelings. No more stress. No more fights. He was alone. With all he'd done in his life to help his friends, his jobs, and his family, at the end he was alone. If he could do it again, would he?, he asked himself. Hell no, he thought. Everything would be different. He would live. He would have a life. He would work to live, not live to work. He would find love. Most importantly, he would give love. He'd finally appreciate and love that someone who loves him most. Himself. Why at the end of life did he now want to live fully?

As he closed his eyes, one final thought haunted his consciousness. Had he been poisoned?

***

"Todd, there's a fire outside."
"Todd? Are you sleeping?" he heard faintly.
Oh great! Not Lori, he thought.

THE END?

Volume 2
Featuring Bianca

309